The Iron of Souls

Emma Bradley

"No more Forgotten. No more suffering."

DEDICATION

For Katina, who for some weird reason loves these characters almost as much as I do (thank you so much for your support and endless enthusiasm right from the beginning!)

A Few Days After the War of Queens

CHAPTER ONE
BLOSSOM

The new queen of Faerie didn't have a throne. She didn't have a functioning court full of grandeur and frightened maids scuttling about either.

No, what she did have was a random common room at Arcanium, the hub of the FDPs that often guarded the realms of Faerie. Even worse, it was full to the rafters with mismatched chairs and piles of paper.

Blossom eyed a huge palm tree in one corner that housed a very unimpressed looking lizard. If she was hearing right, the lizard was snoring.

Even though Demerara had been queen for over a week now since the War of Queens, she sat on a faded armchair that had scratches on the wooden legs. She wore a hooded black sweatshirt with her thumbs poking out of the cuffs and dark green jeans that wouldn't even be used for rags in any kind of respectable establishment, let alone a queen's court.

Facing said queen of Faerie wasn't how Blossom had imagined her day to go, especially considering she was standing there as a potential traitor, but she straightened her cream blouse and forced herself to stand tall. She had no right to expect the queen would even agree to see her, let alone listen, but it had to be done. She had to speak for herself and choose a side. After the war and the things she knew about the Forgotten, being part of the new queen's version of Faerie was the only way she might survive this with any sense of dignity intact.

Blossom tensed as the new queen's aide rushed up to her, his cheeks pink and a harassed look on his face.

"She'll see you now," he huffed. "No more than five minutes though. She has a whole load of stuff piling up she hasn't bothered to sign yet."

The announcement was pointless considering Blossom could see the queen already, and the queen was well aware of her waiting there to be seen. But as the young man rushed off down the hall, Blossom could appreciate his sense of ceremony even if the new queen couldn't.

"I don't think we've ever properly met," the queen announced. "What's up?"

What's up.

Blossom tried not to grimace at the casual tone. A queen should command a room with a single look and patronise her subjects accordingly. But as she risked a glance toward the far end of the room, she realised that Queen Demerara might look casual, might sound and act like it, but there was something undeniable about her, a stubbornness that sent out a subtle warning to those around her.

It took all of Blossom's inner strength to walk those last few steps to stand in front of the queen, and even more to kneel. As a once-princess of Faerie with her future hanging uncertain, she had to shift for herself. Even her mother, the Oak Queen Tavania, had refused to interfere in Demi's new ruling.

A soft scoffing noise echoed from the corner of the room, but Blossom bowed her head and didn't dare look toward the king consort. He sat with his legs flung over the padded arms of a chair in the far corner. She couldn't hope for any mercy from him either, the half-brother she once delighted in tormenting.

"I'm surprised you agreed to see me," she said stiffly,

her chin still bowed to her chest.

Until recently, the queen would have been lower than her in social circles, but now the queen had all the power.

"Is there a reason I shouldn't agree to see you?" the queen asked. "Are you here to confess, or perhaps to take a shot at me?"

The king consort grumbled under his breath at that but didn't raise his voice loud enough to intervene.

Blossom drew a strangled breath and forced the words out.

"I need to pick a side, so this is me picking one. My family, those I aligned with, are either part of the Forgotten or vowing not to get involved anymore."

The admission didn't come easily. Supporting a new queen over the old, and a fairy's modern ideas over her family's more traditional Fae ideals, screamed rebellion. She risked a glance at the king consort, who likely understood as much as she did about betraying family ideals, if not more.

He was as casually dressed as the queen, something she remembered about him from their shared childhood. Not only was Oakthorn, or *Taz* as his friends apparently called him, in grubby boots, jeans and a faded *Demon Babies* t-shirt, but he also had his fiery wings furled, as though she was no threat to them at all, someone with absolutely no power.

"You don't sound too thrilled about the idea," the queen said. "You don't have to join any side, unless there's something you want to tell me?"

Blossom hesitated. Doing what she was about to do went against everything she'd been trained for, family over Fae, tradition over new ideals.

"Nothing that you won't have already figured out," she

admitted. "Your- the enemy won't take defeat lightly. They might be quiet for a while but they'll strike again. I want to be on the right side when they do."

The queen was silent for a long moment. Blossom kept her place even though the instinctive urge to raise her head raged. She rarely had to bow to anyone at home and the position turned out to be ridiculously uncomfortable.

"What exactly do you see as the 'right' side?" the queen asked. "You mean your own safety?"

Again Blossom hesitated. "In a way, but it goes deeper than that."

"Tell me." The command was softly spoken, one she could refuse if she chose to. But she'd come this far.

"A friend of mine got caught in the war. I think you knew her briefly. She was once one of you, an FDP, but she was bewitched by Elvira and the lure the enemy power."

The queen shifted in her seat.

"Enough bowing. Who was it?"

Blossom lifted her head, relief screaming through her neck and back muscles.

"Alannah Hazeldale. She was my friend but they got to her. She was convinced they could do no wrong in the end, and everyone with any sense knows it doesn't matter what side you're on, nobody is entirely infallible."

A wisp of sadness crossed the queen's pale face, the vivid blue eyes sparking. Then Queen Demerara swiped a hand over her messy dark curls with a sigh.

"What happened to her in the end?" she asked.

"She displeased Elvira, so she was left out as a toy for the all-powerful essences. She wasn't the same after but she begged for death in some rare moments of clarity. Then they…"

Blossom pressed a hand to her chest. She couldn't explain any further but the queen nodded sharply, a mercy that Blossom was sickened to find she was grateful for.

Alannah had been her closest friend, the one person who'd given her some spark of life in the otherwise dreary trudge of her familial obligations. They'd orbed constantly after Alannah had moved to Arcanium, and in her darkest moments, Blossom forced herself to remember that it was her who suggested Alannah would make the perfect FDP go-between for Elvira.

"So, you're not a fan of the Forgotten then?" the queen asked.

Blossom shook her head. "No. I can't say that was always the case, but I'm doing the best I can to not go down the same path now. I don't want to end up like that. If-*when* they regroup, I want to be on the side that doesn't use Fae as pawns."

The queen leaned forward, her elbows on her knees and her expression serious.

"Would you be willing to fight for that?" she asked, ignoring another grumble from the king consort.

Blossom knew Taz had no love for her due to their past, not an enemy exactly but someone who definitely didn't think she was worth anything. The fact he was her half-brother was something neither of them cared to admit to. The strangest urge to prove everyone wrong gave her the strength to remain in place as trepidation set her pulse racing.

"What kind of fighting?"

The queen frowned. "It would depend. But would you be willing to betray the Forgotten while smiling to their faces? Pretend to be one of them and report back to us?"

Blossom hesitated and her skin chilled at the thought.

She had access to the queen's enemies. She only had to reach out and they would welcome her, not with trust perhaps but with hope she'd be mouldable. Useful. She didn't want to be a resource any longer. But to have a future for herself beyond being useful, that could be worth the sacrifice in time.

"I'd be willing to try."

The king consort leaned forward at that.

"Dem." His tone was laced with warning, but the queen ignored him.

"You can back out at any time," the queen added. "But if you betray us, we won't go easy on you. We may be fair but that doesn't make us easy targets, and we won't be kind to traitors either. If you agree to join the enemy and report back to us on what they're planning where you can, keep your true intentions anonymous to them, then perhaps we can start fresh."

As easy as that. Blossom blinked at the queen in surprise.

"You'd trust my word on it? You're not going to expect me to swear to your court?"

The queen laughed. "No, of course not. I'm building a court of people I can trust, and I have nothing to prove you'd fit that description. I'm giving you an opportunity to earn it though. Who knows what the future holds or what your part in it will be? I need to think this through, specifics and things, but I'll have someone let you know what we expect you to do in the next couple of days. Was that all?"

Blossom blinked back at her, all hope of words fleeing. The queen was giving her an opportunity to prove herself loyal. Practiced arrogance at being judged and dictated to warred with memories of Alannah's last few weeks. She could unlearn her habits and her prejudices enough to keep her comfortable life of nobility safe, but not if she was driven mad or dead.

She nodded. That was all she had to say and more opportunity than she'd dared hope for.

"Tell nobody else," the queen added.

She froze. "Not even my family? My mother?"

"No. No family, no friends. Nobody at Arcanium. You speak to me, to Taz or to Milo, my aide, but nobody else."

"Do we need a code word then?" The sarcastic stab leapt out of her mouth automatically.

The queen's lips twitched. "What a wonderful idea. How about 'banana'? If you can fit 'banana' into a sentence without making it seem weird, we'll know it's you talking to us. That'll be all then."

Employed, mocked and dismissed in a few quick minutes.

How humiliating.

With an awkward jerk of her shoulders, Blossom forced a bow, guessing she should at least show willing even though it went against every single thing she'd grown up knowing.

"I'll wait to hear," she said.

The queen nodded. "Okay. Actually, thinking about it there's much to do with the courts of Faerie. Perhaps we should all prepare for a royal visit. We'll start with the Court of Illusions. I imagine you'll have friends there. If not, make some and fast. Perhaps it's time for you to think about certain unions that could be made."

Blossom froze, her mask of indifference slipping. Unions to be made at the Court of Illusions. She knew Kainen Hemlock of course, but by many accounts he had turned traitor to the Forgotten even before she had. Would he welcome her as a prospective bride?

She glanced at Demi. *Assuming he even has a choice.*

Demi gave her an expectant look. "You can go. Oh, if you see a burly looking guy with brown hair and lots of paperwork flapping about, tell him I'll sign the bloomin' stuff now."

So unqueenly.

Blossom fought the urge to insist she wasn't anyone's errand girl and stalked to the hall with a stiff nod. She had no idea what kind of paperwork the queen had to sign if it was blooming, perhaps something to do with the Flora Court, but until the queen gave her further instructions she was left waiting.

She would serve the crown and the queen with everything she had, if only to avenge the one girl who had shown her true friendship over the years.

Errand girl or not, the true danger was only just beginning, because the unexpected queen of Faerie apparently wasn't someone to be crossed after all.

Present Day

CHAPTER TWO
REYAN

The Illusion Court library had absolutely nothing useful in it.

Reyan chucked the final book from her lap onto the teetering pile on the table in front of her. With a ragged sigh, she lifted her arms to her head and scraped her blonde strands into a ponytail.

Seated across from her in the armchair by the fire, Ace gave her a weary look and folded his muscled arms over his chest.

"You need sleep, and no offence but a shower wouldn't hurt." He risked a smile. "As your official aide courtesy of the royal court, it's my job to look out for you."

Reyan pressed her hands to her eyes in torment. Days had passed since they lost Kainen and Demi to Faerie knew where, the portal underneath the human world sucking them out of sight. Reyan couldn't remember the last time she had changed her clothes or showered. She was pretty sure Meri had delivered some food hours ago, muttering about the court needing a leader.

That stung. Reyan had conceded to managing a lot of the paperwork, beyond confused by the specifics and overwhelmed by the sheer intensity of it, but she hadn't made herself visible to the courtiers since addressing them on her return from the human world.

I was never meant to be lady of a court anyway.

But lady she was, Lady of the Court of Illusions, a

position she was failing at while she skulked in the court library hunting anything that might bring Kainen home to her.

Before she could make some excuse to Ace, the air shivered beside her chair and Meri appeared. She had her usual smart grey suit on and her black hair was perfectly in place, but Reyan took one look at the no-nonsense expression on her stern face and scrunched down in her seat.

"There are things that need tending to," Meri announced. Then, as an afterthought, "Lady."

Reyan nodded. "What kind of things?"

Meri eyed her up and down, a disapproving frown flicking over her face, no less severe half cloaked in the shadowed glow from the fireplace.

"Audiences. The courtiers are growing restless, and with the current situation in such a fragile state you need to be seen."

Reyan groaned. The urge to roll herself small, or better yet dissolve into the shadow completely, filled her limbs until she had to tense them to hide the jittering.

"What does one even do at audiences?" she asked. "I never saw Kainen do them."

Ace slid onto the sofa beside her. "Demi tends to listen to people when she holds hers, then she promises she'll think about whatever they're asking. A timescale for a reply is good too, but remember that this is your court now. You don't have to do anything that doesn't suit you." He caught Meri's eye. "Except maybe do the audiences."

Reyan wiped her hands over her face. Kainen had shown a ridiculous amount of ill-placed faith in her before disappearing. He'd believed in her, insisted she was the lady that he and his court had chosen. If she had to hold audiences to keep the court going, she would muddle through somehow.

"Right, I'll do what I can."

Meri nodded. "Good, about time. Tradition suggests the office so we can filter them through one at a time. I doubt you're in any fit state to hold court in the main hall."

Reyan groaned to her feet, sucking in a breath as she swayed. She grabbed a stale pastry from the tray on the table before Meri could vanish it, but surprisingly Meri didn't suggest she shower or preen herself into a court lady before disappearing to another part of the court.

"She's going easy on me," Reyan muttered.

Ace sighed. "Probably. Just do a couple of audiences for today, get the feel of it. Then I insist you sleep and eat and shower. May I escort you, Lady?"

He flourished his arm and she smiled wearily.

"I remember last time you were here," she said. "Protecting Demi."

Ace grimaced. "Demi was her own kind of chaos and this wasn't her court. It is yours though. You can take ownership of it. They'll follow you the moment you prove you're someone who can lead. I know you can do it."

Without Kainen. The words were there even though he didn't say them.

"I'm no good at any of this," she muttered.

"You haven't tried yet. Yes, it'll be hard and there will probably be people against you." He waved his crooked elbow at her, an invitation. "But that's what I'm here for. I'm your support, so use me."

Reyan slid her hand around his arm and visualised Kainen's office, her connection to her Fae side tingling as she wrapped the purple-grey swirl of the nether that formed the in-between fabric of Faerie around them and

13

translocated them through the court.

The swirl of the nether faded and lights flickered on as the dark green walls of Kainen's office formed around them. Reyan had only been in there once since returning to the court, but the sight of his messy desk strewn with paperwork and his black leather chair with the jacket slung over the back of it standing empty made her frantic with heartsickness.

The lights flickered on automatically and she forced her feet to move around the desk, settling on his chair.

"The translocation is getting easier at least," she said. "I'll ask Meri to get you a seat."

Ace shook his head. "I'll stand. One thing I've learned through the FDP route is to never underestimate a silent person standing."

"I guess Demi has Taz for that, not that she needs anyone as queen."

Ace's brow crinkled and he balanced himself against the edge of the desk.

"Demi needs people the most as she tries to do everything herself. The more power someone has, the more they need friends to rely on."

Reyan sighed, slumping back in the chair. A faint whiff of tangy grapes and fragrant, sweet smoke wafted from the jacket behind her head. She closed her eyes, soaking in the scent of it.

Before she could answer Ace, someone knocked on the door.

Tension shot into her shoulders, anxiety winding knots inside her gut. Ace pushed off the desk and strode to the door, giving her a quick glance to check for permission before swinging it open.

That moment gave Reyan the time she needed to settle

a mask of indifference over her face, to relax her limbs until she was lounging on the chair instead of perching on it. She'd seen Kainen do it a million times, snap his court lord mask into place, and she would do the same.

None of that resolve translated to her nerves the moment she recognised the man stalking past Ace and approaching the desk.

Ciel swept a hand over his silky blonde hair and raised his eyebrows at her. Tall and lithe, he was Kainen's court spider, the spy who twitched through all the gossip webs among the courtiers. But he was also a traitor, at least to Kainen if not also to the queen, and Reyan didn't trust him for a second.

He didn't speak but a sneer grew at the corner of his mouth.

Right, he can't address me unless I wish it.

Kainen had sewn up Ciel's ability to hound her nicely after he tried to coerce her into marrying him, but dealing with him more tiresome when he exploited the situation to make life as difficult for her as possible.

"Yes?" she snapped.

"Meri said you were ready to hold audiences." Ciel clicked his fingers and a large sheet of yellowing paper dropped onto the desk in front of her. "Those are the courtiers waiting."

Reyan grabbed the list, her insides churning as heat burned over her face.

"I take it audiences are the same here as they would be at the queen's court?" Ace asked, his tone hostile.

Reyan looked up to find him glowering at Ciel, broad arms folded across his chest and his stance wide. Ciel eyed him before shrugging.

"I don't know how audiences are done at the queen's

court. Our lord usually sends- *sent* me to fetch people. Who do you want to see first?"

Reyan ignored his habit of talking to her without referring to her as Lady, because pointing it out would only encourage him to bait her.

Instead she stared at the list. She recognised most of the names, none belonging to people she wanted to have to speak to. Weighing up the possibility of doing it alphabetically to purposefully mess with the hierarchy of nobility and cause chaos for the sake of it, she froze as her finger wisped over one name.

Anger flared, white hot and needling through her limbs. Inhaling sharply, she forced the sensation aside. The feeling wasn't borne from any part of her she knew, not like her shadow-merging self or her transmutation gift. No, this was the unexpected gift that had transferred to her from Belladonna Elverhill, a traitor to the crown and leader of the Forgotten and the newly named Blood and Bone court. Reyan had no idea what the gift did, but it felt fiery and powerful.

"*Him*," she whispered.

Ciel sniffed. "Sorry?"

He flinched when she looked up, his eyes widening at the pure vengefulness in hers. She tapped the name and Ace moved over to stand beside her. He seethed through his teeth, his sentiments echoing her own.

"Are you sure?" he asked.

"Absolutely. Ciel, call Lorens in first would you? Also, tell him he really should have the common decency to declare his family name if he's going around demanding audiences with courts."

Ciel blinked. "You want to see him first? Why?"

She braced her hands on the desktop and stood,

gathering a protection warding around her. She forgot often because she could dissipate into shadow when she needed to, but it would make her look weak if she kept dissipating at the first sign of conflict.

"Oh, sorry." She frowned, then smiled with sweet cruelty. "I didn't realise the court hierarchy expected its lady to explain herself. Lorens first, *if you'd be so kind.*"

A scowl flitted across his features before he could school them, but she continued smiling with her teeth gritted until he left the office.

Sagging over the desk, she groaned quietly.

"This is going to be a disaster," she said. "I'm so overwhelmed. I bet I'll end up running the court into the ground. Anything you feel is noteworthy, take it straight to Milo for me, please?"

Ace nodded. "Thank you. Warding up and safety first."

"Lorens can't harm me. Kainen made him vow he wouldn't move against me, same as he did with Ciel. He thought of everything it seems."

She chuckled sadly and Ace rolled his eyes, resuming his wide-legged stance behind her chair as she sat down.

"The boy is absolutely crazy about you. He said as much on our way to rescue you from the human world. I doubt I've seen any man quite so tormented, and I've seen Taz with Demi."

Reyan wiped a hand over her face and settled back against the chair. She didn't have Kainen, but she had his court and his foresight protecting her. She didn't have him, but she had Ace and while it wasn't in any way the same, it was still a huge comfort.

The door swung open again, Ciel entering with Lorens right behind him. Reyan leaned forward to clasp her hands on the desk.

"You'll knock and wait for my permission before you enter from now on," she snapped at Ciel.

He froze, then pressed his mouth thin as he nodded. She waited until he had left again before looking Lorens over.

His brown hair looked longer than it had been a few days ago during the fight with the Forgotten, the ends now lining his jaw. But the narrow, emotionless eyes set in the suspiciously perfect bone structure with flawless Fae skin were obvious signs he was holding a glamour. He was at least honouring the colours of the court in charcoal grey corduroy trousers and a black shirt, but somehow the gesture from him was pure mockery.

Reyan eyed him for a few more moments, drawing out the silence. Lorens stared back with the same irritating smirk she knew him for. Vague memories of screaming, rocks falling and him contorted in pain filled her head, but those hours during the fight in the human world were hazy from panic.

Possible formalities filled through her head.

What can I do for you? Opens up the floor for him to request things I don't want to give. I definitely don't want to waste time on pleasantries.

"Why are you here?" she asked.

Lorens inclined his head, a mocking bow of sorts.

"I find myself in need of a place to stay. I thought where better-"

"You have the whole of Faerie. You also no doubt have an entire host of wiles to trade on and victims to prey on. Why are you really here?"

He didn't react to the interruption, holding himself with no sign of nerves or tension.

"A court is the natural place to seek sanctuary."

Reyan snorted, the incredulous laughter bubbling up.

"And you thought here would be the first place?" She interpreted the truth even as he opened his mouth to answer. "No, the Revel Court is loyal to the queen now, and the Flora Court. If I understand it right, you can't go near the Nether Court again. Tira probably wouldn't allow you to step foot in the Word Court. So that leaves Fauna and us. How am I doing so far?"

He smiled. "Immaculately, Lady."

"Well then. I suppose if Fauna is already under Forgotten control, which I know is the truth after Belladonna kidnapped me there, you wouldn't have anything to gain by lurking around. So you're here hoping to undermine my rule and get information on your enemy. Why would I allow someone like that to take refuge in my court?"

He faked a morose frown, eyes wide with pretend torment.

"Do you really want your first act as a supposed lady to be turning away those in need? I swore to your lord that I would never harm or cross you. How much damage could I do?"

Reyan forced her hands to remain still on the desk even though she wanted to grab the nearest pen or something, anything to fiddle with. The energy roiled under her skin, fighting to obliterate him.

"I'm sure you could manage plenty of damage without doing it yourself."

She glanced at Ace, interpreting the weary rise of his eyebrows.

Kainen would tell me to keep the enemies close, she knew that much. *Actually, Kainen would threaten to destroy him, then follow me around with a warding over my head.*

The thought made her smile, a mix of love and unresolved grief twisting inside her chest.

"Let me put this plainly because I have a lot to do," she said, fixing him with a look. "I'll keep you close and keep you watched. I'll know every person you whisper to in dark corners of my court. I'll learn through you who your allies are here and judge their futures accordingly."

"You'd threaten members of your own court for a mere acquaintance?" he asked, amused.

Reyan leaned back in her chair.

"Oh, I won't threaten anyone. I'm not like your lot. But rumour can be a wonderful thing and nothing passes information around like the gossip mill at a court."

She knew that was definitely accurate. Even in her recent isolation since returning to court and announcing she was their lady until Kainen returned, the courtiers and staff alike were laughing at her, mocking her and doubting her.

Lorens smiled wide. "True. I suppose there's no sense in us discussing any possible advantages of colluding-"

"None," she snapped. "I don't know whether you're against the queen because of the whole traditional blood-traitor nonsense or you simply think it should be you somehow. Maybe you're the kind of royalist that thinks Belladonna should be next in line, or maybe you'll reveal you were somehow the long lost son of the Old King here to claim your "rightful" title. I don't care. Cross me, or my court, and you're banned."

He laughed, his eyes sparking with an unnerving amount of consideration.

"Consider me warned, Lady. We'll play the necessary games. My own agenda reaches much further than the petty squabbles of courts."

Reyan nodded. "Oh don't worry, we all know exactly how far-reaching those are. Off you go then. We'll be watching you."

Lorens gave her a disbelieving look and walked to the door. She thought he'd give some parting shot but he simply walked out and closed the door behind him.

Reyan let her body drop forward, her head thudding gently on the desk.

"You held yourself really well," Ace insisted.

Reyan grunted. "He was toying with me the whole time."

"They all do that though so consider it an introduction. The nobles will probably expect a lot more pandering to."

Reyan lifted her head, horror filling her face. Ace took one look and chuckled.

"Come on, I'll be beside you the whole time."

She shook her head. "I'm grateful you're here, but I keep trying to work out what Kainen would have done."

"Shout at people?" he suggested.

"Flirt with them until they conceded or passed out more like." She rubbed a hand over her face. "Everyone's right though. You, Meri, the rumour mill. I'm not being a great lady of a court at the moment."

"What would he have told you to do?"

She had been trying to figure that out for every tiny situation she faced, but as she sank back against the chair and inhaled the already fading scent of him from his jacket, she knew what he would say.

"He'd tell me to give them something to gossip about. It's all a show, the whole thing. A pretence. But I've been trying to pretend to be him, who he pretends to be."

She stood up and eyed the multi-way door that would take her anywhere in the court she needed to go.

"I'll be back in a few minutes. If Ciel reappears, I'm taking a brief break."

Ace hesitated. "And after that?"

She stalked to the multi-way door and swung it open.

"After that, I'll hold the rest of today's audiences in the main hall. They want to whisper in corners? I'll give them everything to whisper about in plain sight."

She didn't give Ace a chance to answer, stepping through to Kainen's bedroom and letting the door slam behind her. She ignored Kainen's bed, still mussed up from her sleeping in it earlier, and the general opulence of the rocky walls decorated in dark green. She only had eyes for one part of the room. The jacket had given her an idea and she opened the door to his wardrobe, choking down a half-hysterical laugh.

The insides of the wardrobe had one side neat and folded with shirts and jackets hanging. The other side was a complete chaos pile of jeans, socks and t-shirts.

She reached into the chaos side and pulled out a smoky charcoal shirt. He'd obviously worn it once, thrown it on the floor and someone, Meri probably, had refused to wash it after a short use and thrown it onto his messy pile instead.

Reyan tugged off her cardigan and pulled the shirt on over her vest top. The shirt was baggy but she could roll up the sleeves well enough with the bottom hems knotted over her ribs. She would wear a piece of Kainen if she couldn't have the real him.

Her fingers settled over the pendant around her neck, the dark onyx stone wrapped in silver that all ladies of the Illusion Court wore. He'd chosen her. The court itself had chosen her. Giving her grubby trousers a weary look, she went back through the multi-way door into her own

22

bedroom that adjoined Kainen's.

Moping around won't help anyone, least of all him. He needs a court to come back to.

She changed into fresh grey jeans and pulled on her sturdiest boots. Eying the dagger Kainen had gifted her a while ago, she deliberated over not taking it with her, but in the end she tied the holder to her belt loop and scraped her hands through her lacklustre blonde hair.

Ace was right about the need to eat and shower, but she would give the court their show to hold them until she could lead them from a stronger place.

By the time she returned to the office to find Ace spinning around in Kainen's chair, her misery had settled to a simmer. There would be time in private to worry later.

"Ah, now that looks like a she-devil of the Illusion Court," Ace teased. "Much better."

Reyan sighed. "If you don't have it, fake it. I just hope wherever he is, he's okay. Demi too."

Ace stood and held out his hand. Reyan hesitated, but even Kainen would trust her with Ace. Probably not anyone else, but Ace was safe. She took the outstretched hand.

"Trust me, I don't envy anyone that comes up against Kainen these days, especially now he'll be trying to get back to you," he promised. "Demi will do anything for her people as well, especially not leaving them alone with Taz while he's throwing a tantrum."

Reyan had heard the legendary extent of Taz's tantrums, but considering she was missing Kainen she could easily understand where he was coming from.

"Ready?" Ace asked.

Reyan nodded. "Let's give them an entrance then. Hold on."

She gathered the nether around them, the grey-purple swirl obscuring her vision until the main hall settled around them.

The underground cavern was lit by firelight which meant another day had already passed her by. She glanced up at the skyholes hewn into the ceiling, but there was no sign of sunlight. Banners in the Illusion Court colours of charcoal and silver hung from balconies, each one now piped through with strands of pale lilac. Kainen had done that for her so soon after they started their supposedly fake engagement.

Was it still fake back then for him?

Whispers flew across the crowd, the rustle turning to a buzz as she dropped Ace's hand and stalked toward the pool in the centre of the hall. Lit by the firelight, the pool had miniature wooden decks floating on the water, a circle of them surrounding one larger raised platform covered with charcoal grey drapes.

It was the official seat of the lord of the court, Kainen's personal chair a king-size lounging recliner. Reyan knew he'd never used it, refused to point blank because he never wanted to be like his father who had loved meting out cruelty from his high perch. He'd even gotten rid of them initially, but the nobles made such a commotion about losing their decks that he'd conceded and brought them back again.

She didn't have Kainen's pedigree or his natural charm to trade on, but she had one or two assets still. As she walked up the couple of steps to the wooden platform with her head held high, she called through the shadows.

I know I told you to look for Kainen, but if you're around, I could use your presence.

She reached the enormous bed on the main deck and

24

considered lounging on it, but sank cross-legged instead.

"Sit with me," she told Ace, letting dominance coat her tone.

He nodded. "Of course, Lady."

He sat beside her, his knee firm against her thigh. She had his support and he knew that her persona in front of her court was only for show.

Ciel strode toward them, stopping at the edge of the bed. Reyan wrapped her warding tight around her and raised her eyebrows up at him.

He grimaced and conceded to a tiny bob of his head.

"No bow?" she asked, her voice filling the hall. "Something you'd like to raise instead?"

Ciel's eyes narrowed but after a tense hesitation, he lowered his shoulders.

Reyan caught the subtle tension in the crowd before she could address him again, her sharp hearing picking out sudden squeaks and huffs of alarm. The shadows shivered around her and she smiled, reaching out a hand to the shadow-snake wisping over the bed to curl beside her.

She nodded to Ciel, taking strength from Betty in her shadow-form on one side and Ace as a solid added protection on the other.

"I'm feeling chatty today," she announced. "Ciel, why don't you show me who you think should have the next audience, and I'll judge your choice accordingly?"

Present Day Somewhere Entirely 'Other'

CHAPTER THREE
DEMI

Being a queen is exhausting. Being a queen in a place that doesn't feel like part of my realm deep in my bones is scary as hell.

I sat up with the memories of how I ended up in this situation swirling around in my head, pissed that I didn't think to keep clear of the painting portal without Taz beside me.

He'll be going absolutely frantic. I clutched my arms around my knees as the unfamiliar world swayed around me. *Come on Demi, FDP training – think and act calmly. First step, figure out why I feel weird and if I have my gifts still. Second step-*

A soft groaning noise caught my ears and I lifted my hand on instinct, the relief pluming in my chest like a blessing as a shaky protection warding knitted around me. With my panic levelling out, I scanned the immediate area.

Trees towered above with pinkish brown trunks, wider than I could wrap my arms around and with some kind of lumpy bark I'd never seen before. Far above, gold and yellow leaves formed a thick ceiling that kept warm air in and any wind out. Not the weirdest thing I'd ever seen in Faerie, but again that subtle chime came from deep inside me that whispered I wasn't even in Faerie any longer.

I grabbed my orb out of my pocket, sliding my thumb through the keychain loop and holding the large white marble in my palm.

"Taz?" I waited but no face appeared. "Message Taz:

Are you getting this?"

Nothing.

Taz, can you hear me? I sent my thoughts through to him with the mind-speak link we shared.

Still nothing, which left me alone in a random place with no idea where I was or how to get home.

A scrabbling noise filled the air.

Not alone after all.

I scanned the area with nerves biting at my insides. The forest surrounded me in a swathe of pale green grass and light brown undergrowth, but there was one blot on the otherwise peaceful landscape.

Kainen Hemlock, Lord of the Illusion Court, scrambled to his feet with one hand on the nearest tree trunk, his other hand already holding up a black orb. His brown hair was usually artfully mussed, part of his court lord persona, but now it was an absolute mess, much like his pinched, startled face and the rips in his clothing.

"Reyan? Rey?" Kainen scrunched his face up. "Reyan, in the name of Faerie, answer me!"

Memories swirled, my head spinning as I remembered the fight with the Forgotten and the painted wall in a tunnel underneath the human world. The painting had turned into a skip-way and dumped me and Kainen in wherever the hell we were.

He stood with his eyes tight shut as an ooze of blood leaked out of the gash in his leather jacket. I gave him a few more seconds before clearing my throat. He twisted around in alarm, his gaze spinning across the forest until he found me. A thrum of foreboding trickled through me and I kept my warding strong. For all his recent redemption, I had no guarantee that would remain without Reyan there to soften him.

"We went through the painting," he mumbled, realisation dawning on his face.

I nodded. "Life and death, light and shadow. We had all four in the same place, Lolly's earth gift and Tyren's ability to cling to death. Faerie knows how deep his power runs with that. Then Reyan has the shadows."

"What about light?" he asked.

I noticed how he was hesitant to approach me, but I couldn't guess whether it was because he didn't want to alarm me or didn't trust my strength as queen. My gifts felt scratchy under my skin which wasn't normal, like they'd taken on tiny lives of their own and were exploring me for the first time like their new playground.

"Tira." I remembered the flicker of flame at her fingertip. "She can conjure flame. Put those four together and apparently whoever was nearest got sucked in."

Kainen glanced around again, his face twisting with anguish.

"We need to get back then. Belladonna won't stop until she wins, and Reyan still hasn't been fully accepted by some of the court."

The panic in his voice sounded real enough, his worry for his girlfriend encompassing all else.

Fake girlfriend technically, although the only people stupid enough to believe that now is them.

I couldn't dredge up a smile at that but the thought was there somewhere. I clambered to my feet with a grunt and pulled a wad of cloth for wrapping wounds out of the worn satchel hanging across my back.

"Here, take this. Your arm's bleeding."

Kainen looked down at his wound and frowned at it. With a wince and a shrug of his shoulders he eased out of his jacket and inspected the damage.

"Arrow went clean through the side of it," he mused. "Oh, thanks."

I held myself firm as he walked toward me, then doubted myself and threw the cloth the rest of the distance. If he guessed I was uneasy about him getting too close he didn't show it, catching the cloth and winding it around his arm.

"What now then?" he asked.

His guess was as good as mine but as queen I technically overruled him.

"We start walking," I suggested. "Once we find someone to ask, we figure out how to get home. There's something the enemy want here, whether it's people to fight for them or a new place to tear apart, I'm not sure."

Kainen nodded. "Alright, I'm following you. Which way though?"

With absolutely no idea and no way to see through the trees, I shrugged and pointed in a random direction.

"Seems less woody that way," I said. He didn't look convinced. "At least we didn't land in a bog."

I expected some kind of argument, maybe an element of him trying to pull rank or sound like he knew better than I did, but he only inched back into his jacket and set off in the direction I'd pointed to.

Uneasy, I set off after him with my body aching and my gifts rioting in my limbs. We hadn't spent more than a couple of minutes alone for a long time, not since I'd spent a week being trapped and tortured at the Illusion Court. I still woke up with nightmares sometimes, but he didn't need to know that. Whenever he'd admitted to feeling guilt over his part in it he sounded genuine enough.

As we trampled over the roots and briars amid the tangle of grass, I sought for something to break the silence.

Other than a strange, swooping birdsong now and then, we were utterly alone.

"Are your gifts feeling… odd?" I asked.

He nodded. "I usually feel them restless if I've been holding court for too long without using them, but this is a wholly different type of irritation. It's like they're tattooed on my bones and fighting to get out."

At least it's not just me then.

I tried to keep my thoughts on the situation and my gaze trained on our surroundings, but worry kept spiking into my gut every time I thought about Taz at home. He would know to get everyone out and back to Arcanium safely, or Cheryl would at least, but he'd be panicking without me.

"I have to ask," Kainen asked, then hesitated. "Is it 'my queen' or 'Demi' while we're here?"

I frowned, unnerved by the sudden formality.

"Demi's fine. I don't hear 'my queen' as often as you might think. Not at home anyway. Also, no mentioning who we are or who we were fighting until we know a bit more."

"Got it. If it's any consolation, I just want to get home. No evil plans or designs or anything. Figured it'd be worth saying in case."

Assuming lies still aren't possible here, wherever here is. The thought hit me followed by a huge swell of guilt.

"Thanks. She'll be okay, you know, Reyan. She's strong-willed and sensible."

He grimaced. "I don't know. The court don't exactly accept her yet and with the Forgotten sniffing about, some might try to overthrow her without me. Will Taz be okay do you think?"

"Um, pass." I snorted loudly. "He'll be going crazy, I know that much. Whether he'll be sensible enough to do all the stuff he should be doing, we'll have to see. Assuming we make it home. But I have Milo and Ace and a whole bunch of protocol Milo got all excited about for that, and at least we have someone on the enemy side now."

It slipped out without me meaning it to. Kainen stopped dead and it took me a couple of paces before I found the strength to turn back.

"You have someone on their side reporting back to you?" he asked.

Crud.

I stared at his shoulder, not great with eye contact at the best of times, let alone when he was staring at me like I'd grown two heads and sprouted horns.

"Yeah, kind of." I wondered if that would be enough, but then perhaps he of all people deserved to know who.

"Is it Blossom?" he asked.

That distracted me. "Blossom? Why her?"

He shrugged and slid his hands in his pockets. I tensed. Even with my warding up, there was still a section of my mind on high alert.

"Why else would she be rolled in as my supposed bride?" he asked, his tone glib. "To keep an eye on me and my court while still being Queen Tavania's daughter. I never considered it, not really. I figured she was being sent in as a test of our loyalties. But now you've said that it's kind of obvious."

I bit my lip. "Yeah, okay. It was an idea she had floated in those first few days after we won, Queen Tavania I mean. She wanted May to go to the Word Court or the Fauna Court to strengthen our positions there. When Blossom came asking for safety, I told her she was bound for the Illusion Court. Then you kind of hijacked that plan."

Kainen stayed silent and I wondered if he was waiting for me to explain or to brush him off, to dismiss the question.

"How… when? And why?" he asked eventually.

"Where and what and who," I finished. He didn't laugh. "Blossom approached me shortly after I became queen. Said she wanted to be on the right side because of what Elvira and her lot had done to Alannah."

Understanding dawned over his face. I couldn't help wondering how close he'd been to Blossom in previous times, but I had bountiful experience of saying the wrong thing so I kept quiet, letting him process it.

"It all fits now," he mumbled. "I saw Blossom with Belladonna at the Nether Court and she seemed to be fumbling. Then she made a couple of mistakes fighting as well and she's never usually careless, not from what I remember anyway. I never even considered any of them might be trying for their own kind of redemption."

He grimaced in apology and another wash of guilt hit me. Taz told me over and over that I had nothing to feel guilty about, that the torture I'd experienced at Kainen's hands and in his court wasn't my burden to bear. But Kainen had been trying so hard to redeem himself since, and he hadn't exactly had much of a choice back then either.

Unless he really is as good at acting and playing the long game as I always feared.

I pushed the thought away, the fear sinking back down where it joined a whole pit of other potential fears. Rehashing our past wouldn't get us back home.

Firming my warding around me, I set off again through the trees. Even with his admissions, I wasn't risking letting my guard down, not yet.

The land dipped but the forest seemed endless. We had no way of knowing if we were headed in the right direction or if we'd get any kind of favourable reception when we finally found someone, but we had to get out of the forest before nightfall. Even with my gifts still inside me, I didn't want to risk using them while they felt weird, not unless I had to.

"Shhh." Kainen flung out an arm in front of me.

It bounced against my protection and recognition flickered in his eyes as he lowered it, but I didn't see any sign of him looking upset at my mistrust. I could hear the subtle crunch now, footsteps in the undergrowth.

"Behind a tree," I whispered.

I'd intended for us to use the same tree but I moved left and he moved right, splitting us apart. I summoned my fairy connection to the fore, unnerved at how powerfully it tingled through my hand. Kainen had his hand aloft too, a swathe of shadow and black sparks roiling around his fingertips.

"Hello?" A hesitant male voice echoed through the silence.

I pressed my finger to my lips. Kainen nodded and we both peered around our trees at the same time as I thanked every single blessed entity I could think of that part of qualifying as an FDP was being given the gift of linguistics transference. I had no idea what language we might be hearing, but it would come across as English to us all the same.

"I- I'm- I can protect myself," the wavering voice insisted, not sounding entirely sure. "If you're bandits, I don't have anything of value. If you're not, you really should get out of the forest before nightfall. You know, because bandits."

There was a strange, lyrical lilt to the accent which belonged to a skinny teenage boy with black hair and round pink cheeks. He might have been my age or a year or two younger, with brown trousers and a faded matching waistcoat a few sizes too big for him over a tight grubby shirt.

"I am going to walk away now," he announced.

He might be the only person we saw for days and we were running out of time as it was.

"Um, hi."

I stepped out from behind the tree with my most reassuring smile, determined to get him on side given how uneasy he sounded.

It was a good plan, all things considered, until he saw me and jumped about six feet in the air.

"Oh, sorry." I frowned as he pressed a hand to his chest. "I didn't mean to startle you."

He stared wide-eyed as Kainen stepped out as well.

"We're not bandits, if that helps," I added.

Kainen's smile must have been way more reassuring than mine, his natural gift oozing out of him as he relaxed his gaze and held both hands up.

"We're honestly not," he said. "We ended up here and need to find the nearest safe town or village. Even a passing inn would do."

As the boy finished huffing at the mere sight of me, I dropped my hands into my sleeves and tapped my thumb over my fingertips irritably.

I'm not that scary am I? He doesn't even know I'm a queen yet.

But one thing being a queen had taught me was when to concede to better skills than mine, and Kainen had charm in spades when he needed it.

"Can you tell us which way to go?" he asked.

The boy nodded slowly. He was taller than me by half a head and maybe even had an inch on Kainen too, but he also looked like he hadn't quite grown into his ears yet.

"The nearest place of any importance is ages away," the boy said. "But there's a wise woman who lives not far from here. She sometimes lets me stay in her barn if I don't get home before night comes."

Kainen nodded sagely. "Very sensible. We'd be delighted to meet her. We're very far from home, you see."

The boy didn't look very convinced but he pointed through the trees in the direction we'd been walking.

"It's this way. You can follow me, if you want," he offered.

I tried another gentle smile, apparently not my forte. "What's your name?"

"I, um… M-Muriel. My friends- well, people who know me, call me MC, because my middle name is Curdle."

He blinked at me in some kind of awed terror and I glanced down to see if my skin was glowing or sparking or giving off some kind of sign that I was in any way powerful. I'd been to realms in Faerie where magic wasn't common and if this really was the fabled prime realm, they might be similar.

I wasn't glowing or sparking. I couldn't see anything unusual about me, but Kainen was already striding toward our new friend with one arm held out.

"Lead the way then, MC. It's nice to meet you. I'm Kainen, and this is Demi. So, where exactly are we?"

CHAPTER FOUR
BLOSSOM

The remnants of the once lively Revel Court were deserted. Blossom wandered past stalls with tattered awnings that had once been full of wares and cafes that no longer rang with the merry sounds of people.

She lifted a hand and let it trail over a brown hedge surrounding one of the pricier ateliers. It hadn't taken long for the pristine topiaries of the priciest establishments to go to ruin with nobody to prune and water them. Mere days after the Lord of Revels had been denounced as a traitor, the market magically upped and moved. Almost literally like magic, because one day they were there and the next the air was almost silent. Some had remained of course, those loyal to the new Blood and Bone Court that had crept into the marketplace and taken over the castle further up the hill. But most of the original Revel Court had fled to the Flora Court's realm. Blossom envied them.

I shouldn't even be thinking these things. She frowned at a pile of broken crockery in front of her feet. *If anyone realised I'm doubting, I'd be flayed or worse.*

But doubt was there all the same, or rather the gritty knowledge scratching under her skin that she was playing a very dangerous game by staying at the Blood and Bone Court. She'd played her part well enough for the past year, but she hadn't had any instructions from anyone linked to the queen in a long while now.

"Blossom."

The unyielding tone she'd once tried to imitate as a

child now sent chills rippling right to the bone. She took a deep breath and exhaled slow and steady as she turned to face Belladonna.

Similar in their honey blonde hair and brown eyes, Blossom had spent her entire childhood trying to be like her sister. She'd copied the fancy fitted suits and kept a similar long hairstyle. But now she feared the very sight of her, the shivers breaking out over her skin whenever she heard Belladonna call her name.

"What are you doing out here?" Belladonna demanded.

Blossom shrugged, fighting the urge to play with her bracelet, a nervous reaction Belladonna would notice and take interest in immediately.

"Wandering. Thinking."

"Well don't. You're not here to think, especially after what happened in the human world."

The accusation would have stung once, the implication that she was useless, but now it rolled aside before the barb could take effect. She had to act a tiny bit hurt though, or Belladonna would wonder why she was so calm, so collected.

"I apologised over and over for that," she said. "What are you doing out here? Can't imagine you're looking for me of all people."

"So what if I am? You start wandering places and people will ask questions."

People like you. Blossom started walking toward her sister.

Peace was a hard thing to come by for Fae, but getting time to herself around Belladonna was proving to be harder than she remembered from before her moral 'awakening'. Appeasing her sister with the utmost petulance took so much mental effort, but Blossom had no other choice.

Not since-

"Lorens will be leading the charge on the Illusion Court to redeem himself after failing at the Word Court," Belladonna reminded her. "But our brother still has mother in his pocket, and the Word, Flora and Fauna courts. Revels barely counts after their treachery. But if we can take the Illusion Court from that low-born nothing, we can grow. We can storm Arcanium and turn the tide while the queen is gone."

Blossom thought of the last time she'd seen their brother. Taz had been glowering at her, not a wholly unusual occurrence considering he used to be their punching bag when they were bored as kids. With the courts in disarray and the queen disappeared, presumably to the prime realm, Belladonna's time to strike had finally come.

Blossom had done her best to help a couple of servants escape over the last two days, the odd slip of a key in the wrong place, or leaving the wrong door open. Belladonna didn't even notice, but Lorens would if he was going to be returning for any length of time.

She said none of that as Belladonna clamped a hand on her shoulder.

"Take me to the Fauna Court," she demanded.

Blossom pulled her Fae connection close and wearily focused her efforts on realm-skipping. As the nether wisped around them in a swirl of purple-grey haze, she didn't whine about being dragged somewhere without being told why. She simply obeyed.

The landscape of the Fauna Court settled around them, the warmth of the sun beaming down on the rolling fields and fertile forest. Blossom eyed the place with a sinking heart.

The main entrance, a large wooden structure with two open sides like a tunnel, was deserted. A few people scattered as they noticed Belladonna, and her too probably, but she couldn't blame them. The last time she and Belladonna had been to the Fauna Court, Belladonna had impersonated Lord Rydon's daughter and stolen the lady of the Illusion Court.

"What's the matter with you?" Belladonna snapped. "Is this because of the whole humiliating you in front of the court thing? You know I have to set an example. If I show favouritism to family, it makes me look weak. Do you want to be a sitting target?"

Favouritism to family was basically ramrodded through Fae genetics and Belladonna used it obsessively when it suited her. The moment they'd returned from the human world after escaping from something called a police station, Belladonna had gathered her minions and tortured Blossom personally.

Aside from the agonising pain, Blossom had taken the public punishment with shame burning inside her as Belladonna's Blood and Bone Court laughed and sneered at her. Even deeper down though, the whole thing only fanned the tiny flickering flame that told her she was doing the right thing.

After what had happened to Alannah, the doubt had settled in. She'd watched the almost cultish mania drive Alannah to support Elvira and the Old King in the hopes of reinstating her disgraced family line. Watched as the adoration turned into sycophantic hostility. Watched as she became the puppet of the Apocalyptians at Elvira's insistence, a mere resource to be used. Watched as the essences of lust, pride and greed sucked the life out of her for fun, then diligence and virtue shamed the last vestiges of her mind for it until there was nothing left of her. Death had been a kindness in the end.

But Belladonna had laughed and called Alannah weak. That turned Blossom's head in the opposite direction because one day she would be next. She didn't like her brother or the new queen but the chances of them torturing her, mentally or physically, were slim.

So, betraying the sister she once idolised became the only way to end the war and the insanity it was causing.

She opened her mouth for a suitably bland answer but never got the chance.

The air shivered in front of them and Blossom's heart sank ever further to see Lorens materialise. Not many people could realm-skip into various courts at will, only court lords or ladies and regents, but Lorens seemed to have many gifts.

With Queen Demerara stuck Faerie knows where, the courts are almost leaderless. I doubt mother will bother getting off her throne either, too busy raising May to be her identical doll.

Blossom pushed aside the age-old bitterness, barely even feeling it sting anymore. As the youngest, May was the apple of their mother's eye, the sweet-hearted innocent that shouldn't be exposed to the avaricious mores of Fae society. As the crown prince and only one year older than May, Taz had been fed to the wolves in preparation for his future instead.

Lorens strode toward them and cast a glance around to check for any potential eavesdroppers.

"How are we doing?" he asked, his voice velvety.

"We're awaiting your update," Belladonna said, her voice rising a note. "I've been playing with the captured Fae back at our court, but we need to attack Arcanium as soon as we can. Will you be joining us?"

He flicked a dismissive glance at her, one she actually preened into with amusement, as though his dismissiveness were as affectionate as flirting.

"I've made myself known at the Illusion Court," he said. "I can't personally move against her, Kainen saw to that, but I can create some discord so that others do. I've introduced myself to her of course, made it known I'm lingering, unsettled her. She should fold easily enough."

Blossom crunched her hand into a fist, knowing that would make enough of a statement to them about her feelings on the matter of Reyan, the supposed Lady of the Illusion Court. Having to go there months ago and pretend to be obsessed with Kainen Hemlock was a totally embarrassing pain, but thankfully her animosity for Reyan was real. Some might call it jealousy but Reyan's family lineage was non-existent now, and someone like that would never be fit to rule a court. No training, no upbringing, no breeding.

Bad enough we have a fairy as queen now, even if I have to be loyal to her, let alone a low-born Fae dragging one of our oldest courts through the dirt.

"I can't talk to you like that," Belladonna huffed, her tone straying perilously close to whining. "Take your glamour off."

Lorens smiled, his mouth curving wide and dangerous.

"Trying to trick me into proving my true identity, Belladonna? And what if I say no? Are you going to make me? Oh of course, you can't. Your gifts are gone."

Belladonna's shoulders stiffened, her arms vibrating with tense energy. She glanced around to make sure nobody from the Fauna Court had heard, but they were giving her an exceptionally big space.

Blossom grimaced as Lorens mentioned Belladonna's missing gifts. Another reason for Belladonna punishing her was that she'd 'accidentally' summoned all Belladonna's Fae gifts into Reyan. They were supposed to go to Demi, but she'd stumbled because Reyan was trying to impale her on a sword at the time. Wildly inconvenient, but still safer with her than with Belladonna.

Lorens laughed. With a shudder of his shoulders, he dropped his glamour. His brown locks wriggled, disappearing until only a head of short, greying hair remained. The willowy figure shortened until the three of them were almost the same average height, and the agelessly handsome face widened into a wizened one. Even the stylish frock coat and flouncy-hemmed trousers morphed, the dark blue boilersuit looking out of place in the derelict court grounds.

"Ah, now you look like Emil again," Belladonna said.

Emil nodded, shaking off his Lorens persona as easily as breathing.

"I am more comfortable in my natural form," he admitted. "I've spoken with my contact in the Prime Realm and told him to keep an eye out for Demerara. In the meantime, we should continue our plan to gain control of Faerie."

Belladonna smiled. "Oh, we are. What brings you here anyway? Are you going to accompany us back to the Blood and Bone Court? I have a few souls I haven't interrogated yet."

Blossom clenched her gut muscles as a wave of sickness bubbled up. Belladonna had such a gleam in her eye at the thought of people she hadn't had a chance to torture yet.

Emil seemed to be thinking something over, his eyes narrowed as Belladonna stared back at him. She'd always idolised him, and Emil had been around since before both of them were born. Blossom had once asked if Belladonna saw him as something of a father, and Belladonna had sneered that fathers weren't of much use to princesses with a queen for a mother. But in her darkness the last few nights, Blossom had realised the insidious truth. Emil had targeted Belladonna young, seeing ruthlessness and a lack of compassion in the way she'd push her siblings simply to see how badly she could hurt them, or how she'd manipulate and torture creatures and Fae alike for fun.

"I'm going straight back to the Illusion Court to sow the necessary chaos," he said. "But you're welcome to attack Arcanium. I'd say sooner rather than later too. The Fae in your dungeon will keep but Arcanium haven't yet experienced your special blend of torment, and isn't that a shame?"

Belladonna grinned. "Finally."

Blossom kept her steps slow, letting them move a few paces ahead as they reached the kitchen door. With any luck they'd rush off and Belladonna would forget her for a few hours. She hadn't had any opportunity to contact Taz or anyone at Arcanium, not that anyone would know she was secretly on their side if she did. But if Belladonna took her with them when they attacked, she could find Taz.

I should warn them.

She had no way of doing it though, not without Belladonna finding out on the orb-waves. By naming herself Lady of the Blood and Bone Court, Belladonna had very little power to wield from it, but as followers came and swore loyalty to her, the court began to take strength. It was power enough that Belladonna was able to put many safeties in place for herself, including being able to monitor and eavesdrop on orb communications in the

44

bounds of her court.

I don't have a single friend left who would help me take a message either.

The loneliness ate away at her, grief for Alannah and curdling anger at her sister and Emil tangling a sharp web inside her head.

"Are you sure you don't have time?" Belladonna asked, that subtle whine still in her voice.

Emil sighed. "Alright, just one. Then I need to get back. We do have a reckoning to unleash after all. Now, I've heard whispers that Lord Rydon is becoming increasingly belligerent which is why I'm here."

Belladonna nodded. "I've heard the same. Let's go and enquire, shall we?"

Blossom followed a few steps behind. She tried her hardest to avoid being around when Belladonna decided to torment people, but it wasn't always avoidable. Standing there with a mask of emotionless boredom on her face while her insides were threatening to upend her last meal took all her strength.

"Ah, Lord Rydon." Belladonna stalked toward the wary-eyed troll. "I hear we have a little insurrection on our hands."

Lord Rydon, burly shouldered and gruff, folded his arms across his chest. He had scrapes over the moss-brown skin and some discolouration on his cheek suggested bruising.

"Insurrection?"

Belladonna nodded, leaning close. "Yes. I heard *dreadful* reports of a bridge that was sturdy and standing for 500 years being torn down just as some of our supporters were crossing it. Apparently, four of them died."

Lord Rydon huffed. "If they were block-headed enough to march across and ignore the weight restriction sign, that's their doing."

Emil tapped his foot, a similar tutting noise echoing from his lips.

"We've also heard tales of loose animals wrecking the camp we've been building," he said.

"Animals get loose. That's why we don't build shoddy camps."

Belladonna tapped him on the chest with a taloned forefinger. Her nails were painted blood red today, and when the memory of Elvira surfaced in Blossom's mind, the memory of Alannah seesawed up immediately after.

"We may need to consider your 'elevation' to lord then if you can't keep control of this court," Belladonna taunted. "I don't approve of elevations personally, rather than being titled by family and by blood."

Blossom saw the gleeful malice spark in her sister's eyes seconds before the flash of the blade hit the light. Lord Rydon's gaze never faltered, his eyes fixed on Belladonna as he jerked forward and headbutted her in the face.

"You absolute-"

Belladonna pressed a hand to her nose now gushing blood as Lord Rydon choked. Blossom's insides twisted at the same time Belladonna's knife did, until Lord Rydon dropped to the floor.

Blossom breathed in slowly to stem the sudden urge to run, to scream, to do anything other than look supremely unconcerned that her sister was a murderer and a psycho.

"Well, at least that's done with." Belladonna wiped her knife and glamoured the blood from her face. "I'm going to see the healer."

"What about the court?" Blossom asked before she

could stop herself.

Belladonna eyed her for a moment. "You manage it, but from a distance. I still need you for now. I'm sure there'll be some squabbles from the other courts, but our lot here will keep them in line until we've done what we need to do."

A loud scream filled the air and Blossom closed her eyes in torment that it couldn't have waited a few more seconds for Belladonna to disappear.

Nobody moved as Lord Rydon's daughter stumbled onto her knees beside her father. She closed his eyes, sobbing quietly, her hands smoothing over his body.

"Oh get up," Belladonna snapped.

The young woman, Cerys, stilled. Several moments passed and Blossom wondered in that moment whether she should simply let nature unfold. Cerys looked strong enough to fight, and she might even be able to strangle Belladonna before the blade could make another appearance.

Blossom eyed Emil, not likely to allow Belladonna to come to any actual harm unless he wished it, as Cerys stood up.

"I vow you this," Cerys swore, her voice deadly calm. "I will have vengeance for my father." She sped on before Belladonna could talk over her. "You might not care about Faerie or its courts, but if you don't want hundreds of angry nobles on her hands, you'll leave this particular court my care."

Belladonna's finger tapped the hilt of her knife, her head tilting as though she was considering it. Blossom recognised the flickering gaze, a sure sign her sister was assessing the best and most painful way to strike. The thought of another death filled her head with so much anxiety it felt like she might burst, and she garbled out the first thing she could think of.

"You might as well," she drawled, forcing herself to stay in character. "I'm going to be too busy for this to be more than a dummy title for me. Let the nobles run around and the menial Fae care about placating them."

Cerys glared at her, but Blossom only had eyes for her sister.

Nausea rose in her gut, swirling fast because for once in their lives, Belladonna almost looked impressed. Going one further to protect those who apparently were part of 'her' court now, Blossom frowned.

"Didn't you say you had people to torment?" she asked.

Belladonna's eyes brightened further.

"Absolutely. Come on then."

Blossom steadied herself as the hand clamped onto her elbow this time, and it took all her strength and focus to skip them back to the kitchens of the old Revel Court castle.

She wouldn't concede to calling it the Blood and Bone Court, at least not in her own mind. It was a tiny flicker of rebellion, but it kept her from collapsing, or worse, crying.

Emil appeared beside them moments later and Blossom breathed a sigh of relief as he and Belladonna disappeared into the bowels of the castle.

Blossom stayed put in the kitchens. Several frightened Fae were rushing about to get the evening meal ready, not the confident team of professionals that the Revel Court were famed for but leftover members of the court and people who didn't flee the market in time. Blossom wanted to tell them to run while they still could, but she assumed they would have done so already if they had a way out.

She, on the other hand, did have a way out. Belladonna

would want her summoning gift when they attacked Arcanium, so she would be going with them. When she got there, she would find Taz and ask for sanctuary.

With her fingers ghosting over the orb in her pocket, she sighed and turned back in the doorway to look at the derelict market at the bottom of the hill.

If she warned Taz in any way that an attack was coming and Belladonna found out, the attack might not happen and she would be stuck with her sister for longer.

No warning anyone. Nobody else is going to look out for me, so I'll have to do it myself.

Either way, she had a sinking feeling that her part in the whole thing wasn't going to end well at all.

CHAPTER FIVE
DEMI

The strange forest seemed to go on forever and the lengthening shadows suggested we'd be walking through the night. MC insisted we were in the woods, which didn't help in any way whatsoever, but he also insisted that he knew someone who would be able to help us better than he could. Without any idea of what we might be facing, following him was our only option.

Every few minutes I tried sending mind-speak to Taz but our bond was eerily silent. He'd be panicking something savage, storming around at home issuing orders about finding us. I had no fear of that but last time I'd gone missing he threatened to destroy half our friends as well.

"How far is this place?" I risked asking.

MC's wide eyes drifted to me, blinking rapidly. With Kainen between us that provided a small buffer but the boy seemed absolutely petrified by the mere sight of me. I couldn't rule out the Prime Realm having some kind of view into Faerie either, so it was possible people here might recognise who I was.

"Um, it's not far now. Almost there really."

That would have to do. Every particle of my body ached and my head was swimming with exhaustion. I wanted my bed. I wanted Taz. I wanted to go home.

Some queen. I breathed in deep and forced myself to keep going.

"No family around to worry about you out after dark?" Kainen asked.

MC shook his head. "No, I had a mother but she left. I had a sister too, but she left. Camora took me in and lets me stay if I run errands for her. I had a dad too, but he-"

"Left?" I asked, way more grouchily than I should have done.

Kainen shot me a weary look.

"Yes, how did you know?" MC asked.

I decided not to reply to that and didn't dare let my thoughts drift to my own family back in the human world. My sisters thought me being a queen was some kind of huge, disgusting joke. My mum understood but the lines of communication had drifted a lot in the last year. Calls had become the odd message, and I didn't bother feeling guilty any longer when I said Arcanium was home and my friends were my family.

"She was a scary woman, my mother," MC added. "My father used to call her the she-wolf. Then he left. He wasn't a very nice man, or useful, so none of us missed him much."

I understood that. I often thought the same about my sisters.

"What kind of place is this?" I risked another question. "Is it just forest?"

I didn't want to ask about towns and cities in case he'd never left the woods, but we needed to find some way of getting to civilisation, somewhere they might have old histories and records we could trawl through for mentions of Faerie or portals to other realms.

Again he blinked at me in that startled, terrified way and I had half a mind to grab his shoulders and give him a shake. I pushed the urge down, my gifts fighting against it. If they started splurging out we'd have all kinds of trouble.

"There are towns beyond the border," he said. "Um,

I've only been twice before though. Once when I was very young, then not too long ago."

"Is it far?"

He shook his head. "Three days' walk, but they will be able to give you better guidance. Here we are. We can rest here tonight. I'll take you as far as I can tomorrow."

I stared at the tumbling down wooden barn in front of us, my heart sinking. I could cope with rustic. I could even cope with no amenities if needed. But this didn't look like it would have someone here that could help us.

"This is…" I couldn't finish the sentence.

MC nodded. "Camora doesn't like visitors, but we can stay here tonight. I will go to speak to her and get some food."

It would have to do. I inched through the doorway after MC, rolling my eyes when he turned to find me behind him and visibly flinched.

"There are um, blankets here." He hurried to a pile of them and started making three piles. "You can sleep on these."

Ever cautious, I grabbed a pile from the floor at his feet and carried them a respectful distance away. As I sank onto them with a relieved groan, Kainen hovered with his pile in hand, eying it like it might bite him.

He's used to much finer things. I bit down a smile.

Through the open barn door, the dusk falling over the forest was visible, the sky cast as a vast purple blanket with the colour slowly seeping toward the inky blue of night-time as the stars began to twinkle, much larger than they ever seemed at home or in the human world.

"So what exactly are you here for?" MC asked.

Although he spoke to Kainen as he rushed around lighting lanterns with a long stick, he risked a darting glance my way without shaking which was an improvement. Kind of.

Kainen looked my way too, a wordless request for permission which I approved with a slight nod. If he wanted to do the talking, I wasn't going to stop him. He was way better at it than I was anyway.

"It was sort of an accident," Kainen said, dropping his blankets to the ground. "We come from a place very far away and didn't mean to end up this far from home. Now we need to get home again."

MC frowned. "Can't you travel by horse or by foot then? Go back the way you came?"

"Not exactly. It's difficult to explain. We didn't come by... normal methods."

"You must be talking about some kind of land magic then. Not everyone has faith in that these days."

"Land magic?" I forgot about his weird aversion to me. "So most people here don't have gifts?"

He flinched again before staring at me.

"Um, a lot of folk have small ones. As much as Camora says people can move mountains, I've never met anyone who could. Most folk don't have faith in actual magic though."

At least he was talking to me. I leaned forward, bracing my forearms on my knees.

"What do they have faith in then?" I asked, trying my hardest to keep my tone gentle and friendly. "Gods? Deities? Prophets? Some kind of saviour?"

Kainen flicked me an irritated look as the suggestions came out more like worded stabs.

I've spent too long around people who are used to me clearly. Too long playing queen and having a court full of friends.

"Sorry, I just find it interesting," I muttered.

MC blinked and got to his feet. "There is only the one belief that we know of: the word of the Great Obe. It has been passed down since the beginning of knowledge and time. Are you not loyal followers of Obe then? You must be from very far away indeed."

"We are." Kainen jumped in. "Where we come from there are a different set of beliefs entirely."

"And beyond that, there's a place with many beliefs at once," I added, thinking of the human world.

MC's mouth dropped open. "I cannot envision a place with more than one belief. How does anyone get anything done without fighting? Here there is only the Great Obe and people fight over that all the time."

"People fight everywhere no matter how many belief systems there are," I grumbled. "But I reckon people would find something to fight about even if there were none. It's in our nature."

"Hmm." MC seemed to forget it was me he was talking to. "There is some sense in that. I'll go fetch us some food."

I frowned after him as he scurried out of the barn and out of sight.

"At least he's talking to me. Do I have the queen glow turned on or something?"

Kainen moved to stand by the doorway staring out, his arms folded over his chest. He didn't glance at me once but I saw his expression turn withering in the glow from the lanterns.

"He fancies you," he said.

I tensed. "I doubt that. He looks terrified."

"If you say so." Kainen rolled his eyes. "But no, you're not glowing. You look completely ordinary."

I shoved my hands between my knees and scrunched myself small around my satchel. Homesickness swept my breath away but I couldn't let it make me vulnerable. We needed to focus on getting home and if Kainen was right, at least there was less chance of me scaring off our guide now.

"Does any of this make sense to you?" he asked.

I shook my head. "Not really. We may find out more when we get to whatever civilisation he's leading us to, or we might need to do some research there and keep moving. We're in completely foreign territory. We have no idea if our gifts will work properly here, or whether we'll be safe or attacked wherever we end up. We should probably find some space to test them, just in case."

Kainen nodded. "I don't expect you to trust me but I can't lie. When I agreed to help you and support your rule, I meant it. I'll do that either way."

"I won't expect you to put that before your shot at getting home. Reyan will need you."

He scuffed his boot over the dusty ground, his face descending into shadow.

"Reyan will expect me to do the right thing." His lips lifted. "She'll yell at me if I don't. We'll get home to them somehow, and I'll do it at your side for what it's worth."

Awkwardness swirled in my gut but I had to force a weak smile. Even with our past, he sounded entirely genuine.

"Thanks. I need to eat and sleep. Should we take turns to stay awake?"

He nodded. "Probably wise. I'll take first watch. No knowing how much time is passing but worst case we can swap back and forth. It's not like you can't pulverise them if need be though, right?"

"My gifts feel volatile," I admitted. "I don't want to risk that unless I have to. I'm going to stick to my non-fairy skills where I can for the moment."

Kainen chuckled. "Good for you, I don't think I have any non-Fae skills."

He pushed himself free of the doorframe and a moment later MC appeared with a large wooden tray. I wrinkled my nose and closed my eyes as the scent of fresh bread and something sweet wafted over, but I didn't dare leap to my feet or anything dramatic. Knowing my luck, Kainen was wrong about MC liking me and he'd send our dinner flying into the wilderness out of fright.

"Here," MC held out a plate to Kainen first.

He then held mine out without looking at me or making any attempt to walk over, but Kainen grabbed it and brought it to me. Memories flashed as he stood over me with the plate, recollections of dark bars and a chilly vault of a hall around us. He might have noticed my subtle flinch as his lips pressed thin, but I reached through my warding and took the plate.

"Thanks."

He nodded, his expression still clamped down tight.

I bit into a large roll filled with some unknown meaty filler, too famished to care what it was. The last time I'd eaten had been earlier that morning before venturing to the human world, and there was no guarantee how many days might have passed between realms. I tried not to think about returning to find Taz an ancient old man, but the thought plagued me as my stomach filled the stilted silence with ominous growling noises.

"So, what do you do for fun around here?" Kainen asked.

I finished my roll, wondering if I should be taking

personability lessons from him. He sat on his blanket with his shoulders relaxed and his face full of friendly interest.

MC raised his brow in surprise. "Me? I walk the woods. I whittle figurines. There aren't many folk that venture out this far. Sometimes I talk to Camora about her experiences of the land."

"No friends around nearby?"

"I do not have friends." MC shrugged. "My sister would play *pitak* and cards, but I never had the skill for either."

"I used to be like that," I admitted against my better judgement. "My sisters both played hockey, but I was never very sporty."

MC's brow wrinkled. "Hoh-kee?"

I looked around for a suitable stick and stone to use for a demonstration but decided it was safer not to attempt it.

"Yeah, it's a game with sticks and this flat disc thing."

"Ah. It sounds much like *pitak*. A wooden disc is swept through the air with nets on sticks to hit the markers for points."

I shook my head. "Not exactly. With hockey you have to get the disc into the other team's net. It's quite rough though, lots of barging each other out of the way."

I shunted my shoulder sideways to imitate shoving.

MC stared wide-eyed. "That sounds very uncivilised."

Kainen gave me a look which suggested he agreed but I was more concerned with our future task now that MC seemed to be relaxing around us. Or around Kainen at least.

"It is a bit," I admitted. "Is there anything we need to

be wary of where we're going? Weird things in the woods kind of thing? Actually, where exactly are you taking us?"

MC grimaced and his hands began to twist in his lap.

"The spire is the best place to ask questions, so I'm taking you there. We have bandits in the woods but I know how to hear them coming. Some of the animals are a bit beastly too, but they keep to themselves if you don't stomp all over their lairs."

At least we don't have to deal with anything monstrous then, except maybe other people.

I caught Kainen's eye, the same relief swimming on his face.

"Oh, and there is also the Bone-Wolf," MC added conversationally, suddenly comfortable enough to reach for the final roll on the tray. "It tends to come out at random times to eat folk for their bones and leave their skins behind. But nobody's seen it in almost a season now."

CHAPTER SIX
REYAN

It took Ace insisting that she didn't have to see every single courtier to tear Reyan from her duties. The court was a sea of nobles all hovering with demanding stares, waiting for their turn to be called. A headache needled behind her eyes and she had to take several deep breaths to quell the dizzying waves of nausea.

Ciel appeared in front of her, his nose in the air and his lip curling.

"Some of the staff have requested an audience also," he said.

Reyan hesitated. She'd already told him that the audiences were done for the day, yet here he was forcing the issue.

"How many?" she asked.

He pursed his lips. "Only one, but she has a long list. I told her you were far too busy and important for the likes of them now-"

"You *what?*" Reyan sat up, the anger firing immediately. "You overstepped then. I'll see them."

She heard Ace's almost inaudible groan beside her, but she didn't want those she once called friends to think she'd become as bad as the nobles they'd always secretly mocked.

As Ciel stomped off, Reyan focused on relaxing her tense shoulders. She would need a long soak and large plates of something delicious to unwind, but she didn't dare sag or wipe at her face with the whole court milling around.

"You really have done enough," Ace murmured. "There's always another tomorrow."

"I've spent Faerie knows how long listening to complaints about gambling debts, sleights and insults, shady deals, and all sorts of horrors I really don't care about. The staff of the court I do care about."

Ace chuckled. "You sound like Demi. She tries to get away with telling the nobles she'll send them an orb message, but the moment anyone from Arcanium asks for something she bends over backwards."

Halfway through laughing at the thought, Reyan stiffened as a young woman ascended to the platform and bobbed a stiff bow of her head.

"Amba," Reyan hesitated, lost in a sea of awful formality and now inappropriate casualness. "Ciel said you wanted to raise some stuff?"

Amba nodded. "I'll speak plainly, if I can."

"Brilliant, you'd be the first."

That earned her the tiniest flicker of a smirk. They'd been casual friends once, laughing in the combat training classes the court provided, occasionally sitting together during meals or sharing tasks. Reyan hadn't seen her since taking on her role as Kainen's fake fiancée, but she guessed Amba had given her an equally wide berth.

Amba tucked a strand of black hair behind her ear, then folded her arms across her chest.

"Rumour has it the deck we were given was your doing," she started. Reyan nodded. "Thanks. We want permission to have music some nights."

Reyan frowned. "You need permission for that?"

"Apparently it's too close to some of the nobles' rooms and they don't like our choice of music. They threatened to have us all dismissed."

Amba wrinkled her nose in disgust and Reyan tried not to smile. She knew the push and pull of the court well enough from her time in service. Nobles thought they ran the court because of the money and prestige they funnelled through it. But without people to manage and keep it running, they'd be forced to clean their own rooms and make their own food, find their own entertainment. Realising she could at least have the tiniest smidgen of fun with her new role, Reyan tilted her head, pretending to look confused.

"Did they? I'm interested to know who thinks they have this kind of power in my court," she hummed loudly, drawing the attention of the entire hall. "Kainen gave you that deck to use as you saw fit. Anyone who wants to threaten to fire his staff can take that up with him. Sadly, until he returns, they'll have to take it up with me, and I'm less lenient than he is with gross entitlement."

A mutter ran through the crowd but Reyan held Amba's gaze, refusing to doubt herself.

"Keep it down after two in the morning. Anyone who wants to move their room to an alternative part of the court can request it. Anything else?"

Amba smirked. "Nothing that Meri wouldn't scalp us for not taking to her first. But we did want to give you this."

She pulled a small item from her pocket and held her hand out, a flash of shining grey on her palm.

"It's not much," she added, lowering her voice. "But we wove some protection into it. As much as we staff can support someone noble, we've got you."

Reyan reached out with tentative fingers to snag the scrunchie. Small and stitched from strands of satin, the pale lilac, silver and dark grey fabric glimmered in the firelight. A gentle hum of calm thrummed through the fibres and Reyan reached behind her, securing her hair in one fist and winding the scrunchie around it.

"Thank you." She forced a smile. It was either that or cry. "I'll honour it."

Amba retreated into the crowd and Reyan held her hand out to Ace. He took it and helped her stand to look out over the crowd.

"It seems my court supports me, even if the nobility are undecided," she announced. "Go play while you still can."

The crowd noise rose as Reyan dragged the last elements of strength into her resolve and folded the nether around her and Ace. As they translocated back to Kainen's office and blessed silence fell, she sagged in his arms.

"Okay, straight into bed," he demanded.

Reyan opened her mouth to argue but bed did sound irrepressibly enticing. She'd been sleeping in Kainen's since he disappeared, a mad manifestation tactic to get him to come back if only to tease her ragged about it.

She didn't even blink as Ace tugged the shirt off her shoulders and guided her out of her boots, leaving her in jeans and her vest top. She clambered into bed and wiped a hand over her eyes.

"We still have Lorens to consider," she said through a wide yawn.

He hesitated. "We do, but not right now. Can you do that clicky thing to summon food?"

Reyan nodded and lifted her arm. It took her a moment of concentration, but she still had a squish in her chest when the glittering black smoke appeared to wreath her hand. She'd always thought of it as Kainen's ability, but whether it was a part of him the court had then claimed, or a part of the court itself, she couldn't remember.

She thought of the kitchens and clicked her fingers.

"Can we have some dinner, please?" she asked.

A buzzing sensation through her hand let her know she'd been heard, so she dropped her hand and the smoke disappeared.

"Food's on the way."

Ace sat on the edge of her bed, toeing off his boots and settling cross-legged.

"You did really well," he insisted. "Firm with the nobles but kind to your court. They'll remember that. It's all about appearances sometimes to keep yourself safe."

He didn't need to say 'when the time comes', but Reyan understood the meaning. She was a fool if she thought the nobles would take her ascension to lady of the court without a fight. They might try to undermine her and drive her out, or with Lorens sniffing around and Ciel poking his nose in too, she might have to deal with all-out war on her leadership. But she couldn't let them see her rattled.

"Appearances are tiring," she mumbled.

Ace nodded. "They are, glamours too, but sometimes we need them for safety too."

"Speaking from experience?"

When he hesitated, she gave him her full attention.

I actually don't know anything much about him, other than he's Demi's most trusted friend and a qualified FDP.

Ace sighed and stretched out his arms.

Reyan eyed the black skin there, not getting the point, but then-

She gasped as he dropped the hint of glamour. The smooth skin, previously unmarred, shivered until harsh lines appeared. Scars littered his skin in stripes, too neat to be anything other than self-inflicted.

"Yeah." He sighed again, the resignation a second

nature. "Milo had much the same response. Some things are better hidden behind appearances, but none of us are invincible, no matter how good we are at pretending."

Thoughts thundered, of reassuring him, of asking questions, of doing something, anything to help mend… something that wouldn't go away with any kind of simple 'fix'.

"No fresh ones?" she asked instead.

Ace raised his eyebrows. "Not for a long while now. When my dad died, I tried to look after my mum and my sister the best way I could. I always felt like I was two steps behind him though, never quite 'getting it' somehow."

"That should never have been your responsibility, but you did the best you could. Sounds like a hellish pressure you put on yourself."

He nodded. "It took me a long time to realise that comparing myself to my dad was pointless. He was the best man, but I can be the best at something else."

"Well, you're doing pretty great at the whole supporting me thing, and I know Demi would say the same about her."

He smiled, his eyes darting down to his hands. Reyan had never seen any emotion on him other than occasional anger, not that she'd known him long or well yet. But this sudden awkward shyness was him laid bare. She wanted to hug him tight and tell him he'd be okay.

"I appreciate that. The urge never truly goes away," he admitted. "If life gets really bad it's always lurking, but we all have ways of coping."

"Some drink," Reyan said. "Some drink and gamble themselves to death, to the point of selling out and endangering their kids. I get it."

Ace settled back against the post of the bed, letting his glamour drop back over his arms.

"Your dad, right?"

She nodded. "I couldn't even hate him for it in the end. He sent me here and got a good deal out of it, but me being angry won't change him or my situation. I don't see him now but he still benefits from the court thanks to Kainen. Like you say, everyone has their ways of dealing with things."

"I used to say at least mine isn't hurting anyone else," Ace added. "But it took me a while to realise that I was allowed to be a person too, that hurting myself was still hurting someone."

Reyan sat up and matched his stance, cross-legged and leaning forward.

"That's what Demi said once, something about needing to see everyone as people. That all this type and title stuff of courts and nobility is just fakery to hide the fact that they've got nothing real to trade on."

He chuckled. "She says that a lot. It's basically her whole manifesto, hiding behind family lineage and titles is a sure sign of someone who doesn't know who they really are as a person and are too scared to find out."

Reyan flinched as the air shivered beside the bed and Meri materialised with a tray.

"She rests and asks for food, it's a miracle," Meri said drily. "I debated with myself whether to tell you this in case you go charging off again, but someone called Lorens is stalking the halls demanding privacy. I thought you should know."

Reyan swung her feet out of bed before Ace could even finish groaning. She closed her eyes, feeling out through the court and the shadows, hunting for that sense of threat that Lorens seemed to carry with him like an all-powerful aura.

"Near the library," she said.

Meri sighed. "I'll take this food back to the kitchen to keep warm. Be careful."

Reyan grabbed Kainen's shirt and pulled it back on while stuffing her feet into her boots, her weariness on hold. If she could find any reason to banish Lorens from court without losing face in front of the nobles, she would take it.

Or we might even get some information about where Kainen and Demi have gone.

That put more energy into her step as she grabbed Ace's hand without waiting and skipped them through the court.

"Wait here," she whispered. "I'm going to shadow nearer."

She dropped Ace's hand and dissipated into shadow, leaving only the outline of her head visible. Underground and mostly lit with firelight for effect, the Illusion Court was rife with shadowed corners and alcoves. She snuck into the nearest one, bemused to see Lorens hunched near a random statue of some old lord. She shifted her position a bit more and eyed the mirror that he cradled in both hands.

"I haven't seen or heard any whisperings here," an unfamiliar male voice insisted, coated with disdain. "From the way you describe them, I doubt a fledgling queen and a mere Fae court lord could cause me much trouble."

"Don't underestimate them, Loth," Lorens insisted.

"Why not? It took you this long to find the entry point to our realm, and now two folk who aren't of your following ended up here by accident. That's assuming they ended up here at all."

Reyan's gasp echoed only in her mind, the noise inaudible through the shadow. She didn't know if Ace

66

could hear from where he was, but whoever Lorens was talking to sounded like he was in the Prime Realm itself.

All this time, Lorens has been the one pulling so many strings. Belladonna doesn't even know about this I bet.

"I'd advise you to stop fooling about," the man, Loth, added. "From the ancient tales we've heard of Fae, if you lot glamour long enough, you don't change back."

Lorens huffed. "For minor fae and those with human blood that might be true, but rarely. You hold the power with your iron resources currently, but we're still the race to be feared. After all, you had to banish our kind from your realm for a reason. I'd advise *you* not to forget that."

Loth chuckled and Lorens straightened up, inhaling sharply. Reyan flinched deeper into the shadows but he didn't turn around.

"Either way, my glamour comes in handy for my own ends," Lorens added. "I am the most feared Fae in all of Faerie and being able to move with anonymity makes life much easier."

"Well then, oh feared one, don't let me delay you. Remember our bargain. If you queenling crosses my path I will deal with her, but you will owe me for that also."

Loth's mocking tone rang through the hall as Lorens dropped his hands to his sides, the mirror clenched in one fist. Reyan kept herself fully shadow as she flitted back to Ace's side, reforming in time to clutch at his arm.

"Challenge him?" Ace whispered.

Reyan hesitated.

Would secrecy be better? There's no sense telling Taz and having him storm my court to tear Lorens to pieces for answers he might not have.

She frowned. Lorens was in *her* court and he was up to something. The longer they waited, the more chance there might be of that Loth person finding Kainen and Demi, and he'd likely have the power dominance in his own realm. That alone made her next decision.

"Lurking in corners?" she called out.

With Ace beside her, she walked toward Lorens, getting the satisfaction of seeing him tense at the sound of her voice. His cocky smile was firmly in place when he turned, and she noted he had already vanished the mirror somewhere else.

"What better place to lurk in dark corners than the Court of Illusions?" he countered.

She shrugged. "A suitable answer that says nothing at all, how boringly predictable. But whoever you are with your little glamour, the supposed 'most feared Fae in Faerie' title is taken. When Demi returns from wherever your Forgotten friends accidentally sent her, she'll have absolutely no problem dealing with you. Assuming Kainen doesn't get you first."

His expression flickered with malice and she reinforced her protection, sweeping it over Ace and his also. She was strong in the court that had chosen her and her retort had clearly hit a mark, but Lorens didn't descend to baiting her back.

"Just remember," she added. "Court lords and ladies can do glamour washes of their court whenever they choose. Keep one eye on your back and stop thinking of crossing me."

He took a step forward but a loud hissing sound swished through the hall. Reyan smiled as Betty glided across in her flesh-form, an enormous beast with shining black scales.

"No eating him," she told Betty. "Not yet. But if he's so intent on playing games, see how far he can run."

Lorens took a step back, his eyes widening. Betty hissed happily and slithered toward him. He glared at the three of them before translocating somewhere else, another worry. Translocation was a rare gift, and him being able to do it only proved he had seriously powerful friends.

Then again, he knows Belladonna and seems to come and go as he pleases, so she probably favours him.

"It's the ability to suddenly strike," Ace muttered.

Reyan frowned. Realising he meant his fear of snakes, she chuckled.

"She's harmless to anyone who doesn't want to hurt me," she insisted.

Can you shrink to shadow again please? She sent her thoughts through to Betty. *Ace is scared of snakes.*

She held her hand out as Betty obeyed, becoming a mere wisp of shadow like she had been when Reyan had chipped her out of her egg.

I won't eat him. He's nice to you, smells of loyalty, but I will go and hunt soon.

Reyan frowned, remembering she'd asked Betty to try and find anything she could about Kainen's disappearance or where he might be.

For food?

Betty's laughter hissed through the shadows.

For many things.

CHAPTER SEVEN
BLOSSOM

Wandering the deserted halls of the old Revel Court's castle wouldn't delay the inevitable, but Blossom wanted to avoid going outside, not only because there seemed to be a hideously strong bee problem infesting the market and the court itself, but also to avoid facing Belladonna. Even though she knew going with the court to attack Arcanium was her only shot at freedom, to get to Taz and beg him to take her in, the actual reality of betraying Belladonna still made her uneasy.

She almost missed the sound of voices approaching, so used to the insistent buzzing of random bees. There was no apparent cause for it, but the bees seemed to move in certain formations, chasing certain members of court more than others. She had to count herself lucky that she didn't seem to be one of the unlucky chosen ones so far, but it was almost like the realm itself was fighting back against Belladonna and her hostile takeover.

As the voices grew louder, she dipped into an alcove.

Moments later, Emil came into view. He'd not bothered with his Lorens glamour since returning from the Illusion Court, but Blossom couldn't spare much thought or compassion for Reyan having to deal with him. She shrank into the shadows as Emil spoke to something cradled in his palm. It wasn't an orb, but a mirror, the surface of which seemed to be moving.

"Remember our deal."

She didn't recognise the voice coming out of the mirror. Emil frowned, his shoulders set with tension as he came to a halt.

"I am well aware of our deal, Loth. I orchestrated it."

A dry chuckle leapt from the mirror.

"If you say so. You can only have access to our iron if you complete your part of the deal. Open the portal and rid us of our earth guardian."

"Yes, yes, I know all that," Emil snapped.

Blossom shrank further into the alcove, determined not to be caught eavesdropping. Whoever Loth was, it sounded as though he was calling the shots. She didn't know who he meant by 'earth guardian' either.

"The opening of the portal will benefit us both," Loth added. "So get on with it."

A moment of silence filled the hall before Emil huffed and slid the mirror into the pocket of his trousers.

"I'm going to have to do something about them," he muttered, rubbing a hand over his chin. "She'll be busy ransacking Arcanium and distracting everyone, but I need to find a way to reopen the painting. There must be a way. If Blossom has the ability to summon… hmm."

He started walking again but Blossom stayed pinned in place against the alcove wall, her heart pounding uncontrollably.

She needed to get to Belladonna and fast. If Emil insisted she stay behind, if she didn't get herself to Arcanium, she could realm-skip out but there probably wasn't a single place else she could hide where Belladonna wouldn't find her.

She took a deep breath and pulled her orb out of her pocket.

She had to orb a message to Taz at some point to warn

him about the attack. The chances of Belladonna checking the orb-waves so close to leaving were slim, but before anything else Blossom had to make something right.

"Cerys at the Fauna Court," she requested.

Several moments later when she was about to give up waiting, Cerys appeared, the image of her looming large against the far wall. Blossom twisted so that the orb projection was smaller against a nearer wall as a couple of people walked past.

"I want a report," she demanded.

Cerys gritted her teeth in a snarl. "The sooner your lot is gone, Lady, the better for all concerned, there's your report."

Blossom knew she deserved that, at least in terms of her proximity to her sister. She nodded and peered out of the alcove to check she was really alone.

"Then leave me to my affairs and I'll leave you to yours. The Fauna Court is in your hands." She lowered her voice. "And yours to command if anything happens to me, let Faerie be witness to that."

Cerys stared back, shock written all over her face. Blossom wondered if there was something too honest in her tone, but after a tense moment, Cerys nodded.

"If you say so," she said, confusion marring the hostility.

"I do."

Blossom hung up before she could risk any more telling mistakes.

If something happened to her, Faerie would recognise Cerys as the Fauna Court's next lady. Then Cerys could call in all the other courts for support to oust the Forgotten from her realm if she needed to. It wasn't any kind of repayment or penance for Lord Rydon's death, but it was the only thing she had in her power to do to make amends.

Slipping her orb back into her pocket, Blossom hurried through the familiar halls and out of the kitchen door. She stumbled to a halt, staring out over the assembled crowd of Fae standing on the hill in front of her. There were so many gathered that they tumbled down into the fringes of the marketplace. She pulled on her best attempt at an expression of vapid intrigue as Belladonna strode toward her.

"I'm going to need to amplify my voice," Belladonna said, smug confidence written over her face.

Blossom nodded and pressed her hands in the pockets of her jeans. Fear cloaked as nonchalance, she'd perfected that at least.

"What's the actual plan?" she asked, keeping her voice low.

Belladonna flicked an impatient look her way. "We have someone who is ready to open a skip-way into their library. Resurrecting the *Maladorac* was to retrieve the shadow-snake egg as a go-between to test the waters in the prime realm, but it also allowed Emil to create a skip-way to Arcanium's library. He's brilliant really."

He's gifted, that's all, and fiendishly minded.

Blossom frowned. She would have respected that once but now it held no appeal for her.

"You aren't getting cold feet are you?" Belladonna's eyes narrowed. "We are so close to achieving a win over them."

Blossom shook her head. "I'm still coming with you, don't worry. The attack will catch them off-guard, and with Demi gone they're weaker."

It wasn't hard to word-tangle in vague half-truths. She was still going with them to attack, she just wouldn't be on their side if she could avoid it. The attack would overwhelm Taz and his lot even if she warned them first. And they were weak without Demi, whether anyone wanted to admit it or not.

"Demi now is it?" Belladonna snorted.

Blossom shrugged. "Would you prefer I called her queen? It's her name. No sense giving her titles she doesn't deserve. When do we leave?"

Belladonna eyed the group assembled, getting restless and starting to squabble in small factions, several of them closest still swatting away mini swarms of bees. Left long enough they'd start their own wars and vendettas, but it was the mood Belladonna seemed to want them in because she didn't make any move to capture their attention.

A harsh wind whipped across the hill, fluttering the hastily made Blood and Bone Court banners. Two blades coated in blood and a black crown in between them. She guessed Belladonna would crown herself the Nightshade queen, as that was always what she'd insisted when she was younger.

Probably why mother never wanted her to take the throne.

She let the thought slide away and focused on her hand around the orb in her pocket. What she was about to do was dangerous to the extreme, but a night awake listening to Belladonna torture Fae until their screams tore through half the castle had made her restless. She wanted to claw and bite and punch people. One person in particular.

But fighting Belladonna in combat was near impossible. When she fought with gifts that was beyond difficult too, but at least now she was currently giftless with nobody she trusted around to gift her.

"I'm surprised you didn't ask Emil to gift you,"

Blossom murmured.

Belladonna froze and Blossom tensed, waiting for a blow in reply.

"I can't trust him," Belladonna muttered. "I respect him, a high honour from me, but he would laugh and he has no intention of doing anything other than crowning me while he rules behind the scenes."

Blossom stared at her sister in astonishment, so much so that Belladonna laughed.

"Did you think all that eyelash-batting was real? My poor, simple sister, I know people. I know when I'm being betrayed, when I can risk trusting."

"Why are you telling me this then?"

Blossom folded her arms, her gaze narrowing as she reassessed the gathered Fae.

"Emil doesn't know I'm giftless, nor does anyone else. Why do you think I had to torture those who went to the human world with us? It's fun of course, good practice, but I can't risk anyone else finding out."

Blossom squeezed her hand tight around her orb. She just had to work the conversation around to saying that one name she needed. It would likely be the end of her if Belladonna found out, but she'd become surprisingly skilled at playing the fool.

"You haven't tortured me," she said. "Much."

"I would have thought your loyalty is undoubted. Isn't it?"

Blossom held in the startled squeak as Belladonna whirled toward her. A forearm clamped across her throat, the force shunting her back against the castle wall.

"Of course my loyalty is undoubted," she choked. *It's just not yours anymore.* "Who do you think it would belong to? Arcanium? What am I going to do, message

Taz?"

She prayed to Faerie and the nether and anything that might be listening in the seconds that followed, her pulse thundering through her body enough to make her limbs shake. If her orb had understood her command, it would send whatever was said next as a message to Taz's orb.

Belladonna's furious gaze flicked over her face, but Blossom almost cried out with relief at the subtle burn of warmth on her palm. Her orb had picked up her command and now she had the determination she needed to see this through.

Belladonna released her. "Even you wouldn't be that stupid."

She turned away, the brief moment of violence giving her the adrenalin hit she'd apparently been lingering for.

"Amplify my voice," she barked.

Blossom pushed away from the wall with the orb curled in her fist. Transmitting the next few minutes to Arcanium through the orb-waves would likely be a garbled string of words, but hopefully they would get the basic idea.

Amplification gifts were a simple gift for members of a court, one their mother had gifted them all with at a young age. They'd used them mostly for calling the servants to random parts of the palace for no reason at all, but with Belladonna losing her gifts she couldn't even do that now.

Blossom clung to the warmth in her hand and passed her other fingers over Belladonna's throat, pulling her amplification gift into her fingertips.

"Done."

Belladonna nodded. "*Attention!*"

Her voice blasted through the air, the entire crowd swivelling to face her with stunned expressions. Many of them were high-born and unaccustomed to being hollered at, and others were from fallen or current noble families. But they obeyed. When someone like Belladonna commanded, Fae obeyed, or else.

"We are going to attack Arcanium. They can have no idea we're coming for them, and our retribution will be unending."

A raucous cheer rolled around the crowd and Belladonna sucked in a satisfied breath. Blossom focused on the burn in her hand, opening her fist slightly in case that allowed whoever was reading the message on Taz's end to get it clearer.

"Take no prisoners but leave the king consort for me," Belladonna added. "Once we step through these castle doors, we will be in Arcanium. Oh, and have fun!"

Another cheer rattled the ground underneath and Blossom pocketed her orb. The message would end when she let go of it, her connection broken, but hopefully it would give Taz a few valuable moments to prepare his people.

"Shouldn't you get them to bring some captives back?" she asked. "Give them some intel on who to target? Or where the entrances are?"

Belladonna's irate gaze turned on her and she softened her expression. The crowd were gearing up, ready to charge through the doors at Belladonna's command, but Blossom intended to buy Taz as much time as she could.

"Underestimating an enemy is the surest way to make things difficult," she added. "Wasn't it you who once said that?"

It wasn't but posing it as a question would get around the lie and it had Belladonna hesitating.

"It does sound like something I would say." She raised her voice to the crowd once more. "There are a couple of others you should bring back if you can. Consider them high-prize targets." She glared at Blossom. "Go on, project the images then."

Blossom lifted her orb out but couldn't risk pausing to read the reply message now swirling on the surface. If Belladonna grabbed it from her, she'd be done for. Projecting a blank screen from the orb onto the castle wall, she waited for Belladonna to name her targets.

"Milo, their librarian, a close personal friend of the bloodless queen," Belladonna announced.

The orb reacted to her voice at Blossom's will and projected an image from a recent article in the *Faerie Net*. She swiped her thumb across the surface of the orb to move the indicator circle and put a red ring around the boy with the worried look on his face. "Ace, I don't know his surname. Diana Hemlock, once Forgotten, now traitor as we haven't heard a peep from her. The Eastwick sisters. The Hutchinson brothers. The Arcanium director, Queenie. If anyone can get her back here, I will give you double the accolades of the other ones."

Blossom clenched her gut muscles tight to avoid the gasp creeping up and out of her mouth. Their aunt Queenie was supportive to their mother and always had been, but she'd sided with Demi enough to offer her Arcanium as the home for her court. She'd been Taz's protector even with Emil sniffing around for years.

She was always fair to us when mother wasn't.

"The library is a central chamber with levels." Belladonna glanced at the projection, then at Blossom. "We don't have actual visuals? Really? Orbs alive."

Blossom dropped her hand in reply and cancelled the projection. She didn't dare check the message that had been sent back to her. It might have even been showing on the projection but she couldn't risk Belladonna seeing any potential reply from Taz. She swiped the message aside and slid her orb into her pocket. A few more minutes and she would be inside Arcanium with the others.

"We believe that they move around different levels and rooms by lifts," Belladonna added. "If you can get yourself into a lift, go hunting wherever it takes you. Anyone who returns will be respected, and anyone who returns with one of the captives will be suitably rewarded." She darted a sideways glare at Blossom. "Anything else?"

Blossom shook her head.

"I don't want you to leave my side," Belladonna muttered as they turned to face the doors. "You will protect me and work your gifts for me."

With that command sinking like a stone in her gut, Blossom nodded. She would protect her sister and she would use her gifts, until she saw an opening to reach Taz.

She stepped up to the double doors and raised a protection warding over herself and Belladonna, realising that while she was warding both of them, Belladonna was warding herself, soaking up two protections alone while leaving Blossom with one while expending the effort of two. Despite losing her gifts, protection wardings were the one element of magic that were innate to Fae, unremovable.

She sighed. There wasn't even any guarantee that Taz would protect or support her but she had to hope, because after all, he was the good one.

A brush of nether wisped around them as they walked into the darkness, swirling purple and grey before dumping them into overpowering silence. Blossom stared around through the soft amber glow of various lamps, taking in the circular platform she stood on with the huge gap in the centre, signs of other levels travelling both up and down around them. A wide walkway leapt across a central chasm that tumbled down into darkness with a statue of their mother made from pale marble in the centre. She couldn't see the statue's hands from where they stood, their forces crowding through behind them, but she knew that was where the Book of Faerie was housed.

If they've moved the book, Belladonna will know someone told.

Belladonna glanced around, her lip curling in disgust.

"Is this it? This is the grand library of Arcanium? Where are the towering sculptures? It's just a bunch of dusty old books. And where are the people?"

Blossom scanned their level once more but couldn't see a single soul. Had Taz evacuated somehow in the few moments she'd managed to give him?

"What if they know we're coming?" someone shouted from near the back.

Belladonna hesitated, a death-sentence when leading a bunch of power-hungry Fae. Mumblings radiated like wildfire.

"They can't," she snapped, then lowered her voice. "The only people who knew were me and Emil. Unless he's crossed me."

She forced a look of steely determination over her face immediately, but standing right beside her, Blossom had heard the soft wobble in her voice. She might have given a good show before about not trusting Emil, and she was wise not to, but the attachment lingered all the same.

"Should we go back?" Blossom asked.

It had the intended effect. Belladonna glared at her.

"Why should we? They can't fight us, even if they are FDPs." She lifted her head, her eyes bright. "Time to go hunting, everyone. Spread out and do your worst."

She started toward the walkway and Blossom hurried a step behind her. If the book wasn't there, Belladonna would either assume they'd moved it or that Emil had betrayed her for some unknown reason of his own.

She has no reason to suspect me. She doesn't think I'm smart enough.

They stopped in the centre of the walkway to stare up at the impassive face of their mother, the oak-leaf crown woven with gold the only thing not made of pale marble.

"Where are you now?" Belladonna sneered.

Blossom tensed as her sister breathed in deep and spat up toward the unseeing statue. It landed on the shoulder and Blossom glanced around for a distraction. If Belladonna noticed the empty plinth covering the outstretched marble hands, she'd realise the Book of Faerie was gone.

A brief slash of colour flickered at the edge of one of the bookshelves near the main desk, the merest hint of purple. It could have been a trick of the light, a simple optical illusion as the lights flickered around the room.

Belladonna's gaze dropped down to the plinth.

Blossom took a step back.

BANG.

A scream filled the air, followed by several of their crowd shouting. Bursts of red, purple and blue filled the platform, the flashes echoed on other levels both above and below. Splatters of whatever was being cast or thrown rebounded off wardings but she couldn't see any sign of Taz or any FDPs.

"NOT THE ARCHIVES!"

The amplified male voice screeched through the air, grating on every single nerve. Then a loud roaring noise

81

echoed from the chasm in the middle, loud enough to rumble the foundations of the library.

Belladonna stormed to the edge of the walkway but Blossom hung back, inching closer to the marble statue as the distance threatened to sever Belladonna from the warding she had over both of them.

The rumbling grew until the walkway was rattling and she eyed the crowd now spanning the whole circular level around her.

"What the-"

Belladonna jumped back as a stream of bubbling red shot past her, splattering her warding. She growled under her breath but a splash had caught the edge of Blossom's warding too, and the sensation of corrosion bit into it.

How can they have something that eats through wardings? Only metirin iron can do that.

She stared around, panicked as she tried to find any sign of Taz. She could dip into the crowd before Belladonna noticed and get one of the lifts, find a place to lay low until Taz got everything sorted.

As another loud battle cry filled the air and FDPs swarmed from the sides of the platforms, she hesitated.

Belladonna stormed toward her, grabbed her hands and spun her, one arm anchoring around her neck from behind.

She knows.

"What are you doing?" she choked out.

Belladonna's free hand was fumbling at their side, no doubt going for the orb in Blossom's pocket. How she'd figured it out Blossom had no idea, whether she'd seen the orb and waited to take revenge or simply assumed that her precious Emil would never betray her.

"You agreed to serve the cause, so stop struggling."

Blossom didn't stop, shunting her elbow into

Belladonna's ribs, but Belladonna clung on. She clawed at Belladonna's arm until something wavered in front of her face.

"Open wide," Belladonna sang.

Blossom clamped her mouth shut. The vial that Emil had given Belladonna the day before was in her hand, uncorked and tilting toward her lips. She wanted to ask what it was, but Belladonna wouldn't tell her and it wasn't going to be anything in her favour.

Belladonna's fingertips pinched painfully over her nose.

"Open up, or I'll break your nose."

Blossom wriggled, trying to drop herself to the floor like a dead weight on a noose, but Belladonna gave her nose an excruciating twist. The crack echoed in her ears like a gunshot and she wailed through pinned lips.

She was going to pass out from lack of air and from the pain throbbing in her nose. She couldn't draw breath with Belladonna still pinching it, but whatever was in the vial had to be even worse than passing out.

"Don't you trust me?" Belladonna crooned softly. "Wise, but I'm stronger than you. I've always been stronger, fitter, smarter. Did you think I'd come in here to fight without gifts?"

Confusion waltzed with the mix of pain and light-headedness. Blossom managed a groggy moan but Belladonna only pinched and squeezed tighter.

"I admit, your gifts won't be the best for fighting, but they're better than nothing. I'll be able to summon everyone else's gifts perhaps, like you did with mine. I won't ask again. Open. Your. Mouth."

Blossom fought the clawing, roiling urge to breathe straining in her lungs, her fingers losing their coordination and strength against Belladonna's arm.

She would resist until her last breath, not because she wasn't afraid of dying, or of losing her gifts, or of being hurt or punished. She was petrified of all those things, but the thought of Belladonna being able to steal everyone's gifts was the most frightening of them all. She had to realm-skip away, but she wouldn't be able to get back into Arcanium if she did.

"I'm ashamed of you, putting yourself before the cause," Belladonna snapped. "I would have thought-aaah!"

Belladonna jolted and Blossom stumbled into the marble statue of their mother with a resounding thud, dropping to her hands and knees as she huffed in pained breaths through her mouth. She didn't dare try to breathe through her nose, the pounding suggesting the red now on the marble beneath her face was her blood rather than whatever had burned through the wardings before.

"Sorry, I would bow but I don't want to." The most irritating sing-song voice echoed behind her. "See, your princess-ship, I had a day off today and got called in. It's my birthday too, and I am *really* not happy about it."

Blossom rolled to the side, recognising Beryl Eastwick standing in front of Belladonna. As she winced at the pain in her nose, she spied the open vial leaking green goop over the walkway.

Belladonna stood nearby with one hand raised to hold her warding firm, but against the onslaught of what looked like dancing rocks battering against it, Blossom could feel the subtle shake of it. She should raise her warding and protect her mostly defenceless sister.

Belladonna's gaze flicked to her. Then to the vial.

As she lunged for it, Blossom twisted with an agonised

wail and shoved the heel of her shoe into the vial. It wasn't in any way a powerful kick, or even well aimed, but it made contact.

The vial rolled slowly toward the edge of the walkway.

She would have used me. Blossom forced herself up using the statue. *Even facing a fight, she'd have targeted me again instead of running.*

Hurt stabbed deep but Blossom stayed on her feet as Belladonna landed on her front, her fingers grasping after the vial seconds too late.

It tumbled over the edge of the walkway, gone from sight.

"Summon it back!" Belladonna screeched.

Blossom almost laughed but the pain was too bad. Her sister, who had broken her nose and tried to steal her gifts, who had tormented her and called her simple and stupid and weak for most of her life, who idolised a cold, calculated psychopath, wanted her help.

"No." She stood straighter. "You're done using me."

She turned to Beryl Eastwick now standing beside her with an overwhelming aura of someone who would get on your last nerve until the ends of time and Faerie if you so much as looked at her wrong.

"My brother is probably expecting me," she said.

Beryl raised her eyebrows. "Fair enough. He'll be here soon, don't worry. Until then I'm going to keep you both here. You can have a nice little family chat if you like while you wait."

Blossom turned to find her sister shaking with unspent rage. As Belladonna opened her mouth to yell, Blossom made the final step of severing and pulled her warding around herself alone, leaving Belladonna undefended.

CHAPTER EIGHT
DEMI

My feet were threatening to fall off, but we kept walking. MC and Kainen managed to keep up a regular litany of talk about different experiences and parts of MC's realm, but I stayed silent. MC seemed less twitchy that way.

Only when we stopped under the endless landscape of trees did I sigh out loud.

"We should be okay to sit here and rest a while," MC said.

I sank onto the nearest fallen tree trunk, of which there were quite a lot, and took the scant twist of pale bread he handed to me.

"And how far is it now?" I asked.

He frowned. "Not far. I don't read the map distances like some do. I just walk in the right direction."

A gift maybe? I wondered.

His discussions with Kainen made it clear that MC at least knew nothing of gifts and Fae magic, but he had mentioned land magic of a kind.

I leaned forward to snag another twist of bread but Kainen leaping to his feet made me freeze. Before I could dredge up a warding, something cold and pointy tapped against my throat.

With what I assumed was a blade of some kind pressed to my neck, I clambered to my feet as carefully as I could. Any sign of magic and whoever it was might run away to bring a whole army down on us, so I wanted to leave that as a last resort.

"Come on, come on." The voice was female, muffled and extremely snappy.

Kainen stood with more grace and turned to face our enemies. Unable to see what was going on, I shuffled on the spot until I faced them as well.

The woman who'd spoken stood with a dark brown fabric scarf covering her mouth and a matching bandana hiding her hair. I could just make out the thin ridge of her nose between wild, orange eyes. Two hulking figures stood either side of her, also covered with face scarves.

The other two much more intimidating figures flanked her, one on either side. Beneath the scarves that barely covered their beards, one had a hint of brown hair, his figure short and round, while the other, tall and solid like a cart horse, had blond curls.

The woman removed her sword from my neck and pressed the point of it against Kainen's chest next.

With his chin jutting out and his mouth twisted with scathing dislike, Kainen drew every element of his arrogance and entitlement to his face, his brow cocked and his lip curling with amusement.

"We have nothing to give." His tone was drenched with perfect high-born disdain. "You are welcome to share our food and fire, meagre though it is, if you put your weapons away."

His innate confidence pierced a tiny hole in my panic.

He probably expects me to do some kind of queen thing to save us.

Kainen placed his hands behind his back and leaned forward, pressing his chest into the sword's point. The woman's eyes widened as his pressure pushed back against her hold on the blade.

"We'll leave you here to starve then," she growled. "If

you make it a day, the Bone-Wolf will get you instead."

Kainen didn't even flinch, his eyes fixed on hers. "You will not. Go, before the Bone-Wolf eats you instead. It won't get me."

The woman's eyes narrowed and an idea hit me so fast I almost gasped out loud. Aware all attention was on Kainen, I opened my lips the slightest amount.

"Graarrrsnarrrrf." The effect wasn't as terrifying as I intended, but I was only getting started. "AAARRRRRRHHHHHOOOOOOGGH."

Even Kainen's eyes widened with the hint of trepidation. He risked the point of the blade to lift his chin and glance into the forest behind the bandits.

"You'd better run," MC shouted, catching on remarkably quick. "Do you not know who this is? You have crossed the path of um, the fabled Woodsman, er, Ian! Yes, all creatures bow to the Fearsome Ian. The beast will not harm him, but he cannot ask it not to feed. He does not control it. Run, while you still can."

Kainen didn't look remotely impressed at being labelled the Fearsome Ian, and there was a really inappropriate part of me that wanted to howl with laughter. I pressed my lips almost fully closed.

"GGRRRRRRRAAAAAOOOOOUUUUU."

The bandits were scanning the murky shadows between the trees now, their expressions distrustful and confused.

Not scared, confused.

Is this some kind of bandit trick, invent a monstrous wolf fable to scare people away from the forest?

I opened my mouth and dredged up my most terrifying sound. "GRRRAAAA-*oof*."

Someone grabbed my collar and hauled me sideways, the growl in my throat hitching into a startled grunt. I struggled but the bandit holding me was about three times my size.

"This one was making beastie noises," he rumbled.

Kainen had a dagger out in one hand, where from I had no idea, but he looked ready to face anyone that came at him. I considered slipping out of my shirt while the bandit was distracted by him, but running around in my bra wasn't really on my ideal prime realm bingo card.

The woman rounded her blade and squared up to Kainen, one foot placed in front of the other. As she bent her front knee, her trouser leg rode up. A flash of russet gold around her ankle caught my eye. MC's gaze zoned in on it too, his eyes like saucers as he leaned forward to make it out clearer.

No mere bandit would wear a trinket like that, not unless they stole it.

We needed information and given the look on MC's face, he knew something that might help us.

When he caught my eye, panic written over his face and his limbs close to rattling, I sent the command out, putting a tinge of compulsion behind it.

"*Follow me when I run,*" I mouthed.

I didn't wait for him to reply. While Kainen and the woman face each other, ready to fight, I said a silent prayer to whoever might be listening and lifted my arms. I dropped, crouching until I was free of my shirt. Bare to the elements, I left the bandit holding my shirt and hared off toward the trees.

I could hear footsteps pounding after me, but I only needed enough time to settle my fairy connection. It roiled inside me, my more volatile gifts fighting to be unleashed, but I only needed one.

I ran in a wide arc, stumbling over briars as MC

appeared beside me. Huge hands clamped on my shoulders but I wriggled free, my connection sparking in panic and a sizzling ice-blue glow encasing my hand. I sent a zap of it into a branch overhead as I passed, wincing at the crash and the timely yelp that echoed behind us.

I risked a look at MC to find his petrified gaze fixed on my glowing hand.

"You're… you're magic!" he gasped.

I nodded, already out of breath. "You recognised that ankle bracelet. Tell me everything you know."

"It's the symbol of a great royal house from a neighbouring part of the land. The lord and lady lost their daughter a long time ago, but she was said to be wearing an amulet of protection. A bracelet to be hidden. I wondered… but it's just a fable."

I grimaced. "Fables nearly always have at least a grain of truth in them."

Whether the woman was or wasn't part of a great royal house, it was something I could ask of her. I would find some way to reassure Kainen then I would vanish. If he had any sense, he'd take the distraction as a chance to ward himself too.

That doesn't leave MC much hope though, unless I keep him with me.

Thoughts of what Kainen had said the night before in the barn filled my head and if my face weren't already red from running, I might have blushed.

The clang of metal filled the air as we neared the group again, the remaining male bandit standing back while Kainen dodged and ducked her sword artfully with his dagger swiping back and forth. Now wasn't the time for memories of training with him a long while ago, but he always did have impressive grace and strength. It was the ruthless cunning that had unnerved me. I shook my hand and pulled the glow of my power back inside me, forcing the overwhelming urge to let my gifts reign free down with it.

"What was her name?" I asked as we slowed to approach. "The missing daughter?"

"Lady Sabine. You don't think it's her, do you?"

Only one way to find out. I grabbed my discarded t-shirt and hoodie, pulling them on as I charged forward.

"Sabine." I all but shouted it. "Or do I call you Lady? Sorry, I'm new."

The female bandit paused, almost giving Kainen a chance to slice right through her middle. His cheeks were flushed with effort and frustration but he stepped back and I had to trust he knew to ward himself. Lady Sabine whirled out of the way and stared fury at me. When she didn't answer, I stepped in front of MC just in case.

"I saw your ankle bracelet and I do my homework," I paused. "Sorry. The crest on your ankle is the one for a royal family, right? Anyway, you and um, the fabulous Ian are evenly matched in combat. We could suggest a truce. We only need a few days around these parts then we'll be out of your hair."

The woman stared at me, orange eyes not blinking. Then she gave MC an accusing look.

"You said he was the Fearsome Ian."

He did. *Which means he can lie.*

Storing that thought away for future use, I sized up the Lady Sabine. She clearly wanted to establish some dominance back, some remnant of the upper hand. No doubt she was used to getting her own way.

"Oh, yes. He did. Right, well, anyway as I said Lady- Is it Lady? I never know."

91

"You would address a future lady as just that, Lady. I am merely a simple bandit girl." She lifted her trouser to reveal her ankle. "I stole this."

MC shook his head and I tensed as his shaky voice wobbled past me.

"I doubt it, Lady. A trinket like that would have been too noticeable for anyone but the wearer. Your scarf too, very fine, and you round your words like royalty. So, either you spent time with the real Lady or- wait, what are you doing?"

I dodged as the Lady Sabine tried to get past me with the point of her sword going ahead of her, eyes glinting at MC over her scarf.

"Help," MC squeaked. "Do something magical!"

Lady Sabine froze. "What do any of you know about magic?"

I smiled and stepped in front of MC again, forcing her to look at me instead.

"Lower your sword and I'll tell you," I offered.

"Lies."

I snorted. Loudly. "If only you knew how impossible that is. I can show you if you like, but lower your sword first. Also, are you against magic in general? No point me proving anything if you're going to burn me at the stake."

Kainen's closed his eyes momentarily in disbelief. When he opened them again, I knew he was regretting ever agreeing to support me or my crown.

"Burn you? Why would I burn you?" The orange eyes narrowed again and the sword point pressed to the side of my neck.

Neither of us saw Kainen move in time. The male bandit roared in protest as Kainen caught the Lady Sabine around the waist. I squeaked and twisted as the blade swung near my neck.

"Release me, brute!" She flailed her arms and legs against him. "Fiend, barbarian. Help!"

"Stop struggling, I insist." Kainen insisted in his loudest, most commanding voice.

The struggling increased. "No, shan't."

Given the startled look on Kainen's face, he'd been trying to compel her and failed. He caught my eye over her shoulder, possibly about to let me know exactly that, but she threw a savagely placed elbow into his gut. Her hand swung lower and I brought my power forth again, letting the glow dance on my palm.

"Let her go," I insisted.

Kainen stumbled back, muttering something extremely uncomplimentary under his breath.

Sabine raised a hand and pulled down the scarf covering the lower half of her face. Against her brown skin and the delicate line of her nose, her eyes seemed to glitter gold in the evening shadows.

"You may call me Sabine, for now." She offered. "What are your names?"

"I'm Demi, that there is Kainen, and this is MC. We're headed for the spire."

MC flinched when I mentioned our destination but there was no sense dancing around the situation. If Sabine really was a Lady, she might know histories or legends. Her eyes narrowed even further but she sheathed her blade.

"We are going in the general direction of the spire. I'm interested to know more about magic. If you answer my questions, we'll guide you."

I flinched as the bandit I'd brought down with the tree branch came stomping toward us.

There was no guarantee that Sabine wouldn't be out to

use us for our gifts, but if we were smart we could handle it. Kainen gave me a doubtful look.

"They already have a guide," MC said.

Sabine chuckled. "You? Well, you might know how to get there, but do you know how to get in? Besides, there are beasts in the woods, the Bone-Wolf included, and isn't something to joke about."

She eyed me for a moment then flicked a wary glower in Kainen's direction as he replaced his dagger at his belt and lowered the bottom of his shirt to cover it.

"The offer is there," Sabine added. "We'll give no harm to you or yours and you're welcome to share our shelter and food as we travel. We may be able to meet our respective goals better by working together."

With MC looking at Kainen for an answer, and Kainen and Sabine staring at me, I took a deep breath and quashed my gift down. It grumbled but apparently the brief use had tired my connection enough to let it settle a bit.

"A guide we have, but shelter and food we're kind of lacking," I admitted. "If you can lead us to the spire, get us in and let us know anything useful about it, then I will tell you about magic."

Not exactly a hardship to offer, especially as there were no specifics included. I could tell her about magic without including anything useful at all, but then she could lie and avoid compulsions. I forced my gaze to remain near her face and not flick down to her ankle.

If the charm was protecting her from Fae, then she'd be mostly immune to us. I should have gotten a look at the sword as well. If it was made of *metirin* iron we wouldn't be able to protect ourselves from it.

Sabine held out her hand. Kainen started forward but I reached out and shook before he could get beside me. Even though I felt his protection warding nudging the edge of mine, I held firm. Until I was back with Taz beside me, I couldn't truly trust a single soul.

Sabine grasped my hand as a loud growl tore through the air, distant but close enough for us both to flinch in panic.

"Was that you?" she asked.

I shook my head. "Not this time."

"We need to get to safety," Kainen insisted.

Sabine nodded. "There are wolves about that aren't friendly."

"There are wolves that are friendly?" MC asked, possibly without thinking because he gave Sabine the same frightened, wide-eyed look he usually gave me a second later.

"Some, not others," Sabine muttered. "Follow me."

"We'll draw them off," the blonde bandit said. "Get yourself to the spire, Sabine. We'll regroup there."

Sabine nodded and I edged as close to Kainen as I could get.

"Keep MC under your warding," I whispered. "I'll do what I can to protect us but you keep an eye out for him, got it?"

Kainen nodded as Sabine strode off into the trees. Without any hope that we could trust her, or MC for that matter, we set off after her.

The moon cast an ethereal glow as we plunged further into the shadowed darkness, but clouds quickly obscured the view. A brief onslaught of rain earlier had slicked the ground but not soaked it, so we slipped and slithered between the trees. I kept my head down, adamant I would be swept off by a low stout branch or blinded by rogue twigs.

"We can't risk any light," Kainen murmured. "But follow my footing, I've always been able to see through the darkness."

I did exactly that, mindful of MC behind me. I tried not to think of what Taz might do if he knew MC was holding onto the back of my shirt with a shaking death-grip, but I couldn't bring myself to shove him off. Enduring the touch of someone else wasn't my ideal way to spend the night, but I could only imagine how scared he must be.

The moon re-emerged in time to illuminate a glade, little more than a dirt crater. Crops of rock rose up against the hillside opposite. A trickle of foreboding sent dribbles of dread over my back and shoulders that had nothing to do with the rain residue from the trees.

Up ahead, Sabine stumbled to a halt. We might have walked straight into her but Kainen stopped too, his feet slithering on the mud.

"Where are-" Kainen began.

Sabine glared back at him. "Shh, quiet."

Eying each other with territorial dislike, neither of them noticed what lay ahead. I blinked to make sure I was definitely seeing what I thought I was.

From the black, yawning mouth of a dark cavern at the base of the rocks, two orbs of lethal yellow blinked back.

CHAPTER NINE
REYAN

"There might be a slight problem occurring."

Reyan looked up as Amba rushed into the library without knocking, her breath uneven and her cheeks bright pink.

"What kind of problem?" Reyan asked.

She looked for Ace, but he was already speeding across the room to her side.

"Um… that man, Lorens, the one with the permanent sneer on his face. He's holding court in the main hall. Sitting on your deck and everything."

Reyan froze. "He's what?"

"I didn't get much of what he's saying, but Ciel is hovering and Meri is suspiciously absent, which means she's-"

Amba squeaked and fell silent as Meri popped into being right beside her.

"Which means she's been locking down the court," Meri said, her tone snippy. "You need to make a stand, Lady. Now."

Reyan inhaled deep and let the breath tumble loudly out again, her mind working over the possibilities. She would banish him from court, but if most of the nobles supported him, would that sway the court itself?

This is Kainen's court. She stood, her fists clenching. *Mine too.*

"It's lucky I've been doing some research then," she said.

With her hands out in front of her, she focused on the tingle of magic under her skin, calling it to the fore. She could feel the essence of the court, the heat from the kitchens, the wind outside their mountain, the subtle rushing rage of the river, and the uncertainty of her courtiers.

With intent firm in her mind, she let the thought of illusion dribbling away fill her head, trickling like raindrops and roiling back like smoke from the entire court.

"What was that?" Amba's awed voice echoed nearby.

Reyan opened her eyes, the sensation of exhaustion tugging at her from using such power.

"Glamour lift." She held her hand out to Ace, then to Amba. "Meri, keep the court secure. Gather anyone who might consider being loyal to me to the main hall. Be ready to call in favours from other courts if we need them. The last resort will be Arcanium."

Meri nodded and disappeared, but Reyan had to reach over and grab Amba's hand as the woman stood staring at her, too wide-eyed to obey. It was either that or leave her to take the tiring climb down the stairs from the library.

The nether wisped around them, depositing them in the main hall right in the midst of the crowd.

"-traditional leanings-" a familiar was shouting, but the crowd seemed to be drowning it out in a roar of chaos.

Reyan let go of Amba's hand and Ace's, drawing her shoulders straight and holding her head high.

If this ever goes down as a battle in the Book of Faerie, it'll give Kainen something to laugh his behind off about at least.

"SILENCE."

Her voice rang through every inch of the court, the

command wiping the noise clear away. Ace gasped softly and she clung to his hand, pulling him back before he could attack. Because the glamour lift she'd performed in the library had stripped every essence of pretence from everyone at court, Lorens included.

He stood at the top of the platform, her platform and Kainen's, his eyes narrowing with frustration in her direction.

His once-lustrous brown hair was gone, a short spike of grey-brown fuzz growing instead. He'd lost a few inches of height too, and the lithe form had broadened.

Reyan recognised him now in his real form as Emil, once Head Mentor of Arcanium turned traitor, right-hand to the usurper Elvira, and also said to be in league with Belladonna and the Forgotten. Reyan didn't know him in person as himself but she'd heard stories, enough for her to understand what he'd meant by calling himself the most feared Fae in all of Faerie.

"I could kill him," Ace muttered.

She gripped his hand tighter. "He belongs to the queen. Even if he doesn't, we need to reclaim the court. I could banish him but he'd only slink off and hide. Trust me?"

Ace gulped hard and it took a moment before he nodded. She let his hand go. Ace had Faerie and Demi's court, and her rule, to consider. But Reyan had to put her own court first and to do that, to succeed, she needed to prove herself by winning the hard way.

Even Emil seemed to be struggling to speak as she stalked through the parting crowd toward him. She could waste effort trying to hold the silence over him, but he wasn't sworn as part of her court so he would break through it soon enough.

His anger sparkled in his eyes as he watched her, his

shoulders tense and his stance even, a man preparing for battle.

"So this is who you truly are," she said, climbing the steps to the deck. "I bet there are a lot of nobles here who didn't know this."

He stared her down as she drew level with him. Even with her protection around her, she called the shadows close.

"I did what I had to in order to survive, for the betterment of Faerie," he said.

"Or for the betterment of yourself," she scoffed, angling her body so the crowd could see them both. "Since the queen has come into her power, Kainen has sought to run this court fairly and I'm aiming to follow his lead. Could you say you've done the same? Been fair to people? Not lied and tricked them by, oh, I don't know, glamouring yourself and pretending to be someone else?"

She swiped her hand out moments before he sent a wave of burning power to attack her. It hit her warding and she flinched, but her protection held strong.

She laughed even though her insides were roiling with fear, forcing the sound to seem natural as it rolled over the silent, expectant crowd.

They didn't care who won, she realised. The whole thing, the court, the rules and traditions, it was all a performance.

They don't care who wins or leads, only who benefits them. It's all about meaningless appearances.

"Well then, let's do this the fair way," Emil said, his tone lower and rougher than it had been when he was Lorens. "I challenge you to the right of the court by combat. That's an ancient Faerie law that even a court lady can't refuse."

100

Ace stepped forward but Reyan threw her arm out to stop him. In her panic about becoming court lady, and while having to fake it before that, she'd done as much research as she could find time for.

"A bold move," she said. "I have the power of the court still behind me. The other courts won't recognise your rule even if you do best me, which would leave this court friendless and undefended. The nobles would instantly lose most of their social standing by association. Then, when the queen returns, she'll outcast anyone involved. And when Kainen returns, he'll win the court right back."

The crowd began to mutter but she let them. Give them a chance to show their loyalty.

Let them be part of the performance.

She turned her body slightly, keeping Emil in sight as she swept her gaze over the rest of the crowd.

"Tell me, those of you who patronise this court, those of you who are sworn to it, what has he offered you?" She pushed a vein of compulsion behind the next word, not sure it would work for her like it did Kainen but hoping for the best. "Speak."

Silence ran through the hall. Her heart fell.

"He promised us we would have the best rooms at court." Glennoria stepped forward, her movements stiff and her words sounding forced. "Oh!"

Her shock suggested that Reyan's compulsion had worked, her link to Kainen's court still strong enough to let her share and wield his gifts through it.

That also means he's still out there somewhere, even if we can't reach him.

Bold under the strength of that thought alone, she turned to Lord Marquest, who currently had the best rooms at court.

"And I suppose he offered you an upgrade too?" she asked.

Lord Marquest's thunderous face was answer enough.

"No, strangely, he did not."

Reyan laughed. "Typical. The court is mine because I put effort into it. I've fought for it since Kainen chose me. Since the court itself chose me. I fight for the court and for him now, but also because this is my home."

She turned to Lorens, circling him as he kept her in sight. He wouldn't take losing well, and she guessed he could have a host of Belladonna's minions here to take the court by force if he threw enough of a tantrum over it. But she needed her court strong and loyal. For some, she would need to use fear, like the nobility who craved leadership and excess of power. For the staff, she would need to use fairness and kindness.

For Kainen's sake, she would do both.

"How about the rest of you?" she asked. "Have you been promised bigger rooms? More revels? Come on, *speak*."

The silence pushed doubt into her mind, moments spanning excruciatingly slowly. Then a cascade of indignant voices filled the air.

"We were told we'd not have to trade so much of our time."

"Well *we* were told we'd be gifted with more lands around court."

"Not the south lands?"

"Of course, are there any better?"

"WE were promised the south lands!"

Reyan let the court explode in fury for a few seconds. Let them choke on their whims and greed. She kept Emil's gaze locked to hers, forcing her smile wider despite being so tired she wanted to fall over instead.

"As you see, your little machinations seem to have unravelled. Do you still want to challenge me when nobody at court will trust you?" She flicked a gaze to the court. "Does anyone here want to support his challenge? I'm sure he'd be the first to invite people to fight me on his behalf. That's very much his style by all accounts."

Emil's fists clenched and she gritted her teeth as his power swept against her warding. She tensed every single muscle, fighting the push of it that threatened to sweep her into the water.

But other sensations were wrapping around her, shields of protection merging with hers. Ace stood beside her, his eyes ablaze with fury, his hand held out as waves of green energy pulsed from his palm and smashed Emil's warding in return.

Reyan reached through their wardings, his granting her entry based on pure trust. When she settled her hand on his arm, he relented.

"Forgive me, Lady," he said, loud enough for the spellbound, gossip-hungry court to hear. "I know you don't need my help, but that one was personal."

She nodded acknowledgement but almost choked over a startled breath when she saw the fringe of the court closest to them. The staff she recognised well enough, but they had formed a line between the decks and the rest of the court, Meri right in the middle with Amba at her side.

"We make up about half of the court," Amba announced cheerfully. "We serve it and live in it. I wouldn't challenge our lady right now, not unless you want frogs in your toilets and dung in your beds."

Reyan did choke that time, horrified laughter spilling out.

"My court at least gives their loyalty to me, even if the courtiers are too timid to speak up and pledge theirs," she said.

Emil took a step back as Ace took a step forward. Reyan lifted a hand, but before she could find some way to force Emil to stay, he vanished.

"Crud," Ace muttered. "We had him right there!"

She patted his arm and faced the court again, keeping her warding firm.

"As you can see, this is my court. It belongs to me, Kainen and those loyal to me. You've been warned, and that kindness will not come a second time. Now, go make some mischief and don't disturb me unless the walls are falling in."

Orbs, I'm giving them ideas.

She waited until the crowd noise had reached a proper level and the natural echoes of indignant arguments started up. She couldn't risk showing any of them how weak she was after a victory, but her legs were beginning to shake.

"Go back to the room," Ace murmured. "I'll be right there the normal way."

Reyan nodded. He would find somewhere safe and discreet to let Milo know the latest update. She trusted him to be safe in her court, mainly because Meri knew it would cause a war with the queen's court if anything happened to him.

With the last of her reserves, Reyan skipped into Kainen's bedroom and collapsed onto the bed.

His smell had disappeared from the fabric already and she pressed her face into the covers, anguish spilling over as tears burned her eyes.

Where are you? Why did you have to be near that painting? Why you? Taz and Demi should have gone

104

together and then you'd be here.

She slammed a fist into the nearest lump of fabric and forced herself upright as a knock came at the door.

"Come in."

Nobody could enter without her permission, not even Ace, but she relaxed when she saw it was him.

"That could have gone worse," she said.

He eyed her disapprovingly and walked toward the balcony that overlooked the main hall. She kept the drapes shut because that kept the noise out and her conversations safely inside, but Ace seemed more interested now in peeking out.

"You should be less provocative when dealing with those not of our court," he said.

Reyan froze. That was the first time Ace had tried to reprimand her properly. Nag her softly about taking care of herself yes, give her a withering remark about doing things differently, absolutely. But such standoffish condemnation about how she'd taken down their enemy seemed excessively harsh for him.

Is he angry at me for not letting him pulverise Emil?

"You were ready to attack him yourself," she countered. "You did attack him."

"I do what I have to do."

She'd never heard that tone from him before either. He sounded nothing like the young man who'd sat on her bed and shown her his vulnerabilities. Her gaze dropped to his arms. Then to his wrist.

She let the fingers of one hand slide across the bedcovers to her other wrist, to the colourful wire and bead rainbow bracelet Demi had insisted all those she trusted wear.

Ace of all people wouldn't have taken his off.

Yet, there he apparently was, standing with entirely bare wrists and sounding nothing like himself.

Fury gave her the strength when she was running on empty. Reaching out her hand, she sent her intent flying through the air. The magic hit Ace and sputtered, her power all but spent.

It was enough, just a hint to see his black skin turn tanned and his black hair turn blonde, his chin flaring with the wisps of a goatee.

"I'd advise you to be extremely careful talking down to me like that," she seethed, keeping the pretence going. "You of all people don't want to cross me."

'Ace' turned with surprise in his eyes. He seemed lost for words, but then what could he say without lying?

Another knock came at the door and Reyan smiled wickedly. Ciel had clearly cast a new glamour after the incident with Emil, perhaps hoping to come in as Ace and get information from her, or worse. She'd spoken first which offered him a loophole out of the protection Kainen had put between them, but he couldn't actively hurt her. There was no harm in letting him think she was immune to his trickery.

"Get out, Ciel. It's pitiful that you think a glamour would work on me in my own court. Whatever you and your Forgotten buddies are planning, it won't work. This is your final warning. Kainen may have been lenient with your disloyalty, but I won't be. One more move and you're banished from court."

The glamour slipped.

"COME IN." She called out as he took a hurried step toward her.

Ace opened the door and stopped dead, his gaze narrowing.

"Ciel was just leaving," she said. "He won't be coming back into my presence under any circumstances unless called for."

Ciel's cheeks reddened at the threat, but he swept toward the door and almost knocked right through Ace in his hurry to leave.

"Should I ask?" Ace asked anyway. "I shouldn't have left you alone, that was selfish of me."

Reyan shrugged and flopped back onto the bed.

"You can't watch me forever. He came in glamoured as you."

Ace winced. "How did you know it wasn't?"

"That." She pointed to the bracelet on his wrist. "He didn't think of it, or know about it."

Ace looked down at the bracelet, a twin of the one Reyan wore. He wiped a hand over his mouth and chuckled.

"Demi really does think of everything. I'd love to see inside her brain one day."

Reyan smiled wearily. "She'd warn you against it."

"We'll sort out a human signal too then," he said. "If you're ever afraid I'm not me, tap your forehead twice, and I'll answer by biting my forefinger."

"Well, that won't look ridiculous at all." She laughed. "But okay."

CHAPTER TEN
BLOSSOM

Blossom clung to the railing over the enormous, yawning pit of darkness that tumbled down the centre of the Arcanium library. The walkway across shook with the impact of rebounding gifts being cast, but she was more worried about being caught by her sister again.

Belladonna stood red-faced with rage, but she had no gifts to attack with and Beryl Eastwick seemed quite happy guarding her. Extremely gleeful, in fact.

Blossom glanced over her shoulder, searching the chaos for any sign of someone she recognised. She knew the Eastwick sisters by reputation and although she had her own gifts, she didn't want to waste energy fighting Taz's friends if she had to then ask him to protect her. Nobody knew she wasn't the enemy anymore and they wouldn't hesitate to mete out justice for friends they'd lost.

But even though she'd changed sides, the mere thought of begging for favour from her brother made her insides curdle with disgust.

It can't be avoided. We've been pampered with privilege for so long we've lost our ability to fall back on survival.

A flash of orange flitted beside her and she ducked. The walkway shook as something thudded between her, Belladonna and Beryl and it took her a moment of swaying before she could look up.

Taz landed with his fiery wings outstretched, the *metirin* iron blade that had killed the Old King in his hand.

"Where is she," he snarled. "Where did you send her?"

Blossom winced. The first thing he did was ask about Demerara even as his court was at war around him.

"Your pet blood-rat?" Belladonna spat at her feet. "She took my place. She's either flailing around in the Prime Realm, or she's dead. Who cares? Gift me my powers back, or those of equal ability, and I will consider letting you live."

Someone shot past at a ferocious speed. Taz stumbled and reached out to grab the railing, pulling Beryl alongside him. Already clinging to her side, Blossom saw the flash of something arc through the air and into Belladonna's hand.

Not caring what it was, Belladonna threw it at Taz with a triumphant laugh.

Crud. Blossom shot out a hand to summon the bottle. *She really is going to kill me.*

Belladonna snarled as Taz looked up to find a bottle inches from his face and zooming sideways. Instead of catching it, Blossom lashed out and sent it flying down into the abyss below.

"Traitor!" Belladonna roared.

Blossom ignored her and lifted her gaze to Taz, now back on his feet and staring back at her with a strange frown of consideration.

Another round of shaking on the walkway turned them all to face the library and Blossom's heart sank. She recognised Crew and Rayne, two of Belladonna's most sycophantic meatheads. They craved violence as much as Belladonna did, but without her finesse and deviancy. Where she tortured, they smashed.

Taz would leave her to handle herself, Blossom knew that. She firmed her warding but influencing any part of the walkway would leave them at risk too.

"Coward!" Taz bellowed behind her.

Blossom glanced back to see Belladonna already on the run to the other end of the walkway.

"I'm on it," Beryl shouted. "Crud, they're trying to bring the walkway down that end. Harvey! Catch her!"

Unable to follow them as fighting exploded on the other end of the walkway, Blossom faced Crew and Rayne, steeling herself to fight.

Rayne raised her hand and slowed, uncertain.

"You're one of us?" she asked.

Blossom hesitated as Taz appeared beside her.

He gave her a look. "I dunno, are you?"

Blossom glanced between them, stuck. A choice, one she never intended to truly own, fluttered in front of her. She grasped the strand of fate and clung on.

"I'm on my side," she said.

Rayne scowled. "So you *are* a traitor."

She shoved her hand forward, a wave of metal pins flying from her palm. Blossom lifted her arm, knowing those pins were tipped by *metirin* iron and would pierce her warding like fire burning through wool.

The pins shivered before they ever reached her face, dribbling to liquid metal and splatting on the walkway.

"Don't attack my sister," Taz shouted.

Blossom froze. "Sister? Really?"

She gathered her strength from the surprise and summoned a crossbow. She didn't have the kind of gifts that could attack easily, but if she used Belladonna's iron arrows to pierce their wardings, Taz could attack them easier.

"It's weird for me too, don't worry," he muttered. "Hang on."

He clicked his fingers and summoned a wave of fire, lashing it around Crew and Rayne, wardings and all. Forcing them back with it like a reverse lead, he set off toward the carnage on the nearest library level. Blossom followed him.

"We got your message," he said.

She nodded. "I had to. I... well, you know what's been going on since I approached the queen. Belladonna's beyond madness and Emil is pulling her strings."

"You know where he is?" Taz asked, his jaw clenched.

He looked every inch the prince he'd been born to be, his shoulders broader than she remembered and his determination to protect his home clear in his level chin and the piercing swirl of his turquoise eyes.

"He said something about trying to take the Illusion Court with Kainen away. Oh, and Belladonna killed Lord Rydon. She named me lady in his stead."

Taz huffed in fury, whipping the fire so it sent Crew and Rayne clattering into the nearest bookshelf. A ferally indignant scream echoed from somewhere near the main desk but Taz ignored it, so Blossom did too.

111

"Renounce it," he insisted. "That should go to Cerys."

Blossom nodded. "I already told her if anything happens to me, the court is hers. I didn't expect to make it out of this unscathed anyway to be honest. I hoped, but this is Faerie."

Taz rubbed the back of his neck and looked around at the battle raging.

"The sides fairly matched," he said. "If I send you somewhere, will you go? Will you be loyal to us? To Demi? Or is that orb-muncher pulling your strings too?"

She didn't need to ask who he meant. She pulled herself up to her full height and faced him down, determined to carve some essence of respectability for herself once this mess was over.

"I won't betray you or Queen Demerara. If you give me something to do, I'll do it as best I can."

He nodded, a flash of wickedness passing over his face.

"Good. You know the nobles best out of all of us. Go to the Illusion Court. Support Reyan. Get the nobles on her side and Emil out. Dead if you have to, but by choice, I want him alive and wriggling when I get a hold of him."

Blossom wrinkled her nose at the vision that conjured, Emil wriggling on the end of Taz's sword, but then realisation dawned.

"You're sending me to help her? She hates me. She won't believe I'm there to help."

Taz shunted in front of her before she saw the attack coming. He sent their assailant flying with a savage swipe of his flaming wings then gave her a grim look.

"Don't convince her, convince her court. If Kainen returns, he's lord of it but the court itself claimed her so she's their lady now in her own right. The nobles need to fall in line too. Make them. Actions not words."

She didn't dare tell him that Belladonna often said a similar thing before torturing people, that word-tangling and word-play were fun but nowhere near as meaningful as hurting them.

"Alright." She breathed in, pushing down the horror at the mere thought. "If I have to."

Taz nodded. "If you do this, if you prove yourself loyal, I'll make sure Demi recognises it once this is all done. Can't say fairer than that."

He couldn't. She didn't ask how he knew that she could realm-skip by herself and he didn't offer to send or take her, so she took a step back and reached into the nether. She didn't want to see the Illusion Court again, not after that mortifying embarrassment of Kainen choosing an untitled nobody like Reyan Roseglade over her in front of everyone.

As the nether wisped around her, a flash of the library scene caught her eye and she opened her mouth in horror, in warning.

"Watch out for Belladonna!" she screamed.

But as the image of her sister bearing down on her brother with an old-fashioned shield and sword in hand dissipated, her words were lost to the nether.

CHAPTER ELEVEN
DEMI

Facing an enormous beast in the shadows of a realm I'd never intended to visit wasn't how I envisioned spending my evening.

The shadow loomed between the trees before any of us could react, the dark shape of a wolf lengthening, the mouth yawning wide. It was the size of a large horse and twice as broad, even more terrifying when the moonlight hit its pelt and highlighted dark, matted patches amid an otherwise smooth grey coat. Its snarl echoed through the gloom, the rumbling noise rattling the rocks around us.

The shadow lifted its front paws off the ground, standing tall on hind legs. Panic thrummed through me and I wound my warding around all of us, putting every essence of my power into it.

The enormous wolf sniffed. Stilled. And smiled with two rows of glinting, lethal teeth. Fear pounded but I caught the sight of something flitting away, a part of the shadow fracturing free of its host and escaping into the darkness. Thoughts of Reyan filled my head but she couldn't take forms that I knew of, and her pet shadow was a snake not a wolf. But the glimmer of a human-shaped shadow remained as the four-legged darkness shot into the forest, the air and essence of ancient danger around it stabbing my nerves right through.

A loud crackle tore the air and an errant spark flared from somewhere. I flinched and raised a hand to shade my eyes but the spell was broken. The shadow of the person, half-wolf, whatever it was, had disappeared.

In the distance, a feral howl tore through the forest. I clenched my fist around the strap of my satchel as several other cries answered the wolf's call.

I caught Sabine's eye. "We have to go."

Another round of howling echoed, getting louder.

"They are close," she hissed. "We will need to run fast."

I grimaced at that but what else could we do? I couldn't magic up carriages or horses here, and it wasn't like I could just orb Trevor to come and get us or we wouldn't still be here.

"Hurry." Sabine was already bouncing on the balls of her feet. "There's an outbuilding where we can hide our scent until morning. The foundry isn't too far after that."

We had no choice as she set off at a jog. Even with MC as a guide, he wouldn't be guiding us anywhere if we all got eaten, and masking our scent was a sensible plan.

I set off after her, not daring to look at Kainen as he dashed past me at a spritely pace. I would be able to follow him and have MC follow me through the darkness, but while it wasn't exactly my fault Kainen was here with me, he was probably regretting his decision to support me.

Taz would laugh his arse off if he could see me now.

My cheeks burned like they were sunburnt from the exertion despite the rain, and my body ached like I'd been fighting combat classes for a week solid. My mind pounded around and around with worries and doubts, but I forced each footfall to follow the other.

"Up here," Sabine shouted.

I didn't bother to look up until the rain stopped cascading down my face and Sabine and Kainen were standing right in front of me. Neither of them looked more than a little bit puffed out, but I doubled over panting.

I'm going to start running or something when I get home. Ace can train me.

It was a mindless thought because no way was I going to spend time running if I did manage to get home, but it made me feel a bit better when MC stumbled into the barn behind me looking like he'd run the entire length of Faerie in one go.

"I…" He staggered to the wall and leaned against it. "I'm not good at running."

Sabine and Kainen exchanged a doubtful look, but I was too busy realising what exactly was around us.

"Um…" Kainen hesitated. "I get the idea behind covering our scent, but are we actually sleeping in here with the manure?"

Sabine scoffed. "You're high-born, I take it? It'll keep us safe until morning which is more than you'd be if I left you wandering out there. The rain will wash our scent back down the hill and the manure will cloak us."

It wasn't ideal. It wasn't even tolerable really, but it was safe.

"It'll be fine," I insisted. "We can take turns keeping watch in case."

Outside a chorus of howls filled the night air but they didn't sound any closer than before.

"I won't risk starting a fire, but I have rolls if anyone needs them," Sabine said.

She handed out musty blankets from a cupboard in the corner of the barn, giving Kainen a disparaging glance when he took it with a turned up nose.

"We move at sunrise," she added. "Sleep as much as you can now."

Kainen sat on his blanket, eying her with wariness, but Sabine was too busy delving into the large pack she'd been toting on her back to notice.

While nursing my grumbling stomach, I wondered how to question Sabine and get some real answers. If Kainen couldn't compel her, maybe I could. If I couldn't, perhaps the human fallback of actual conversation would work. Not my strength in any way, but given that she and Kainen seemed to have taken a disliking to each other, I couldn't exactly ask him to try charming her now.

Sabine pulled a few things out of her pack before getting up to shut the barn door, plunging us into darkness. Even as queen I didn't have enhanced sight like some Fae did, so I would need to trust Kainen to use his to keep watch. Wrapping my warding around me, I sent another stream of mind-speak out to Taz. For all I knew, he was getting mine but I wasn't getting his, so it was worth the effort to try.

I flinched as a loud snuffling noise surrounded us.

"MC's off to the land of dreams," Kainen said, amused.

"Fnnarrff... Peapot pudding," MC replied grumpily before descending into another round of snoring.

"So, let's talk in truths," Sabine said, her tone guarded. "You can do magic?"

I nodded before realising she might not be able to see me.

"We have gifts. I think MC mentioned people here have land gifts, so it's a bit like that. We can... well, Kainen can summon black smoke and I can wield energy, flame and frost."

I conveniently left out the bit about being queen and that we could compel, although she seemed eerily immune.

"Rare gifts indeed. My guardian was blessed with strong land gifts like yours. But why are you set on reaching the spire?"

I hesitated. It couldn't hurt to tell her we wanted to leave, unless she saw our gifts as a prize to be sold and was planning to lead us into a trap. But she needed something from us in order to tell us what we needed.

"We're not from around here," I said. "We want to go home. That involves magic type stuff, which MC said the spire would be the best place for."

Sabine huffed in the dark. I had no way of reading her reactions other than sound, but again I had to hope Kainen could. And that I really could trust him this far.

"I'm bound to the foundry to see my guardian. She's lived a long time and knows a lot about myth and magic. She would know how to help you. The foundry is also where certain types of folk go to learn the magical arts."

"Then that's where we need to go." I sighed.

Thoughts of getting home to Taz filled my head.

I'll never complain about Milo making me do paperwork ever again if I can only go home.

In that moment, I really meant it.

Sabine moved before my hearing could register the movement, but as Kainen's feet thudded on the floor, Sabine bounced against my warding and fell to the floor.

"Ah, what is that?" she seethed.

I had no idea where Kainen was but I risked a bit of my power and made my fingertips glow. Sabine stood staring up at me, eyes wide and lips parted. Kainen stood beside me as close as my warding would allow, but he gave me a subtle shake of his head, as if to say she hadn't been trying to attack me.

"Who are you?" Sabine whispered.

Kainen reached out and a tendril of glittering black smoke danced in the flickering light from my energy. It pushed against Sabine's forehead and I fought every kneejerk reaction inside me to lunge forward and break her away, to protect her from the same horrors he'd once forced on me.

The smoke dissipated almost immediately, leaving Sabine blinking.

"You're a queen?" she asked.

I glowered at Kainen. "What did you show her?"

"The Battle of Queens."

I grimaced, focusing on Sabine who admittedly had an MC-style wideness in her eyes now as she stared at me.

"I'm not a normal sort of queen," I explained, as if that would solve anything.

When she didn't answer, I dropped onto my blanket and hunched over my knees to the sound of scrabbling nearby.

"Here." Sabine inched up to my warding. "Not much for a queen, but I'm guessing you have the same needs as the rest of us."

I took the roll and gave her a grateful smile, shovelling it into my mouth as quick as I could. I ignored Kainen smirking at my lack of manners and wiped my mouth with the back of my hand.

"I didn't grow up to be a queen, don't worry. That was scrummy."

Sabine frowned. "Scrummy? What does that mean?"

"It means delicious. Yummy, it tastes really nice."

She nibbled at her first mouthful and swallowed before responding.

"Oh, good. We try to avoid wastage here. We have found uses for most of our perishables."

I could almost hear my mum's voice echoing around me, complaining yet again that the council's bin collection had gone down to fortnightly. I thought about my sister Mary throwing away socks that barely had any fraying, and

Jenny's habit of binning dirty clothes rather than cleaning them.

"We aren't quite so conscious where I'm from I'm afraid," I admitted.

Sabine paused with a frown. "What do you mean? We reuse everything, like fabrics that are no longer fit for use are repurposed for cleaning, or banners, or bedding."

"Yeah, we don't so much," Kainen said. "I guess you don't throw out toys once you've outgrown them, or broken furniture?"

Sabine shifted in her seat. "Throw out, as in, put outside? Why would we? Furniture is either broken down for firewood or made into something else. Toys are donated to younger children in the village, although we keep our favourites of course. Food scraps that can't be formed into pies or soups are fed to the animals."

I thought about the amount of games, teddies and handed-down football boots that had sailed straight out of my mum's house and into the bin over the years. The thought of donating them probably never occurred to anyone, and it reminded me that we could always learn so much from other realms if we simply paid attention.

"It's admirable." I decided we would start recycling absolutely everything if I ever made it back to Arcanium. "We just get rid of stuff."

For several moments, Sabine stared from me to Kainen and back again in a horrified sort of wonder. She scratched her chin, as if working out the best way to pose her next question.

"But, where does it go?"

I was ready for that. "Most of it just goes to landfill."

Ironic really that the human and Fae worlds had their similarities in the more mundane things.

120

"Land, fill?" Sabine shook her head. "What is land fill?"

"A big hole in the ground all the unwanted stuff is put in and left."

The deeper I explained, the more ridiculous it sounded. Sabine's nostrils flared as she wrinkled her lip.

"I am not sure I understand. Is it like storage? When do you go and get it back?"

I gulped down a rising sense of hysteria as Kainen hastened to explain.

"You don't, it just stays there until it rots. Some of it doesn't, like the metal."

Oh orbs. I slumped forward, elbows digging into my knees. *Think of all the spoons stuck there rusting and the plastic toys that won't disintegrate.*

Sabine wisely decided not to press the issue, although she gave us both a very baffled look while I stared into the glow of my gift flickering softly over my hand, my mind awash with panic. This was the sort of thing I was supposed to consider as queen, yet I'd been so busy sorting out court matters and trying to implement initiatives that I hadn't thought much about the day to day practicality of Faerie itself and how it operated.

The thoughts stayed with me as I tried and failed to sleep that night, and even as we moved about with awkward efficiency the moment daylight hit the next morning.

We walked on through the forest in silence, Sabine taking the lead with me behind her while Kainen tried to keep asking MC questions he didn't seem very clear on knowing the answers to. If Sabine heard them and knew any, she definitely didn't say.

Only when we stopped to rest and eat in the seemingly endless woods did I start doubting.

"How far is this foundry?" I asked.

Sabine's hands froze around the roll she was holding.

"Foundry?" MC piped up. "Why would you want to go there? I thought we were going to the spire. I don't think I want to go to the foundry."

The sheer disbelief in his voice at the end heightened my worries. I pushed my hands into my sleeves before anyone saw my fists clenching.

"My mentor will be able to help," Sabine said.

I frowned. "And who is your mentor exactly?"

"Her name is Tirzella, but-"

"Oh, you definitely won't find her at the spire then." MC seemed fuelled by obliviousness and his third roll in the space of one minute. "I was told that Tirzella is a great sorceress, so she wouldn't be going anywhere near the foundry."

"Why not?" I asked.

MC blinked at me.

Kainen sighed. "Why not?"

"Oh, well, the Foundry is where the followers of the Great Obe are. They mine the iron that stops the bad folk returning."

He hesitated, staring at Kainen then glancing quickly at me.

"Bad folk?" Kainen asked.

It took all my effort to be patient and silent, my instincts firing with foreboding as my gifts scratched and rioted around my bones. Any question I asked would be met with more blinking and silence, so I'd let Kainen take the lead even if he was going to be excruciatingly slow about it.

"Well, yes." MC finished his roll and grimaced. "Everyone knows that the Great Obe stopped the bad folk from ruling us with their magic. The foundry is where they forge the iron that killed them."

Metirin iron. My brain grabbed the thread and tugged. Emil and Belladonna wanted access to the Prime Realm get more *metirin* iron. If they had an unlimited or even modest supply, they'd be able to torment and control so many.

"Who runs this foundry then?" Kainen asked.

MC froze with his hand extended toward the last roll wrapped in cloth on the upturned tree we stood around.

"His name is Loth, the latest leader of the Great Obeians. He hates magic. It's definitely going to be the spire you want."

Kainen glanced at me, his gaze flicking lightning fast in Sabine's direction. Suspiciously silent, she stood slightly apart from us. I knew what he was asking. I nodded.

"Sabine?" He waited until she looked his way. "Is this true?"

Before she could answer, I reached over, wrapped my hands around the anklet peeking beneath the hem of her trousers and yanked with all my might.

"Loth has been taking over most of the land with his band of fanatics, the followers of Obe," she said. "I've been looking for Tirzella since they captured her. She's our most ancient lady of arcane arts and the only one who knows how to contain Loth and stop him."

She blinked the moment the words were out, her hand leaping to her lips. I had no idea if Kainen had somehow manipulated her into forgetting about the anklet the moment it was off, but she didn't so much as glance down at it.

Feeling hellishly guilty, I slid the anklet and its broken clasp into my pocket. I'd return it as soon as we knew we had the answers we needed.

"You think Tirzella is being held in the foundry then?" I asked.

She nodded, her shoulders slumping in defeat. I couldn't be sure if she knew Kainen was using magic on her, but now she'd started with the truth, it tumbled out of her.

"The Obeians crept into the grounds of her home and took her. They've denounced her as a heretic on all the posters in the nearest settlements and plan to sacrifice her somehow."

I wiped a hand over my face, the lack of sleep and sheer stress from the whole situation draining my ability to do much of anything.

"And you think taking us to this foundry instead is going to help somehow?"

Sabine sighed. "When you explained magic to me, it sounds similar to something Tirzella has mentioned before. But I meant it when I said she would be the one to help you. For her to do that, we have to free her first."

I leaned my hip against the fallen tree with a soft groan. I usually had Taz here to tell me if an idea was nuts or worth going for. I couldn't remember the last time I'd had to deal with anything without his input or the sheer comforting presence of knowing I had him beside me.

"We need a plan then," I said. Because if this Tirzella could get us home, rescuing her would be the best way to convince her she should be kind enough to consider doing it for us.

"Well then." Kainen rolled his shoulders with a grimace. "Luckily, plans is one thing we are excellent at."

CHAPTER TWELVE
REYAN

"Lady Blossom has appeared." Meri at least didn't sound impressed about it after she materialised unannounced in Kainen's bedroom. "Is she still a lady? If not, which room should I put her in?"

Reyan doubled over and groaned. She'd finished an exhausting round of audiences with nobles all clamouring for her favour. It would have been hilarious in any other situation, those who had mistreated her as a servant and mocked her as Kainen's future bride now fawning over her as Lady.

Emil had disappeared and she couldn't get any sense of him at the court, but Ciel was still lurking. She seemed to see him everywhere, as if he was watching her. Thoughts filled her head of Emil glamouring as Ciel waiting for a chance to strike, but she'd had Ace glamour into different people to see if he 'felt' any different. He didn't.

Ciel was a problem that could keep though, and Emil was a problem currently outside the boundaries of her court.

Blossom, or Lady Blossom if she was still titled as such after all her treachery, apparently wanted to throw herself onto the long list of 'things Reyan still has to deal with'.

"Might I suggest greeting her like a friend if you're doing it publicly?" Ace said.

Reyan stared at him. "Nobody would ever believe that."

"Well, she's waiting in the main hall and talking to many of her 'old friends', so I'd be sharp about it," Meri added.

She disappeared immediately after and Reyan fought the urge to cry. Somehow, balancing an entire court of nobles with the wolves lurking inside and outside wasn't as intimidating as facing someone who hated her for being her, rather than for her position or her title.

"Right, come here."

Reyan blinked as Ace opened his arms. "What?"

"It's a hug," he chuckled. "Lean on me, take a minute, then go out and give her hell. I can't actually tell you why I'm telling you this, but trust me when I say it. She might not be the enemy you're assuming."

Reyan checked her bracelet and, feeling foolish, tapped herself twice. When Ace bit his forefinger with a knowing grin, she relented and nestled into the warmth of his chest.

"Think of me like the big brother you never had," he suggested. "And just know that Demi has spies in many places."

Reyan lifted her head. "Are you saying Blossom is Demi's spy?"

Her mind thundered before snagging, Ace's smile widening at the look on her face.

She kept making really dim mistakes. Belladonna even slapped her for it once.

"She… she made mistakes," she muttered, her mind racing. "She let things slip in front of Lolly and Tyren. She fumbled a couple of summonings at the Nether Court too, unless I was imagining it. She gave me Belladonna's gifts, one of them at least."

Ace nodded. "Ask her. Do a glamour lift and once you know she's really her, make her tell you the truth. I definitely can't divulge Demi's secrets-"

"But I can make Blossom tell me hers."

He chuckled. "Exactly. But try and be nice. If she is on

our side, you two should probably put the axes down at least a bit."

"She won't like that."

"Only one way to find out."

Reyan nodded. "I'll see her in the office."

She stepped away from Ace and walked across the bedroom to open the multi-way door to the study. Ace followed her in, shutting the door behind him.

"Where do you want me?" he asked, his tone light. "Looming in the corner? Sitting beside you?"

Reyan snorted. "You can lounge on top of the desk in your pants if you want. I don't want to give her any indication I'm intimidated by her."

"Female pride?"

"Absolutely."

She dragged a spare chair from the corner of the room to the other side of the desk and Ace carried a second one over to go beside Kainen's chair.

Settling into it, Reyan summoned the black smoke and clicked her fingers.

"Ciel, bring Lady Blossom to the office."

She bit down on the automatic 'please' brewing.

Ace nudged her thigh with his knee until she looked at him.

"He'd be so proud of you," he said.

Reyan tensed. "Don't. I can't cry in front of her."

"Then don't cry, but he chose you. I know it was a fake originally but it wasn't by the end. He loves you, and he'd want me to tell you he'd be proud of how well you're managing his court."

Reyan didn't get a chance to tell him off as someone knocked loudly on the door. She inhaled sharply, lounged with a little more purpose to her body and leaned her head

127

back against the chair, contemplating toying with her dagger for effect.

"Come in."

Ciel opened the door and Blossom stalked past him. When he made to enter after her, Reyan gave him a dark look and he slunk out again.

"You wanted to see me?" Reyan asked.

Blossom nodded. "Believe it or not, my brother sent me."

Reyan trusted Ace's judgement, but she didn't feel easy having Blossom in the court no matter the reason.

"Did he? Why?"

She would let Blossom tell her version before pulling the truth out of her, see how easily she omitted things.

Blossom eyed the vacant chair.

"May I sit?" she asked, her tone stiff.

Reyan nodded. "If you want."

Blossom sat but there was a tension to the elegant posture and the delicately folded legs. Taking comfort from that, Reyan waited with her best attempt at a no-nonsense expression.

"Will we be overheard here?"

Reyan shook her head. "Not by anyone I don't trust, and Ace has my confidence."

The irritation began to build, itching through her limbs as Blossom delayed the inevitable.

"I suppose there's no sense in avoiding things." Blossom sighed. "After the last war, I approached the queen and asked for forgiveness of a sort. She sent me back to my sister as her spy. Since then, I've been doing my best to leave clues about what Belladonna has been up to-"

"You left the door open."

Blossom's cheeks tinged pink and her brow creased,

possibly at being interrupted.

"Excuse me?"

"At the nether court, you left the door open to the tunnels where Be- that shadow-snake was."

Blossom hesitated, then leaned forward the tiniest amount.

"I did. I saw the shell starting to crack but Belladonna didn't, so I found an excuse to get her out and left the door open. I thought if it managed to escape it'd be safer in the tunnels than with my sister. How did you know that?"

"I found the door open. Then..." Reyan hesitated. "We found the snake too."

Blossom sank back in her seat with a gentle huff.

"Is it safe?"

Reyan nodded. "Yes, and that's all I'll say."

"Fair enough. There's little else to tell, but now that Belladonna has attacked Arcanium-"

"What?!"

Ace exploded out of his seat and Reyan flinched in alarm.

Blossom blinked at him then turned back to Reyan.

"My brother seems to think the sides are evenly matched, but he has it in hand. At least, I think he does. He told me to come here and support you. If I prove myself loyal here, he'll ensure I'm not forgotten about once the war is over."

If she was who she said she was, none of that would be a lie, but she'd been surprisingly frank without any hint of word-tangling over her reasons. Reyan glanced at Ace's panic-stricken face.

"Do you need to go?" she asked.

"I... it'll be okay," he said. "My job is here."

"Take whatever time you need to orb home then," she

insisted.

He pulled his orb out. "Milo?"

Reyan's heart squeezed tight in her chest as they waited, seconds ticking by.

Milo's face loomed into the middle of the desk between them, Ace's relieved breath huffing over it.

"We're a bit busy right now- NOT THE FOLIOS!"

"Are you okay?" Ace demanded.

Milo's image bobbed with a nod. "Enough. Taz has been spoiling for a fight for days, so this will keep him occupied if nothing else. Are you okay?"

"Yeah, we're fine. I heard… you know what? Check in regularly."

"You too," Milo said. "Oh orbs, THOSE ARE PRICELESS YOU ABSOLUTE BUFFOON."

He disappeared and Ace sank back into his seat with a grunt.

"He seems okay," Reyan said.

Ace chuckled. "I guess so. He's feral himself where the books are concerned, but he doesn't exactly know how to fight."

Blossom cleared her throat, whether out of awkwardness or impatience, Reyan couldn't be sure. Irritated by the interruption, Reyan cast a glamour lift over her in retaliation.

Blossom's eyebrows rose but apart from that she remained the same.

"I suppose that was warranted," she said with a sniff. "Taz has sent me here with the instruction to get your nobles on your side. Many of them are friends and acquaintances of mine."

Reyan folded her arms across her chest.

"And how thorough are you intending to be?" she

asked. "You don't exactly like me."

Blossom shrugged. "I don't know you. I played the part I had to play when I had to play it. I don't particularly care for your lack of lineage, it's true, but if it helps I meant it when I said I have absolutely no interest in Kainen Hemlock. Or this court. I definitely don't want responsibility when the title of princess has enough freedom for frivolity."

Reyan's anxiety unwound slightly. Taz had sent her a lifeline, no matter how unexpected. Blossom did know the courtiers, and she would be able to convince them that Reyan's rule was the sensible one. Then Reyan could focus on proving herself reliable and strong and above all, finding Kainen.

"You will tell me anything you hear that goes against me while you're here," she announced. "Or against Kainen, the queen, Arcanium, any of that. Any plans for moving against us, any insurrections. We've already had Emil here trying to overthrow us."

"He revealed himself already? I thought- he was very determined that as Lorens…"

Reyan smiled. "Ah, so you know who he is. I'm not surprised. Yes, I did a glamour lift of the court and several nobles found themselves on the unreliable side of his not-so-honest promises. He left the court straight after."

Blossom rubbed a thumb over her lip, her shoulders lowering slightly.

"We may not share views on the rightful traditions of Faerie," she began. "But I of all people know that my sister is unhinged and needs to be stopped. Emil too. He's perhaps a little less unhinged but that makes him all the more dangerous."

"On that at least we can agree."

131

Blossom nodded. "Courts are full of Fae that are all the same. They don't care who's in power, only that they are benefiting from it."

Reyan tilted her head, letting the brush of Kainen's jacket over her temple calm her.

"What would you advise then?"

Blossom raised her eyebrows at that, hesitating as she gave it consideration.

"Play the game. Convince them that you could flatten them easily but it's more fun not to. Be strong by all means, be cruel definitely, toy with them for all to see, but also offer potential gain too."

"She's been doing a great job of that so far," Ace said.

Reyan chuckled. "You're *too* loyal I think sometimes. I'll keep doing it though if it keeps the court secure." She eyed Blossom then, letting the first tendrils of compulsion spool through the air. "Do you know what happened to him? Does Belladonna or anyone?"

Blossom pulled a face. "No, only that they went through the painting, presumably to the Prime Realm. Belladonna was adamant that was where it led."

So we already know more from overhearing Emil's little mirror chat than Blossom or Belladonna do.

"What about Ciel?" she asked.

Blossom frowned. "What about him? He hates you, I know that much. The fact you rejected his proposal has dug so deep into his ego it's surprising he can move."

"And you? Are you in league with him in any way?"

"No." Blossom laughed. "I did what needed to be done to keep Belladonna and Queen Demerara happy, but he's inconsequential to me. I can tell you that he is afraid of his family though, so if his family side with the Forgotten, so will he and happily."

Reyan had expected that, but the sheer size of Ciel's aforementioned ego, from wanting to marry her after so many years of carefully prepped friendship on his part to wanting to destroy her so quickly and easily, it was frightening.

"Well, assuming you mean no harm to me or mine, I'll be glad of your help." She admitted it grudgingly. "I've been holding audiences and since the nobles discovered Emil's tricks, they've been fawning accordingly. I've placated a few with potential promises, others with actual promises. The staff are just happy that I'm prepared to listen to them."

She lifted her hand to the scrunchie keeping her hair back from her face, a subtle swell of pride tingling at the thought.

"That is more than many court lords have done before you."

Blossom sounded disgusted at her own surprise, pulling a face and glancing around at the office instead.

Ace gave Reyan a teasing grin and stood up, holding his arm out to her.

"I'm probably supposed to remind you about things like paperwork, Lady, and your dinner reservations," he said.

Reyan had no idea what he was talking about, but given the wickedness crossing his face, he was giving her a way out of doing any more audiences. She stood and moved to the multi-way door with him at her side.

"Of course." She turned and bid the normal office door open out onto the hall. "I'll be interested to hear what rumours do the rounds now that you're here as a guest, Lady Blossom. Really interested."

CHAPTER THIRTEEN
BLOSSOM

The most jarring thing about the interaction with Reyan—*Lady* Reyan, was that Blossom had the slightest inkling of respect kindling deep in the pit of her bones for her.

She wasn't titled by birth, not from any great family full of prestige or wealth, yet here she was a lady in her own right by choice of the court and therefore Faerie itself. She'd even managed in the few moments after their meeting to have her aide appear to escort Blossom personally to the type of suite appropriate for a visiting member of the royal family.

In short, Lady Reyan was scarily like Queen Demerara.

Which means either we've all been lied to as a society our entire lives and Faerie itself actually appreciates all Fae regardless of title, or the low-borns are merely remarkably clever to climb so high.

Blossom sucked in a breath and forced the usual waft of indolent royalty around her, smile in place and glamour touching the edges of her appearance with extra shine to her eyes and flutter to her clothes. It gave her strength to know she had this power.

And Belladonna with all her vengeance and macabre cruelty has none left.

Ignoring the swoop of discomfort at the thought of the sister she had essentially betrayed, Blossom strode into the court's main hall. She knew it well, taking comfort from the towering rocky walls, the many hewn balconies and the gentle glimmer of the firelight glancing off the pool in the middle of the room.

As several nobles flocked immediately to greet her, she let herself settle. This was what she enjoyed most, the sport of flirting and playing with people's egos.

She sought through the excitable faces around her and reminded herself of the hierarchy.

"Lady Blossom." Lord Marquest was undoubtedly first. "It's an honour and a surprise to see you here. You were not a firm favourite of the lady before."

Blossom laughed, letting the sound tinkle over the noise of the crowd and draw their attention. She tilted her head to the side and shook her hair a little before meeting his gaze.

"Things change, my lord. Situations change. Lady Reyan has done surprisingly well from what I hear to hold onto a court she's not been raised for." She raised her eyebrows to intimate the possibility of an insult. "But for all those *inadequacies,* Kainen is lord of this court. He chose her. The court itself then chose her in his absence. When he returns, there will be two strong-willed nobles leading the Illusion Court. Even I would need slight preparation time if I were to challenge that."

Everyone laughed and she soaked in the familiarity of it. This was what she revelled in being, what she was suited to. She had no head for war and no taste for battles. The only secrets she liked were ones that were shared verbally, and occasionally physically.

"And do you know when Lord Kainen is due to return?" Glennoria asked.

Blossom shrugged. "Oh, I couldn't possibly say. I've missed patronising the Illusion Court and the last thing I want is my wine tab on hold because I've spoken out of turn."

Another round of laughter more raucous than the first.

"We would happily share ours, princess!" someone chortled.

Lord Marquest flourished his elbow. "Well, let us hope it will not come to that. I must insist that you join our table for dinner tonight, and our table for cards after that."

Blossom had no idea whether she had any access to funds anymore. She hadn't dared contact their mother while working for Demerara, and Belladonna had been sketchy about where the meals and supplies of declining quality at the Blood and Bone Court were coming from. But perhaps if she suggested Reyan sent Taz a bill, nobody would bother to question it.

"That is the best offer I've had all day, and I've had a few already," she said. "We all know the Illusion Court has the best hospitality, whatever the new or old Revel Courts might brag about."

"That is true," Lord Marquest agreed. "Another mark in the lady's favour, I will admit. She did cut quite a... surprising figure holding court over the challenger earlier."

Blossom widened her eyes, gasping as delicately as she could fake it.

"I did hear a whisper and I simply had to find out. I have things to see to, but you must tell me every single detail at dinner tonight."

Lord Marquest bowed his head and she inclined hers in recognition, nodding to people in the crowd as she made her way to the wide staircase leading up to the halls.

She would have to collar a servant and ask them to contact her mother's court and have some clothes couriered over. Perhaps it would also be an ideal time to word-tangle some alliance out of Ciel too, purely for information purposes. His hatred of Reyan made him an extremely easy target.

She swept down the hall but a tingling sensation of warning in her mind had her casting a protection warding. She slowed to a halt and turned.

"Hello, Emil."

He stood without his Lorens disguise, his arms folded and for the first time she could remember, he looked visibly tired around the eyes.

"How should I greet you, Blossom. Hello, traitor? Princess? Or are you so deep in machinations for Belladonna that even I misjudged your uses."

Blossom pushed aside the irritation blooming in her chest, holding her stance firm and meeting his gaze. She had to be careful, but if he had already challenged Reyan and lost, and she had Reyan's permission to be at court as a guest, he had less opportunity to harm her without consequence.

"Oh dear." She gave him a withering look. "Do you really think Belladonna doesn't have all sorts of plans and fail-safes going on? Are both of you really so arrogant that you believe the other is so easily led into trust?"

A small smile spread across his face and she had the burning urge to reach out and punch it.

"Questions answer nothing, princess."

She shrugged. "Neither do vague statements. I'm not my sister, but even though she's bordering on sycophantic in her admiration of you, she doesn't fully trust you. Here I am, and isn't it a coincidence that here you are too?"

She let that sink in as he started to laugh.

"Do you have aspirations of your own now then?" he asked.

Time to take a leaf out of the 'goodness' book Reyan and Taz and the rest of them seem to be reading from. She

137

almost shuddered at the thought. *Time for the truth.*

"I never wanted to be at the front of the war with the stresses it provides," she admitted. "No, I want to be part of the game itself, a player, taking fun from sweet talking and tricking where I need to. I have no need of a queenly title when I have princess by right of birth, and the rest I can do on my own wits."

"A *noble* pursuit," he mocked.

She shrugged. "Both your side and the queen's will win, lose, win, lose, fight fight fight. Whether it's for honour or power or ego, you'll go round and round winning and losing. This way, I don't exactly win everything, but I rarely lose everything either."

He folded his arms, eying her in a way that made her blood crawl inside her veins, the urge to run screaming in her mind.

"All this time and only now you become interesting," he said.

She forced a laugh. "I'm not any different. The interesting fact is that you're only now starting to notice. That must mean you're getting desperate, which means your pull is waning."

His shoulders stiffened and she reinforced her protection around her, smiling sweetly.

"The nobles already realise it," she added. "How about I don't run to the lady of the court right now and tell her you're here, and you leave me out of your egotistical nonsense."

Emil hummed under his breath. "If you are still on your sister's side, *my* side, then perhaps you can prove your loyalty with a little task."

He'd heard everything she said and disregarded it completely. She was a pawn to be used or discarded, barely even Fae to him. She tilted her head, indicating he should continue. Whatever he suggested would be going straight to Reyan. In that moment, even without her agreement to spy for Demerara and her intention to choose the safest side, her survival instinct knew Emil needed taking down, possibly even more than her sister did.

"I'd hear you out," she countered. "I wouldn't guarantee I'll obey mindlessly."

Emil chuckled. "The stubbornness of the royal oak line is alive and well I see. Well, let's see how you handle this then. We're arranging a little event for the lady of the court."

"An event?" Blossom forced her face to remain impassive.

"She stands in opposition of us, so we need to remove her. Are you going to run and tell and declare yourself against us?"

Frantic, Blossom sought through the potential word-tangling that would put his fears at rest. It wouldn't be an idle threat either; Emil couldn't lie.

"Lady Reyan is no concern of mine," she said. "That display over Kainen was purely what was needed at the time. I'd rather patronise the Illusion Court than lead it. I repeat, leave me out of your war games."

He took a step forward but she held her ground with her pulse pounding, stuck for something to dissuade him with. Belladonna used to simper, but Blossom had never worked out if that was legitimate adoration or a necessary admiration that required equal flattery.

But it worked.

"In some circles, you've been called the most fearsome of all Fae," she said quickly. "If you're worried about me going against you, I'd be extremely foolhardy to risk it. It's safer for me here, and more luxurious than retreating to the Fauna Court. I wouldn't be much welcome in any other at the moment."

Emil nodded. "There's truth in that. I'll be watching you, princess. Until you declare for a side, you're never truly safe."

"You're never safe even if you do."

She turned her back on him and walked a couple of paces before looking back.

"I won't be in any danger personally, will I? This event of yours?"

He rolled his eyes then and any interest he had in her vanished like quicksand. She shuddered.

"Not unless you've taken to sharing her bed, no."

CHAPTER FOURTEEN
DEMI

The stone funnel of the foundry furnace towered above everything around it, shrinking trees, buildings at the base and even a crop of mountains in the distance to toy-town size.

We'd waited for dawn to stage our entrance, but Sabine was being worryingly vague about why exactly dawn was necessary. Clouds scudded above and obscured the moon, but I could make out a low wall surrounding the village at the base of the foundry. Even though we'd managed to evade the wolves, their chorus of howling sounded almost behind us now.

"Here we go," Sabine whispered.

She started down the hill toward the village and I set off after her, aware of Kainen close to my left and MC a more respectful distance to my right. Another howl rent the air and morbid curiosity made me slow and turn back.

The border of the woods was still cloaked in darkness, but I could make out large shapes moving just beyond. The shadows formed and broke through the forest boundary. There were more wolves fringing the trees than he could possibly imagine belonging to a single pack. Amid the thick wall of fur, a pair of glowing yellow eyes watched us. None of the other wolves had eyes the colour of burning lava, or ones that belonged to a beast that tall. The leader towered over his pack. When he growled a feral warning and the enormous pack charged, I ran.

I plunged down the rocky hillside after the others as

another feral howl echoed. The responding war cry of the pack must have woken the whole village.

"We won't make it!" MC shouted, his legs pumping even faster than Kainen's in his panic.

I stumbled over the long grass snaring my feet and sent a chaotic flash of energy behind me but the responding snarl sounded like I'd just made the pack angrier.

Moving as one they shook the ground behind us and I wondered madly if I should sacrifice myself to get the others away safely. Kainen would be able to continue on without me and get back to Reyan. Sabine would have a chance to get her guardian back and no doubt someone would factor MC in too.

I didn't see Kainen stop dead ahead of me. My warding flickered weakly around me and melded with his at a startling force moments before I slammed into his back.

We tumbled to the floor and he twisted free of me like I'd burned him, stumbling away. But his attention wasn't on me and his face wasn't awash with horror, but delight. I scrambled to my feet and twisted around in time to see the entire wolf pack come to a rippling halt in the face of a giant, black-scaled serpent.

I took a healthy step back. Then another.

To my horror, Kainen was walking the other way, headed directly for the chaos as the wolves snarled and slunk away before the snake could strike.

I almost screamed as the enormous tip of its lethal tail flicked at Kainen's middle, but it turned to shadow as it passed through him.

"Betty! Thank Faerie." He turned to face me with the widest, dopiest grin I'd ever seen. "Reyan sent her with a message. Shadow-snakes can pass through pretty much anything it seems. They're looking for us. I can send her back with a message."

I had no idea what or how or why, but all I heard was that the massive demon snake thing could take a message back. I'd be able to reassure Taz we were safe, that we were on our way back to him. My heart lifted as Sabine appeared beside me.

"Whatever that thing is, it's saved us," she said. "We need to move quickly. While the wolves are out, everyone will be indoors hiding. This is our chance to sneak inside."

I nodded. "Kainen, send a quick message back to Reyan. Tell her to tell Taz that we're getting closer to a way home and we're safe, okay? Then we need to move."

He didn't make any sign to show he'd heard, but he laid a hand on the snake's scales. A moment later I realised he was speaking into its mind. The snake hissed softly at him, almost dismissively, and he shrugged his shoulders before joining us.

"She says Reyan has the court in hand apparently but I'm not sure she can take a message back. Maybe she has to rest first. We should get on with our plan, whatever that is."

His entire face was more alive than I'd ever seen it, his brown eyes sparkling and his shoulders relaxed. The snake began to fade until it was a bulk of shadow shrinking fast and then just a small curl of darkness on Kainen's outstretched palm.

"You heard her voice?" I asked.

He nodded. "She leaves imprints of it in the shadow and Betty carries it, I think. But it was her. Orbs, I've missed her."

I didn't see where he put the snake or whether it had disappeared, but I didn't push him for answers as we set off at a jog toward where Sabine and MC were waiting by a low wall. I didn't even think to hesitate when Kainen held out his hands to give my foot a boost, or to reach back and help him up. We scrambled over and dropped, our feet landing in something soft.

And smelly.

"Again?" MC groaned. "What is it about you and manure?"

Sabine grinned. "It has many uses. Soft landing, cloaks the smell, helps grow many crops. We're going to need to pick up something a friend of mine has kept ready for me, then it's literally a case of sneaking into the foundry."

She set off without waiting for us to agree, but I flinched instead of following as something shadowy wisped over my face. Kainen reached out into thin air and the shadow-snake was once again visible on his palm a moment later.

"We're safe enough here," he murmured as the snake wrapped around his wrist.

I wanted to ask if he was going to be sending it home anytime soon, but I was too astonished by the soft tone he was crooning to it in, scarily similar to how Taz spoke to our chameleon, Leo, when he was sulking over food.

"You go back to Reyan now, okay?" Kainen continued. "Oh, you can't? The way is blocked. Okay, stick with me then. No, we can't turn to shadow and follow you sadly. If this works, we'll be home soon. Clever girl."

We should have been darting stealthily through the streets to avoid the tinge of dawn now creeping over the top of the buildings clustered around the spire. Instead I was gawping at Kainen, Lord of the Court of Illusions, ex-Mage of Nightmares and accomplished FDP of Arcanium's elite baby-talking to a snake.

Sabine and MC reappeared, Sabine carrying something bulky over both arms.

MC sniggered as he caught the tail-end of Kainen's cooing, but Betty slithered into Kainen's pocket a few moments later and my heart lifted at the thought that Reyan was able to get a message through. Even if we couldn't send one back it meant there was a way out there somehow, even if it was only through shadow.

"I don't know what you're laughing at." Sabine faced MC. "You still need to get into your costume."

MC's laughter, and possibly the ability to laugh ever again, died as Sabine held up pile over her arms.

"Er, my what?"

I squinted through the gloom but Sabine flourished the pile until it hung in front of her, a crudely stitched wolf outfit. I tried to hold in my urge to laugh while Kainen gave him a smug grin and a thumbs up.

MC folded his arms.

"I am not wearing that."

"You are."

"I am not! Why can't one of them wear it?"

"She's a queen, and he's… I don't trust him." She gave Kainen a dark look. "It'll fit you best."

MC blinked at her. "She's a *what*?"

It took ten minutes of whispered cajoling and hissed threats in equal measure to convince MC as we walked through the silent village toward the foundry. While Sabine was still arguing with MC about his future opportunities, and how slim they would be if he didn't stop complaining, I inched closer to Kainen.

"So, Betty."

He nodded. "I never even thought of her as an option, not that I could call her at will. But Reyan clearly did. I'm sorry you couldn't hear from Taz too."

It really sounded like he meant it.

"Leo can't turn to shadow or I probably would have done," I conceded. "I'll see them soon enough. We need to get through this in one piece first."

"Do we have an us plan, or are we going with the flow?" he asked.

I frowned. "An 'us' plan would be survive and try not to screw anyone else over while doing it. Sabine hasn't told us much about how she's getting inside or in front of her guardian, but if she's who we need then we follow her lead. Stick together."

"Like I said, I'll follow your lead and you have my loyalty."

Strange how things can change. I almost said that, almost confessed to him that I was glad that we could be friends in the end, but we'd reached the front of the foundry and Sabine was marching a silently resisting MC through a side door with her hands on his shoulders.

"Should we stick up for him?" Kainen asked doubtfully.

I grimaced. "If she actually starts putting him in danger we should. Then again we're all in danger. We wing it."

He stood aside to let me go through the door ahead of him, but I made a choice in that moment and let my warding creep through his. He gave me a surprised look as I waited for him on the other side, but he didn't say a word about it as our combined protection merged over us.

Sabine beckoned from a side door and we slipped inside, Kainen closing the door behind us. Immediately confronted by a pair of bare male legs, I looked skyward until MC was fully swamped in what turned out to be a wolf suit.

"Someone is going to owe me big for this," he muttered.

We stood in a large cloakroom surrounded by the cloaks and outdoor wear of grand lords and ladies and my heart sank as I assessed what we were likely about to face. Posh clothes suggested people who might be able to afford protection, which likely meant we'd be fighting against a lot of strength.

My panic was momentarily dimmed by the sight of MC tugging at his grey fur-trimmed gloves as he stared at his reflection in a nearby mirror. The wolf-pelt at least looked realistic, because it was, but the believable bit ended there. MC twisted to look back at the fake rear-end stuffed full of straw, right down to the wispy tail.

"You literally have to show up behind the pillars around the edge of the main hall and growl a lot," Sabine insisted while straightening his ears. "We've timed this exactly right, the morning exaltations are about to begin."

"Exaltations?" I frowned. "Are we in some kind of worship place?"

Sabine's grin turned wolfish. "Welcome to the Grand Oratory of the Great Obe."

My brain hitched, instantly seeing patterns as Kainen scoffed down a laugh.

"The GOGO?" I asked, fighting to keep my tone innocent.

Neither Sabine nor MC seemed to get it, but a loud gong filled the air and Sabine jumped.

"This is it. Are you ready MC?"

"No."

"Good. Create some carnage in the crowd and we'll slip through the halls to free my guardian. Then she'll be able to see about getting you two home."

MC thudded his paws together. "How come everyone else gets what they want out of this?"

"Well, what do you want?" Sabine asked.

He hesitated. "I want to apprentice somewhere I can

147

make friends."

Pity swelled through me. He had the raw end of the stick the last two days with us about, and I knew what it was like to be outside looking in, wanting friends. Arcanium had been that dream for me and it had delivered sixty times over.

Kainen caught my eye and shook his head. Even he knew the promises that were about to roll from my lips.

"Get this done, and I'll get you into any apprenticeship you desire," Sabine promised. "Now go, quickly!"

MC's eyes widened. He seemed to take her at her word, pawing at the door handle and slipping out into the hall. Sabine bounced on the balls of her feet, clenching and unfurling her hands.

"When the screams start, we move," she insisted.

I braced a hand against the nearest wall as a soft vibration juddered through the floor, closely followed by a lot of determined yelling.

Sabine threw open the door to the main hall in time for us to hear frantic cries of panic. We darted toward the noise even though the chaos seemed to be coming to us, people already streaming out of the hall, trampling over each other.

I flinched as a dark blur slunk past my vision and the crowd turned in one juddering swoop, charging back the way they'd come. Betty slithered after them, her jaws snapping happily.

"She won't eat anyone, will she?" I asked doubtfully.

Kainen grimaced. "I don't think so. At least, we've not noticed any disappearances at court yet."

With Betty loose and causing havoc, we charged through the main hall in time to see MC tear off his wolf costume, ripping stitches and huffing a relieved breath as he emerged into the free air. He kicked the costume into a pile of cloaks thrown unceremoniously on the floor and looked around for us.

A young guard in pale grey uniform got knocked to the ground. I turned in his direction, worried he'd get stamped on, but MC rushed forward and helped the man to his feet before I could, one eye fixed on Betty as real wolves streamed into the hall.

"Go!" MC raised his voice over the din. "Get as many people to safety as you can in houses with the doors locked, or up high."

The guard nodded and fled, leaving MC to battle through the chaos toward us.

The enormous doors that led outside slammed shut and my blood ran cold to see how many of us were still trapped inside with the beasts.

"We need to draw them off the crowd," Sabine said. "But how?"

The wolves were separating into packs, corralling sobbing, screaming people against the walls.

"There's always a heroic deed of some kind in the stories," MC insisted.

I thought for a moment. "Okay, but what kind of heroic deed?"

"Um, Demi?" Kainen prodded my arm.

I flicked a quick frown at him. "I'm thinking."

"Okay, but might you think a bit quicker? We are about to be eaten."

I lifted my head and came face to snarling, teeth-baring snout with one of the wolves. The stench of something coppery, probably from the beast's diet of rotted meat and blood, hit me right up the nose and I gagged.

"I have an idea," MC said. "Sabine, run in the direction

149

of your guardian to show everyone the way. When we get there, we can separate. You go rescue your guardian and someone can keep the wolves chasing." His face fell as the three of us stared at him. "Um, not me. I'm actually really bad at running."

"I'll do it," Kainen offered. "I'm a fast runner and I have a few tricks still about me."

Mad thoughts of him grabbing Betty and running to somewhere he could safely use her to get himself home filled my head, but I forced them aside.

"Are you sure?" I asked. "What if the way home is there and you're not?"

He grimaced. "Come find me. If you can't do that, go home without me. You're the queen, Demi. Faerie needs you."

I opened my mouth to protest, but Kainen flashed a suitably heroic grin and climbed up onto a nearby platform of stone. Someone had broken the door open again and the numbers had thinned but by no means cleared. A few bewildered people were still tumbling out, but most of the remaining crowd had turned to watch the wolves corner us instead.

Never underestimate morbid curiosity for potential blood sports, I realised. *Fae, fairy, human, whoever these people are, we're all the same deep down.*

"Good people, fear not." Kainen's voice echoed through the hall. "I shall draw off the hideous beast."

It was then that I noticed the cake beside him on the platform. Whether we'd stumbled onto someone's wedding or the Great Obe required a sacrifice worthy of sixty odd bags of sugar, the cake was a thing of beauty.

Kainen grabbed a handful from the top of the sixteen tiers, perfect in silver icing. Even the piping was silver, as were the flowers, birds, butterflies and so many other fancy depictions. With no amount of ceremony or thought for the cake at all, Kainen took aim and threw his handful at the wolf's snarling head.

The cake splattered against its snout. Icing covered its head and shoulders, dripping down onto its paws.

"I'll find you," he insisted. "If you have to go without me, tell Reyan I love her."

Kainen gave me one final grin and launched into a mad dash toward the back of the hall.

The wolf charged.

People gasped in delight.

A woman in a ridiculously large silver hat fainted before peeking through one eye to see the rest of the show.

The rest of the wolves turned as one unit, their innate genetics reducing Kainen to a huge speeding tennis ball. As they all gave chase, one person started clapping and quickly stopped when nobody joined in.

A concerned muttering started in patches and then grew to a communal hum.

"Hello little queenling."

I froze at the masculine voice echoing through the hall, stilling everyone around us. Even the wolves hesitated before snarling even more ferociously. But this time they weren't snarling at us. I took a step back as the entire pack twisted around to face the man stalking toward us. His ice white hair had a pale blue sheen to it, the strands cut short to frame an angular but rugged face. Tall and broad-shouldered, he would have towered over me and Kainen too.

He kept a short distance between us but my senses sharpened as I stared. I was not only certain that this was the mysterious Loth that Sabine had mentioned, but also that he was as Fae as Kainen or I were.

"I'm sorry?" I asked, playing dumb. "Were you talking to me? I'm not sure who you are."

He smiled, sharpness and malice glimmering in his vivid green eyes and the tight press of his lips.

"How rude of me. My name is Loth, and I am the Grand High Priest of the Great Obeians."

He smiled wider as Sabine spat on the gleaming marble floor.

"You're an abomination," she snarled. "You ravage our home of everything good. You lie about those who wield land-magic and turn folk against them even though you possess it yourself."

Loth sighed, the sound carrying across the hall. Most people had fled outside but the remaining few still visible were sturdy bodies cloaked in grey, all ready with lethal looking swords or metal pikes in hand.

"Magic is not good," Loth said calmly. "It corrupts and ensnares the mind with promises of riches that never last."

Sabine leaned forward, one foot sliding in front of the other, a stance ready for battle.

"And killing our folk in the name of your cause? Taking away anyone who speaks? Anyone who's born different?"

Loth shook his head, but I already knew his type. He wouldn't listen because he already believed that if anyone was to control any kind of magic, it should be him and him alone.

"You have a superiority complex," I told him.

Sabine's gaze flicked toward me but she didn't say any more as Loth turned his attention my way next.

"It has been a long time since I've been around the arrogance of Fae," he said, lips twitching.

I drew myself up tall. "Weird, considering you are one.

152

Is that what this is? Self-hatred so you hunt anyone who shows signs of gift-magic? Or perhaps it's a control issue. I've met your kind more times than I can count."

He lifted a hand but before the zing of power could reach us, Kainen appeared and swung his arm out in front of me to swipe Loth's attack aside.

I contained my surprise and let my fairy connection ripple through my arm. The subtle crackle of my energy gift leapt to my fingers, encasing my hand in a white-blue glow.

As I scanned myself, my power, I realised that the irritability of my gifts wasn't because they were more volatile, but because they were unhampered by greater ones.

Not a shred of my power as queen remained inside me because I wasn't in Faerie, or the human world I'd been born in. Here in the Prime Realm, I stood with only the powers I'd been gifted by others, not any that Faerie and the nether had gifted me as queen.

My energy gift and the gift of giving were all I had left.

"Do you want me to attack?" Kainen asked.

I shook my head. "Not unless he does. I'm more intrigued by this whole set-up."

I faced Loth. If I had to do this as not a queen, I might as well be the most pain-in-the-behind version of myself as possible while I had the freedom to do it.

"I know that someone from Faerie has been in touch with someone here," I began. "I'm guessing if I say the name Emil, or maybe Belladonna, you'll know who they are. To be honest, I'm not a huge fan of either of them. Far too self-centred and mad for power. We also know that they're hoping to use you to get more *metirin* iron so they can get a better control over Faerie. Ringing any bells or do you need me to draw you a diagram?"

Kainen groaned under his breath.

"Is this really the time to be so... so *you* right now?" he muttered.

I grinned, even though there was nothing to grin about with armed guards and a potentially powerful enemy in his own domain standing against us.

"Who else am I meant to be?" I asked. "No. We know why our side are doing all this stuff. But question is, why are you, Loth? Did they promise you a one-way ticket to Faerie? Riches? Or did they promise you all the gifts if you gave all the iron?"

Loth's expression didn't flicker once, that smug smile never hitching or fading.

"Emil has promised many things to many folk, but whether he delivers on them is no concern of mine. An old debt binds us together and I will see my part of it done. There'll be no mercy and no rest otherwise."

I hadn't been expecting anything quite so personal. I hesitated, my mind racing.

If I offer him any kind of help, he won't believe me. I could make a deal but that would leave us even more vulnerable if Emil can use that against us.

"We fight," Sabine insisted.

MC squeaked behind us and I heard him shuffle backwards until there was a low thud.

"She has a point," Kainen added. "Diplomacy doesn't work on everyone."

I thought back to the enemies I'd faced before. Elvira, self-absorbed and hungry for vengeance on the whole of Faerie that hadn't given her the due she thought herself entitled to. The Apocalyptians, pure essences of vice and virtue that couldn't think of anything but fulfilling their individual desires. Even Belladonna and Emil were both drenched in so much entitlement that talking to them or making any attempt at reason had achieved nothing.

Taz's words filtered into my head then, so solid and sure that it almost felt like he was with me, his voice back inside my head.

It isn't the fighting that's the problem. It's the killing.

Belladonna, Emil, Elvira, the Apocalyptians, and now Loth, they all saw people as expendable. Even Queen Tavania, Taz's mother, thought that most Fae were resources to be used.

I refused to let that same mindset be my legacy.

"I think you're probably right."

I lifted arced my arm through the air and sent a wave of crackling white energy zapping through our warding. It hit Loth square in the chest and I flinched back, severing the connection immediately.

"He's not warding."

Kainen grimaced. "No, he's not."

"This isn't a fair fight."

Loth staggered to his feet but as his guards lurched forward, he waved a hand to keep them back.

"This is exactly why we banished your kind in the first place," he said, triumph shining across his face. "You think gifts make you immortal."

I couldn't exactly disagree with him there, but short of using gifts we were outnumbered in all other physical senses, and Loth wanted us to look like the villains.

None of this was helping us find Tirzella or our way home either.

You can't fight everyone else's fights, Sparky.

Again I heard the memory of Taz in my head. We were trespassing on a realm we never should have been able to

155

enter, and whatever was going on, I wasn't queen here. The urge to do good, to meddle, to fix things warred with my desire to get home and let the Prime Realm sort its own problems out.

But then, there was one part of me nobody had considered. A part even I had all but forgotten.

"Sabine, MC, go find Tirzella," I murmured. "We'll be right behind you."

Sabine hesitated for a moment before turning without a word and grabbing MC's wrist as she jogged past him. His alarmed squawking echoed behind us but I didn't look back.

"Follow me and keep the warding up," I told Kainen.

He nodded. "If you say so."

I led us backwards with Loth prowling after us. He glanced around at the hall now filling up with people again. I had no idea where Kainen had led the wolves but they were clearly the least of our worries now.

Several gawkers filled the windows and doorways, all wanting to know what was going on and utter delight spread across Loth's face. He knew he'd trapped us, because using our gifts now would only prove his point. I eyed the guards keeping two paces behind him. No crossbows, but I'd put my entire FDP savings on their swords and pikes being forged from *metirin* iron.

"It's inevitable," Loth said, his voice carrying for the benefit of his crowd. "We bested the Fae once, drove them out of our world, and we'll do so again. Resisting me now is pointless."

"Don't know about resisting, but doing anything at all would be helpful right about now," Kainen hissed.

I nodded. "Agreed. Hands out and when I say 'push', shove with all your might."

Kainen frowned but lifted both hands in front of him. I fought the urge to remark on the unerring obedience, the desire to be me rising at the worst possible time.

Instead I dodged around the vast food table with him at my side.

"There's a tiny problem with your strategy," I called out, inching sideways while keeping the table between Loth and us. "It's the same arrogance trap the Fae always end up falling into, especially when it comes to me."

I lifted my hands into position in front of my chest and Kainen copied me, his body tense and his expression uneasy.

"Do tell." Loth inched toward us.

I gave Kainen a look and darted sideways behind the enormous many-tiered cake.

"I'm part-human, and we're the most infuriating of them all."

I shoved forward with all my might, swinging my entire body behind the movement. Kainen was a fraction of a second behind me, his weight bulldozing alongside mine into the cake until his hands punched right through it.

I grabbed his hand and stumbled back as the cake teetered toward Loth. Then back our way. Then forward again.

Loth's scream tore through the air, a second of scandalised noise cut tragically short by an avalanche of what looked and smelled suspiciously like Victoria sponge and honey.

I ignored the horrifying feeling of Kainen's hand in mine and dragged him toward the doorway Sabine and MC had disappeared through.

"We have no idea where we're going," Kainen reminded me.

I nodded. "It'll be somewhere nearby if this Tirzella person was going to be the sacrifice. I'm guessing that's the reason for the cake anyway. We find Sabine and MC, get all of us out any way we can. Then hopefully they can send us home."

He nodded. "Nice idea but the cake trick will only slow them for a second."

"The guards maybe but it was a hefty cake. With any luck, it'll knock him out for a bit at least and they won't know what to do first."

Kainen shook his hand free of mine as we jogged along.

"I honestly don't know whether to be impressed or petrified," he said.

Neither did I, but I decided not to tell him that.

CHAPTER FIFTEEN
REYAN

Reyan lifted the spoon of stew to her lips. Meri had insisted it was Kainen's favourite, a sure sign that Reyan was in her good books. Meri seemed to be using information about his childhood and anything else about him as rewards for whenever Reyan completed a particularly gruesome decision or piece of paperwork. Reyan would have revolted at the idea of being treated like a child, but it was Meri so she was used to it.

As she sucked in the stew, a smart hammering on the bedroom door had her choking it back out into the bowl.

Ace slid to his feet and went to get the door while Reyan patted down her shirt. It was another one of Kainen's and she couldn't get herself out of the habit of wearing them. She'd run out of the ones that smelled like him soon, but luckily he had a cavernous wardrobe.

"Lady Blossom, was she expecting you?" Ace asked, his tone formal.

Blossom huffed past him and strode across to sit in his seat. Reyan bit her lips together to quell a smile.

"Can I help you?" she asked.

Blossom frowned. "It's more how I can help you, perish the thought. Are we in complete secrecy?"

"As much as we can be, why?"

Blossom still glanced around before answering and Reyan sat with tension leaking through her, and not just because the stew was getting cold.

"Emil is lurking about the court still," Blossom said.

"He cornered me a while earlier but I thought it best to go about my own business a while before coming here."

"Sensible." Reyan frowned and felt her way through the court. "I can't sense him now though. He must be skipping in and out, which is infuriating."

Blossom nodded. "He has always been able to realm-skip at will, a distinct rarity. But either way, he cornered me to question whether I'm a traitor to him and my sister or not, then hinted that there will be an 'event' for you, his wording not mine. Apparently, I shouldn't be anywhere near you at bedtime."

Reyan shrank back in her seat. She had expected some kind of attack but even so, hearing about it was somehow worse than it randomly happening to her.

"We'll be ready," Ace insisted, perching on the arm of her chair. "Whatever happens. If I have to glamour as you and take the risk, I will."

Reyan smiled weakly. "Milo would kill me."

"Emil won't trust it to anyone but himself most likely," Blossom added.

Ace sighed, reaching across the table and snagging his stew.

"I can believe that. But not to worry. Demi gave me certain gifts, so we'll have a plan before bedtime, leave it to me."

Reyan got the veiled message there; they wouldn't discuss any actual plan in front of Blossom. The awkward silence settled and Reyan realised she should be inviting Blossom to stay and eat with them. With any other princess of Faerie, she would have tumbled over herself to be polite, but somehow with Blossom she couldn't bring herself to bother. Guilt warred with dislike until Blossom stood.

"I have been asked to dine with Lord Marquest tonight,"

she announced. "I won't be around when anything happens. But here, if these are of any use, have them."

Reyan winced as Blossom clicked her fingers and a pair of iron shackles appeared in her hand. She dropped them onto the table with a loud *thunk* and started toward the door.

Reyan watched as Blossom seemed to be having some kind of internal argument with herself. Then she turned, awkwardly nodded her head and swept from the room like a horde of frost cats were behind her.

"Well, that was…" Ace didn't finish.

"Awkward?"

"Yeah. But still, these may come in handy."

He picked up the shackles, testing their weight before laying them back down again. Reyan swallowed against the growing lump in her throat, the sight of them bringing back memories of her imprisonment and the day she lost Kainen.

"You have a plan?" she asked.

Ace nodded. "I do. If you can time your shadow-merging for when he strikes, I can trap him momentarily. The moment I have him, the shackles go on."

"He might not strike tonight though. Might not for weeks."

The thought of waiting with an assassination attempt or similar hanging over her head was a horrible one.

I should be used to it after my father kept sending people to threaten me to keep Kainen's protection over me, but I'm not.

That was an old fool meddling to keep himself in trades and rose liquor. This was an extremely powerful and vengeful Fae wanting to kill her and take her court.

"He'll want it over quick," Ace said. "But if not, how

161

about we force his hand? Give him a perfect opportunity to strike?"

Reyan frowned. "What, like distract everyone else for him?"

"Yeah. How about you hold a revel to welcome Blossom to the court and to cement your leadership of it. Doesn't have to be a big one, just some dancing after dinner. Put that dress on from that first night we were all here. Be seen, then slip away with a headache or something."

"It's a good idea, but where will you be?"

Ace smiled. "You can gift people as court lady, right? Well, how about giving me temporary invisibility? You can make it conditional, like only when I'm holding something specific. There was this human story I read as a kid where there was a ring that made people invisible. That'd be so cool."

Reyan heaved out of her seat. It was the least she could give him, and bestowing a gift was something she could have considered doing for him before now. He was doing his FDP job of course, but he was doing it as her friend. She dug through Kainen's drawer that had a bunch of old junk in and came up with a smooth gold ring. It wasn't like any of Kainen's other jewellery, all of which was silver or black, and she had to hope it wasn't somehow sentimental to him as she held it out to Ace.

"Like this?"

He grinned. "Absolutely like that."

She held the ring in her hand and his in the other, lifting up on her tiptoes to press a soft kiss to his cheek.

"I gift you with the ability to turn invisible whenever you wear this ring, but this ring only, and it wears off after about five minutes. It won't work for anyone else either."

She hesitated, trying to see if she'd left any wicked loopholes that someone else might be able to compel or manipulate him through, but she found none.

"Try it out," she said.

Ace took the ring and slid it onto a couple of fingers before it fit over his thumb. He blinked at her expectantly, then he wasn't there at all.

"Whoa, you're gone." She gasped. "Are you still there?"

"Yeah, can you hear me?"

Reyan nodded. "I can. That's weird but also very cool. Okay, you have fun with that and I'll let Meri know we're being social this evening."

She clicked her fingers. "Meri, do we have capacity to attend dinner tonight? Kind of to welcome Blossom but I guess it would be a good idea for me to dine with the nobles a bit."

She froze as a distant shrieking noise echoed.

"Was that..." Ace's disembodied voice asked.

Reyan gulped. "I think I either really peed her off, or I've made her very happy."

She sat down but only managed two mouthfuls of stew before Meri steamed in without knocking, Amba right behind her under a mound of clothing with a large bag with what looked like shoes tumbling out of it.

"About time," Meri said by way of greeting. "Now, we have some dresses for you to try. Put the spoon down, we can have stew anytime. Dinner is served in half an hour and you're nowhere near ready for holding court."

Reyan yelped as she was dragged out of her chair and forcibly undressed.

"Um... Ace are you turned away for this?" she asked.

"Absolutely," his voice echoed. "Nothing I've not seen

before but not that bothered about seeing it again either, no offence."

"Where is he?" Amba asked.

"Invisible."

"Oh. Cool. Stand still, your hair's like a sheet of noodles right now."

Reyan succumbed to being fussed over, her only insistence that she wanted to wear one of the dresses Kainen had commissioned to be made for her.

Meri provided one without much grumbling, although she insisted there were plenty of new ones that needed trying on. By the time Reyan was professed ready, Ace had reappeared readily glamoured into black trousers, a black shirt open to the chest and a lick of black liner under his eyes.

"Escort you, Lady?" he teased.

Reyan nodded. "Yes, but after this I intend to sleep for a week. I want everyone out there so drunk they don't want to talk to me."

"Except the staff," Ace whispered. "I had a word with Amba earlier and she said if anything happens, you've got half an army of staff at the ready."

Reyan let that thought comfort her as she prepared a ready smile and swept into the main hall on Ace's arm. She greeted Blossom first as was the necessary custom, then conceded readily when Blossom said she had already agreed to dine with Lord Marquest.

"I would readily defer my invitation, if commanded," he said, looking put out.

Reyan smiled. "No need. I'm sure Lady Blossom and I will have time in the coming days and a promise is a promise. Take what wine you need for your table with my compliments."

Lord Marquest's eyes widened. "That is very generous, Lady."

She gave him another smile and let Ace lead her to her deck where the day-bed had been transformed into a table. She knew the rumours that would likely be going around too, that Ace was her new toy or spy for the queen's court. She could weather those rumours with actions, but every time she hit a lull in conversation as dinner was served and courtiers came to chat and pay their compliments, she thought of Emil biding his time.

"Ready with the headache, I would," Ace muttered.

Reyan leaned closer. "No need. I apologise in advance for what I'm about to do."

She stood up, surprised when the court's attention was drawn to her as if by her mere change of position. Silence fell.

"I intend to enjoy my evening," she said, her tone light with forced amusement. "I advise the rest of you do the same. Our lord may be elsewhere for the moment, but he would agree with me that the show must go on and Fae must find their fun wherever they can. Enjoy yourselves."

The round of applause was an obvious necessity but she thought it sounded less thin than necessary, as if some of the nobles were actually relaxing into her rule, accepting it. She kept hold of Ace's arm, clinging on as they walked through the hall and up the staircase to her room. Only once they were inside with the door shut did she let Ace go and push away from him.

"Sorry. I had to intimate that we… it was better than the headache excuse."

Ace chuckled. "You're not my type but I've had far worse suggestions thrown at me, it's fine. Now, into bed. No idea what the plan is but if this room doesn't let anyone in without your permission, you should be safe."

Reyan had considered that. If Emil really could realm-skip anywhere, there was nothing stopping him entering her room whenever he chose, or…

She leapt toward the wardrobe and threw the doors open. No Emil. She also peeked under the bed, but the space was bare.

"Come on, once it's done, it's done," Ace soothed.

Reyan left him there while she used the bathroom, making sure to keep the door ajar. She finished washing her face and settled into bed after checking Ace's bracelet and making sure he was definitely still him. The pull of exhaustion made it impossible to consider taking out a book to read, but the worry kept sleep away too.

In a rare, apparently never-before-seen move (according to Tira at the Word Court), Marinda Silverfern, author of the famous *Carrie's Castle* books, had sent the courts an advanced reader copy of the latest book. With all the stress, Reyan hadn't been able to bring herself to sink into it. Once she started, she wouldn't stop, assassination attempt or not.

Probably a cool way to go though, death by 'too busy reading'.

She shuddered as her orb flickered on the bedside table. Swiping at it, she peered at the script scrolling across the smoky surface.

He's coming. They were discussing it at dinner.

Reyan put the orb back on the table and glanced at Ace, who was busy murmuring to his own orb, no doubt sending messages to Milo.

"Showtime," she said.

He hurriedly put his orb away and wriggled into bed beside her.

"What are you doing?" she hissed.

He gave her a weary look. "I'll be under the covers. When he comes in or we feel any movement, tap the blanket and I'll put the ring on. The moment he strikes, become shadow and I'll feel you vanish. Then I'll stun him."

"Oh." Reyan nodded. "I guess that makes sense."

She lay tense beside Ace, the weirdness of it giving her the most inappropriate urge to giggle.

Would Kainen be angry if he came home right now? I'm not sure how he feels about gay friends in the bed.

She closed her eyes tight to quell the urge to laugh and focused on reaching through the shadows, sensing nothing unusual. The fire flickered, the room dimming in response to her closed eyes.

The shadows around the door were still, relaxed. *Tense.*

Movement shivered, displacing the darkness until Reyan's link to the court screamed danger. She softly nudged her finger against Ace's arm but she didn't feel him vanish.

Invisible must be literally no longer visible rather than him actually vanishing.

Her heart pounded, her anticipation climbing until she could barely stop her legs from twitching and kicking out. The shadows wrapped around the sensation of malice that appeared beside her, but she held herself calm, her eyes closed.

A subtle intake of breath and the twist of the shadows was all the warning she got. She dissipated her body into the shadows, keeping her face flesh as she opened her eyes.

Emil hovered over her, his narrowed eyes murderous as his hand plunged down at her body. His froze when the covers depressed too far, and she dissipated the rest of her into shadow, moving across the room before reforming.

Emil kicked out and she heard a muffled grunt, but the wriggling stopped immediately. Emil stood frozen, his arms outstretched and one leg still halfway back in a second attempt to kick.

The iron shackles whirled out from under the bed covers with no sign of anyone carrying them, the metal clasping around Emil's left wrist, then looping around the bedpost before the second cuff captured the right wrist.

Ace reappeared, pausing only to slide the ring into his pocket before he stormed to the balcony.

"Follow me," he muttered.

Reyan did so, her breath pluming in fast, panicked gasps. She owed Ace her life, a huge debt to bear in Faerie.

He swept back the noise-deadening curtain but the sounds of revelry and merriment that Reyan expected to hear were absent. She joined Ace's side and saw immediately why.

The entire court stood downstairs, Meri at the top of the steps that led to Reyan's deck with a projector screen behind her.

"What did you…" Reyan stared at Ace in awe.

"I told you I spoke to Amba and she said the court staff were behind you," he said. "She suggested I keep my orb running live to the court, expose the whole situation."

Reyan pushed aside the realisation that the court might have heard the awkward conversation she had about Ace being in her bed. Or the feed might have been silent. She didn't care.

She pulled Ace out of view of the court and threw her arms around his neck.

"Anything you need, it's yours," she promised. "Aside from the obvious against free will, have my court type stuff."

He chuckled and hugged her back. "Happy to help. Go play lady and expose him. If you don't, I will be tearing him a new one myself."

Reyan glanced back at Emil, now struggling against the bedpost in an attempt to break free.

"Bring him with us for me?" she asked.

Ace nodded. "With pleasure. You know, I once threatened to throw Kainen off this very balcony."

"I do that a lot too, but we won't do that this time. Not nearly a serious enough punishment."

She steadied herself and walked out onto the balcony, standing at the stone banister and staring down.

"Well, we've all seen who Lorens is," she said. "Now we know who Emil is. He tried to kill a lady of a court, and I'm sure we all know the punishment for that. The old laws he loves so much say that his fate is mine to decide."

She turned to face Emil as Ace brought him out struggling.

"These cuffs are *metirin* iron," she added. "That means he currently has no access to his gifts. He's defenceless. As I said, the old ways say his fate is mine but turns out the queen isn't a fan."

She smiled wickedly as the low murmur passed over the crowd, the faces closest below her showing a mix of anticipation and curiosity.

"But the queen isn't here," she added. "How does it feel to be defenceless, Emil?"

He snarled up at her, wriggling with all his might, but Ace was strong and held him back. Reyan caught Amba whispering to a couple of the staff who managed the combat training classes and one of them started forward. She didn't know him well, but he didn't bother climbing the stairs, choosing to climb the rocky wall and vault over the balcony.

When he didn't say a word, she frowned.

"Yes?"

"Lady." He bowed his head to her. "With your permission, I will help."

Reyan nodded then, sparing a real smile for him as he joined Ace in pinning Emil to his knees.

"I will never be defenceless," Emil spat. "I'm the one who's been pulling everyone's strings all along. I'm the one who knows what everyone else has been flapping around trying to figure out for far too long."

Reyan faced him down and let her compulsion gift spool around him before he could realise.

"Is that so? How?"

"The nether is formed of shadow. Belladonna wasted so much time bartering for a shadow-snake, only for her to lose it. Then she went for you but you were all clueless. You might have even managed to cross through yourself without the need for sacrifice."

"Why didn't you tell Belladonna that?"

He scoffed, surging forward only to be forced down again.

"What good would you have done in the Prime Realm? You'd have gone straight back to Demi like a good pet. No, the shadow-snake, then you, were only meant to be conduits for others to pass through."

Which means Kainen… BETTY!

She called out for the snake, reaching her voice as far into the shadows as she could. If she told Betty that, Betty might be able to get through and find Kainen. She couldn't risk leaving the court now because he needed something to come back to, but Betty might manage it if they figured out what direction she needed to go in.

She waited several moments but Betty didn't appear. She'd mentioned hunting last, so she might be outside the court boundaries. Impatience turned to irritation and Reyan bit her lip. For all her fancy words, she had no idea what to do with Emil now. She couldn't kill him. She could send him to Taz, but Taz had enough to deal with fighting Belladonna, and would probably kill him.

"Ace, contact home and see how it's going. If all's good, we need to make a short trip."

Ace nodded, glaring into the eyes of the man supporting him before retreating into the bedroom. Realising she still had the attention of the court, still had to keep the performance going, Reyan turned her attention back to Emil.

"Now, we need to consider-"

She flinched back as the man holding Emil shivered. Even before his hair flickered from auburn to blonde, she had a warding around her.

Ciel dropped his glamour. With one click of his fingers he had a crossbow in his hand. Reyan's breath disappeared, panic roaring in her head. Ciel threw the crossbow to Emil and darted back. Even with the shackles on, Emil rose to his feet with unerring coordination, the crossbow pointed at Reyan's chest.

The shadows curled around her but Reyan's mind thundered over his sneering face, the fury rankling there as she remembered everything he had done. He'd infiltrated her court, challenged her, been part of the group that had killed so many of Kainen's friends. If he and his lot hadn't tried to gain dominion over all of Faerie, Kainen would still be with her.

"I can't catch you with your shadow-merging," Emil

said. "But you're sentimental like the rest."

The crossbow clicked and the point of it turned. Reyan screamed, the note of rage roaring out of her as the crossbow found Ace. He turned in alarm, his eyes wide, his hand still hovering in front of his face with his orb dangling.

A flash of burning seared Reyan's arm, a jolt of power that had her staggering back. She flailed and slammed her hands back against the cold stone of the balcony to stop herself tumbling over it. The flash became a crackle through the air and the wooden frame of the crossbow turned to ash.

Before Emil could do more than gasp, Reyan forced her transmutation power forward. The iron arrow dribbled into a mess on the floor, solidifying again into a misshapen lump. He could still hit her warding with it and potentially bludgeon her to death, but he'd have to get close for that.

Ciel fled. Even before she'd finished with whatever frightening power she was attacking with, he was over the balcony and lost in the crowd.

Ace had Emil pinned in seconds, this time kneeling over his shackled hands and his face wedged against the floor.

"That was wicked, Lady, but I'd use it sparingly," Ace murmured. "It's turned your hair fiery."

Reyan didn't have a mirror but one of the strands hanging beside her face looked decidedly orange out of the corner of her eye.

That must have been the power I got from Belladonna.

Still shaking, she pressed both hands against the balcony to steady herself.

"I am Lady of the Illusion Court," she shouted. "Anyone who supports the Forgotten, the Blood and Bone court, or *him*, Lorens, Emil whatever his name is, or

172

anyone who wants the old ways before Queen Demerara, you have half an hour to get out of my court. Otherwise punishments will begin for any future uprisings."

Of all the people to speak next, somehow Blossom wasn't one of the ones she expected.

The crowd turned as the princess of Faerie stood on one of the decks, cleared her throat and raised a glass.

"I won't bow, it's not my style," she announced. "But I will raise a glass to Lady Reyan. That's the most entertainment I've had in ages."

Silence reigned for several seconds before the crowd recovered. Laughter spilled over, and in that moment Reyan knew she'd be thanking Taz for sending her an ally, no matter how reluctant.

"I'd heed her words too," Blossom added. "When Kainen gets back, he won't take this lightly. He plays the indolent at times, but I've seen his savage side and I wouldn't want to be on the end of it. Then again, Lady, it seems you have claws of your own."

Reyan laughed, the sound rolling dark and low.

"Oh, he'll find it amusing to see how I've been looking after our court in his absence, but if anyone is under the impression that I need him, you're mistaken."

With more sudden energy that she felt was natural, she leaned down and wrapped her hand around Emil's throat. With the help of the shadows mixing with the sparkling black smoke, and mostly Ace's added strength, she lifted Emil and forced him over the edge of the balcony.

"I will only warn you of this once. Make your choices wisely."

CHAPTER SIXTEEN
DEMI

"Demi, over here!"

I skidded to a halt at the end of a long corridor in the foundry, Kainen almost shooting past me.

"It's this way, but we wanted to make sure you found-"

Sabine's voice tailed off, her eyes wide as she looked past us. I twisted around to check how many guards we had to deal with and my heart sank.

No guards, which was a plus. There were several wolves instead, which was a serious problem. If they were under Loth's control somehow, we weren't going to outrun them and I doubted they'd fall victim to another cake toss, not that we had one to toss anyway.

"I'll take care of this," Kainen said.

My jaw dropped. "Er... what?"

He rolled his eyes and took a step back.

"Trust me. Go with Sabine and get us a way home. If you get the chance and there's no other choice, go."

"You can't just go... I don't even know what you're planning to do!"

I stared in horror as he grinned at me, every essence of the Kainen I knew and had once feared gleaming mischief and mayhem in his brown eyes.

"That's probably for the best. It's been... an experience." He bowed low. "My queen."

I stared as he turned and set off toward the wolves. The one in front, large and bulky with lethal teeth, snarled a warning. Kainen lifted a hand and with a startlingly loud yell, summoned a cloud of black smoke to his hand.

Then he smacked the wolf between the eyes with it and carried on running.

The wolf yelped, an injured sound that turned into a terrifying roar. I started after them as the entire pack turned and gave chase, but Kainen was right about being fast.

"Come on, he looks like he knows what he's doing," Sabine insisted.

I hesitated as she set off with MC right behind her. Kainen zigzagged back into the main hall and a second later a chorus of screaming from the crowd started up.

He's not just distracting the wolves, he's causing chaos to distract everyone.

I could just see a flash of him and the hall through one of the wide, glassless windows, and he seemed determined to lead the wolves on a merry dance around and around. I tried to remember what had happened to Betty but I had to hope she would find Kainen and see the wolves off again if he got into trouble.

He thundered on, pulling suits of armour down as he passed to slow the wolves and I turned away. He'd had given himself up as some mad kind of distraction sacrifice, so I would trust him just this once and find us a way home like he suggested.

I jogged after Sabine and MC, my legs stumbling over each other as I tried to keep up.

A stone tunnel extended ahead, lit by flaming brands in brackets on the walls. Almost immediately the tunnel turned into stone steps leading down to a doorway at the bottom. We crept down toward the silence and I winced each time my feet made a noise.

Sabine peeked around the edge of the doorway and hurried forward. MC took a deep breath with wobbly shoulders and hurried after her. Glancing over my shoulder to check we weren't being followed, I inched into the room. It opened out into a wide central area with a table in the middle and four spacious cells against the walls.

"Hello Sabine, dear. Have you not been using the face cream your mother sent you?"

I stared at the tall, willowy woman draped in white robes with shimmering white hair and an aura of light glowing over her skin.

I couldn't be sure if she was Fae or something entirely other, but with her ageless skin and ancient blue eyes that were almost purple, she definitely radiated some kind of otherworldly aura.

Sabine rolled her eyes. "This isn't the time, Tirzella. Demi here and her friend need to speak to you about getting themselves home."

As she set about finding a key or something to unlock the cells with, the woman's gaze fixed on me.

"You are one of the banished," she announced.

"Banished?"

She nodded. "Fae-folk. Your kind were banished from our land long ago and we sealed the way in or out."

I yearned to linger and ask all sorts of questions, like why and when and how, but thoughts of Taz drove me back to business.

"Yeah that's great. We need to get back home, so is there a way to do that?"

Her eyes narrowed and I wondered if I'd offended her. Sabine unearthed some kind of metal key with strange ridges and set to attacking the cell lock with it.

"I am Tirzella. I have watched and minded this land for a long time."

I tensed and shoved my hand in my sleeve to hide my

176

fingers tapping. If she was going to talk in fanciful riddles… there really wasn't much I could do about it without ruining the one shot we had of finding the way home.

Sabine swore as the key dropped to the floor, picking it up and returning to her task.

I firmed my warding around me but with my hand near the bars, a thrumming resistance pushed back against it. *Metirin* iron, if I had to guess. Which meant whatever power the woman had was likely contained. Then the cell gate swung open and I took a step back as Tirzella glided out with a serene smile and sniffed my direction. Her eyes widened a moment later, the rest of her falling still.

"A Fae queen. Interesting. And so young. You say you wish to return home?"

Straight to the matter, good.

"Yes, my people need me to go back." I thought of Taz no doubt tearing Faerie apart, Milo throwing paperwork at him and the courts in absolute turmoil with the Forgotten lurking and Belladonna raging after her defeat. "I'm sure this place is really nice, but I'm not supposed to be here."

And there was the truth of it. None of us were ever supposed to be in the Prime Realm, but Belladonna had wanted to reach this place for something, and I still didn't know what for absolutely sure. Iron most likely, and possibly to use the powers of ancients like the one standing in front of me.

"No, you're not," she agreed. "How did you get here?"

I explained about the painting, about Belladonna and briefly about the War of Queens. Tirzella raised her eyes skywards but didn't interrupt. When I finished, she rubbed a delicate forefinger across her lips.

"There is a way to send you back, similar to the way

you arrived. I protect this land and its heritage, so I will need your word as a Fae queen that no attempt will be made to venture this way again."

I hesitated. It was an easy enough thing to promise from my side, but unless we found a way to best the Forgotten for good there was no guarantee they wouldn't try again.

"You have my word that me and mine will never attempt it, and I'll do everything I can to make sure nobody else does either. I don't control my enemy, but if the painting still exists then I can have it destroyed."

Tirzella smiled, her laughter tinkling through the dungeon. A loud bang echoed down to us and I really hoped Kainen had found some way to dodge the wolves by now.

"Spoken like a queen. Very well, we'll accept and get you home. Follow me."

"My friend is currently playing decoy with a bunch of wolves so I'll need to find him first." I still couldn't quite believe I was calling Kainen a friend, even after everything he'd done for me. "I can't leave without him. Also, we don't have the right gifts for the painting. To get here it was life, death, light and shadow, but I don't have those."

Tirzella shook her head, amused. "Whoever needed gifts for anything other than vanity? Especially when they can be fought with a small bit of iron."

Even though it was beyond time to leave, and I still had Kainen and the wolves to worry about, the question burbled out of my mouth all the same.

"You have a lot of *metirin* iron here then?" I tapped the nearest bar of the cell.

"Of course. It's only iron. Although, there have been strange movements of in the other foundries recently. And since I've been here, I've heard all sorts of rumours."

"From the guards?" Sabine asked, her tone dark.

Tirzella shook her head. "The walls talk, the shadows whisper. When you've walked with the land as long as I have, you learn to listen. Someone is stirring unrest and I intend to find out who."

"The Obe fanatics seem to be excitable as well," Sabine added. "Talks of the next coming of Obe, and they're calling all their forces and supporters here to the foundry."

I let them discuss their own issues with my mind racing over mine. I'd never once thought nor heard of where the *metirin* iron in Faerie actually came from. It wasn't something easily accessed either, but I never considered that we might not 'create' it at all. Normal iron like that which was found in the human world was commonplace enough, but *metirin* iron that could pierce wardings and contain gifts and power, that was rare.

Because it always belonged in the Prime Realm.

Instead of fighting the Fae, these people banished them to Faerie, surrounded themselves with their natural Fae deterrent and closed the door between realms. Much like Faerie had closed most doors to the human world to stop the Fae using it as a sadistic playground in the old days.

Belladonna must be hoping to get metirin iron from the Prime Realm. Or Emil more likely, pulling her strings and setting her off to cause carnage.

I wouldn't let either of them get their hands on any more *metirin* iron. I wouldn't let them wreck Faerie any more than they already had done.

"I think Belladonna and Emil, the ones who wanted to come here in the first place, are after *metirin* iron," I explained. "They've been in contact with Loth, that man who stopped us upstairs, and I imagine they'd do anything to get more as it's not as common at home. I'm sure you

179

already know what it can do."

Tirzella eyed me for a moment before nodding.

"What?" Sabine folded her arms irritably. "What does it do?"

Tirzella didn't answer her and I didn't either. If we could establish an estranged peace between the Prime Realm and Faerie then neither side needed to suffer at the hands of the other.

"I can't promise they won't try to get here once I'm back home," I insisted. "But I will do my best to stop it."

Tirzella nodded, her serene smile never faltering. "Now I am free, I will make sure that doesn't happen. I will collect what we need to send you home. Find your friend and meet me in the main hall."

"What if you get captured again?"

I couldn't help the words springing out, but Tirzella only laughed.

"It would take a lot for them to manage it a second time. They say love usually only strikes once. Find your friend."

She swept out of the room and I sagged with relief. Now I just had to find Kainen.

Kainen, who was possibly still being chased by wolves. Or eaten.

I dashed after Tirzella with Sabine and MC pounding behind me, but while Tirzella disappeared down a random hallway, my first place to start was back in the main hall. My skin was bubbling with chills but I kept going with my warding up. Thoughts of seeing Taz again filled my head, and of going home where I was strong. That alone kept my feet going even as my knees threatened to buckle.

We dashed into main hall and stumbled to a halt. MC crashed into the back of me. I steadied myself and twisted back and forth, scanning the now deserted space.

"What's that noise?" MC asked.

I couldn't hear screaming or growling, just the flurried tapping of someone running.

Kainen barrelled in through a side door, his cheeks bright pink. He spotted us and raised a shaking arm in recognition.

"I have it all in hand!"

He dashed past as the wolves emerged behind him. MC squeaked and I froze. The wolves ignored us, bounding after Kainen with excited yips.

"Lead them around in a circle," MC shouted.

Kainen stared at him like he was mad while still running.

"What do you think I've been doing?!" he yelled.

He hooked left and led the wolves around the outside of the main hall like some garish greyhound race with him as the fluffy rabbit.

"Demi, try to talk to them or something!" he added on his next pass.

I groaned. "I keep telling everyone, my mimicking gift doesn't work like that!"

"Well, try!"

Sabine gave me an encouraging look. "Is this a magic thing? Give it a go."

Despairing at my rotten luck and not able to pull rank, mainly because only Kainen would listen and he had his hands full already, I watched the wolves getting nearer.

"*Grrouff.*" I tried to imagine the noise a friendly dog might make. "*Grrraaaaa.*"

I pointed to myself then the others before holding my hands up in a gesture of peace. I took a step back for good measure as well and tried to appear generally unthreatening.

Taz will insist on me re-enacting this and he'll laugh his head off for decades.

I waited, dizzy with anxiety.

The leading wolf tilted its head to the side, ears cocked and eyes inquisitive. Again I pointed to all of us and, against all my instincts, I stuck my tongue out and panted.

The wolf's tail spasmed. It could have been an involuntary twitch or it could have been a slight wag. I froze as the wolf padded toward me. I tried not to wrinkle my nose or pull a face at the awful stench of rot as it sniffed near my knees and my chest. And my behind.

"The wolf is sniffing my butt," I hissed.

"Um, sniff him back?" Sabine offered.

"Yuk, no! Oh thank Faerie."

The wolf padded away and I tried to unravel the cramping knots in my stomach as the rest of the wolves huffed, gave Kainen slavering glances and slunk outside after their leader.

"How did you do that?" Kainen doubled over.

I took petty satisfaction that at least for once he looked worse than I did, hair all over the place and his face puffy and red.

"I don't know. I don't think I communicated anything, but at least it worked."

I shrugged and wondered if I should try to find him some water or something. Maybe he would fancy a piece of cake from the floor.

"Oh, they won't have understood you, dear. They're wolves. My wolves."

Tirzella swept into the hall and I crossed the few paces to Kainen's side.

"You set wolves on us?" I asked.

She frowned. "No, but they're wolves, not pets. If you

make yourself look edible and walk into their territory, then they'll do what wolves do, especially if I'm not around. Sabine, take the young man outside and wait for me at the cottage."

For a moment I thought she meant Kainen, but her gaze was roving over MC who stood quivering under the power of it. Sabine scowled but didn't argue, turning to us instead.

"May your travels be safe and swift," she said. "It was nice to meet you briefly."

I nodded the same but she stomped off with MC in tow toward the exit. MC twisted at the door to get one last glimpse of us, perhaps framing the memory of the two random people who'd exploded into his life and made him dress up in a wolf costume.

"Now, follow me." Tirzella set off toward a door right at the back of the hall. "We don't have much time before the wolves will need to retreat."

I guessed they were holding back the people for us at Tirzella's command but thoughts of home obscured all else. This realm wasn't mine to govern and Tirzella seemed to have things covered now that she was free.

A flash of doubt filled my head as Kainen tried to straighten up and sagged again with a hand on his middle.

"Here, lean on me." I shoved my shoulder under Kainen's arm.

He snorted, letting me support some of his weight. "Don't let Taz see this."

I rolled my eyes and towed him after Tirzella.

CHAPTER SEVENTEEN
BLOSSOM

Blossom stared up at the balcony, a strange stab of jealousy filtering through her. She'd meant what she said to Emil about not wanting to be lady of a court, mainly because she couldn't imagine it had much to it other than tireless obligations. But in that moment, Reyan held court over the entire room and the crowd was spellbound.

She deserves it, Blossom realised. *What have I ever earned?*

The bitterness swilled like nausea in the base of her stomach, the punch of it so potent she almost missed Reyan stumbling. She tensed, but Emil hadn't risen and Ace's head was still visible, holding him down.

The air shivered. With a collective gasp of horror, the crowd swelled, people appearing in their midst. Nobles were selfish but they weren't always mindless. Several familiar faces, Lord Marquest, Glennoria and others like them were already running for the exits or realm-skipping out of the court completely.

Blossom froze as several familiar faces from the Forgotten masses realm-skipped into the court. She could only assume Reyan's burst of power had disrupted the court's protection, because other than Emil she couldn't think of anyone else who could realm-skip at will. Her instincts tugged at her, insisting she also needed to flee while she still could. She hesitated.

If I leave now, Taz will never trust me again.

She saw Crew and Rayne in the crowd, Rayne with a

big bruise covering half her forehead. No sign of Belladonna, but this could mean that Arcanium had fallen and Belladonna was meting out punishments.

Blossom pushed aside the innate assumption that perhaps she should curry favour with her sister again instead. She'd burned that bridge and wouldn't want to rebuild it even if she had the chance.

Surging through the hordes as fighting commenced, she dodged around the explosions and sizzles of gifts rebounding everywhere. If she could reach Reyan, she could help from a distance. Perhaps Reyan needed someone who could summon things for her, although she could no doubt summon anything in her own court.

"Not in our bloody court!"

A woman with black hair ran forward waving a broom in one hand and a blunt sword in the other. Blossom vaguely recognised her as one of the staff, but she wouldn't have any idea of the woman's name. Several others she recognised for similar reasons were racing forward and… fighting.

Her jaw dropped to see the staff she'd often ridiculed grouping together and lashing out at the Forgotten as though they were real fighters.

Blossom wound a warding around herself and left the staff to hold the court. They clearly knew what they were doing, at least in terms of standing up for themselves, and a battle was no place for a princess. Not one who didn't want to fight anyway.

Even as soon as it started, it ended. Crew struggled against three women holding him with what looked like an array of knotted towels, although the one around his neck like a noose probably could have been a thread of cotton and it still would have done the job the way the woman was tightening it.

Maybe Arcanium isn't falling, she hesitated, surprised by how much hope the thought lit inside her. *Maybe Belladonna's hoping to claw some place to retreat to other than the Fauna Court.*

She didn't see the attack coming.

One step forward and her side spasmed with sudden, radiating pain. It burned and throbbed, and a wave of dizziness hit her the moment she looked down.

The arrow was unmistakeable, dark grey iron sleek in the shape of an arrow. Rayne's hand lifted from the end of it, a savage grin tearing across her face.

"Take that, traitor."

Blossom stumbled to her knees, the pain tearing through her middle as blood pooled over her clothing, dripping onto the floor.

Rayne started to laugh, the sound barking out of her until she froze, eyes wide. Blossom's vision blurred but she recognised the sparkle of black smoke winding around Rayne's head.

Thoughts of Kainen filled her mind as Rayne dropped beside her, falling from her knees to her side and whimpering as she clutched her head.

"You'll suffer that until I'm ready to release you," Reyan snarled, her eyes sparking with ire. "Your own personal hell."

Blossom blinked up at Reyan, who still had hold of Emil's collar in one hand with the black smoke swirling around her fingertips. Blossom almost cried. Reyan stood, lady of her court, as fierce and confident as Blossom had ever seen.

"Ace, get her to a healer now," Reyan insisted.

"No." Blossom choked as she tried to get the words out.

"I need Marthe, at my mother's court."

"I'll take her to Taz, he can take her home," Ace said. "I'll be right back."

Reyan nodded and clung tight to Emil, pressing her hand to his forehead until he closed his eyes tight against whatever personal torment she was subjecting him to.

"Okay, this may sting a bit," Ace said, his tone surprisingly gentle.

Blossom closed her eyes against the pain, the brush of the nether a moment later fading into nothingness. A loud bang and the sound of shouting filled her ears but she couldn't open her eyes.

"What the-"

She recognised her brother's irate voice.

"She said she needs Marthe," Ace said.

A hand curled firm around her wrist and the nether wisped again, dropping them into quiet.

"MARTHE." Taz's voice shattered her ears.

He even sounded a bit frantic, which confused her even though she couldn't remember why it should. Haziness claimed her thoughts, odd fragments of words and feelings she couldn't cling onto.

A sharp pain brought her eyes open and tore a scream from her lips.

"I'm doing my best."

She turned her head to find Marthe beside her, purple light radiating from her wisened fingertips, her lined face pinched and her greying hair askew. Behind Marthe stood Taz with his orb held up.

"I need him here now!" he barked. "I don't care if he's the other side of the Revel Court, get him now."

Tyren. He wants Tyren's death gift.

Blossom squeezed her eyes shut, her breaths rattling in

through her parted lips but never hitting where they needed to.

Death hovered, she knew that much. The arrow had punctured halfway through. If it hadn't decimated her guts, it probably at least took out a lung.

"Taz," she hissed, her voice almost failing her.

She twisted her head to find her mother beside her, Queen Tavania wide-eyed and tight-lipped. What did one say to a woman who was a queen first and a mother merely when it suited her. Blossom forced her head to turn the other way again as Taz dropped to his knees and took her hand.

"Hang on, okay?" he said.

She winced and forced her lips into a smile.

"No point. I- fought, for Arcanium- and your friends in the end."

Taz huffed. "Shh, you shouldn't speak."

She chuckled a laugh and choked on a groan.

"The Fauna Court, to Cerys," she rasped. "Was always rightfully hers."

He looked like he was about to cry. They'd never been close. Belladonna had tormented him and Blossom had joined in more often than not. Yet he'd given her a second chance and now he sat with her like she meant something to him.

"Tell Reyan…" She hesitated but he didn't interrupt this time. "I'm sorry, for the beginning."

Taz wiped a hand over his eyes. "You turned out to be the most honourable of all my sisters."

"Don't lie." She smiled.

"Fae can't lie."

I did the right thing.

She closed her eyes and whatever Taz was saying

slipped away. Something about what she'd earned. She hadn't earned much in the end.

But I did the right thing.

She blinked against the sudden glow of light, except her eyelids weren't there. A sensation, then. Humans talked about a light at the end of the tunnel after death for some strange reason, but this glow seemed to be dazzling soft warmth right through every essence of her body.

And there was a distant voice, an echo of something she felt she should know, something familiar.

"Come along my little acorn, we have all the time in the realm now."

CHAPTER EIGHTEEN
DEMI

I towed Kainen after Tirzella, my head full of thoughts of home. I'd considered the possibility that Tirzella was somehow tricking us, but I didn't get that kind of vibe from her. She wanted us gone so we'd keep the Fae out of her land, and I was more than happy to agree to that.

"Well now, who let you out I wonder?"

I flinched at the sneering sound of Loth's voice even as Kainen straightened up and forced himself in front of me.

Tirzella stood between us and Loth in the wide corridor, but he had no guards with him this time.

"She can handle it," Kainen muttered.

I frowned. "I hope so, we need her to get home."

"Dear me, Lothan," Tirzella made a soft tutting noise. "All this time you've had me contained down there and you didn't once dare to visit. Scared your followers will find out that their Grand Priest is nothing more than one of the Banished wielding magic in secret?"

Loth laughed, but there was no warmth at all to the noise, a mere performance.

"We both know you can't harm me, witch," he sneered. "If you could catch me, you could banish me. But I shan't be letting you near enough to manage it."

I inched closer to Kainen. "I reckon he has gifts but not the knowledge. He didn't ward against us earlier, but they're talking like he has power."

Before Kainen could reply, Tirzella stepped back to

190

stand alongside us.

"Be a dear and hold him for me, would you?" she asked.

I blinked. "Um… okay?"

I gave Kainen a helpless look and he sighed, flicking a hand out. Loth dropped to his knees, his eyes widening in horror.

"There you go."

Tirzella frowned. "You'll need to hold him still for this to work."

Kainen opened his mouth but I stepped forward, summoning my energy gift into one hand. Trepidation pounded inside my veins as I stepped close enough to Loth to touch, my hand landing on his shoulder.

"Now what?" I asked.

A thrum of foreboding jolted through me, but Loth's hand was on my wrist before I could react. He shot to his feet, his body dipping behind mine and a thin dagger pressing against my throat.

Wild-eyed I found Kainen.

"It should have worked!" he insisted. "Demi, I didn't, I promise."

I had no idea if there was some look of accusation on my face, or if he assumed I thought he had pretended to compel Loth to his knees. I hadn't even considered the potential for him to betray me until he said it.

I couldn't do anything about the blade at my throat, and stupidity had convinced me to drop my warding, sheer arrogance that I thought Kainen's gifts had rendered us safe.

"Tirzella didn't tell you?" Loth crowed, his voice like poison dripping in my ear. "I am immune to any kind of mental influence. Now, your little queenling and I will be going."

He took a step back and I had to stumble with him.

"Yeah, that'd be a no." I braced myself, knowing I had to time what I was about to do immaculately. "My boyfriend's expecting me."

"Your wha-"

Loth's voice pitched into a surprised huff as I leaned forward and launched myself backward to attack with the human effect. My head hit his nose and my hand was already prying away the dagger as he staggered back. I kicked out, my boot thudding against his ankle.

The moment I was free, I warded myself and crashed into Kainen's side. I glanced up at his irate face.

"Taz is going to kill you," he grumbled. "Or no, he'll probably kill me for letting you do it."

I pushed that aside and turned to Tirzella.

"Thanks for the warning," I snapped. "If he can't be compelled, how do we contain him?"

She gave me a disapproving look. "Do you have any other abilities? Ones that might keep him from moving?"

"Only one that'll shock him."

Tirzella nodded. "That will do nicely."

I sucked in a sharp breath and fought my kinder instincts. Loth had his dagger aloft again as I flicked out my hand, letting my energy power zing through the air and sizzle into his shins.

"Make it quick."

We watched Tirzella glide toward Loth and tilt her head up toward his pained face.

"May your incarceration teach you some manners," she crooned, pushing the tip of her forefinger between his eyes and pushing sharply.

A loud pop echoed. I gasped.

As Tirzella straightened up, Loth was nowhere to be

seen.

"Where did you send him?" I asked.

If she's somehow sent him to Faerie, if he and Emil find each other before she sends us back, or even after-

"To a distant part of our land, do not worry yourself. He won't be able to find his way back for a long while, and when he does I will be more than prepared to deal with him. Come along. The quicker I get you both home, the sooner I can start sorting out the mess he created."

She strode away past where Loth had been standing and Kainen held out his arm.

"Do you need support?" he asked, his tone stiff.

I pulled a face. "Ideally not. Why, do you?"

He shook his head as we started after Tirzella.

"I thought I was going to see the same thing play out now as I did when the Old King was going to sacrifice you to be honest."

I shuddered. "History always repeats in one way or another. That's why I'm determined that there will be no more secrets, no more suffering of our people."

He didn't answer but we were both trying to keep up with Tirzella so I didn't let it bother me. The moment we were home, he'd be off back to the Illusion Court and I'd be back at Arcanium. Taz would probably threaten to chain me in my room, Milo would have drowned under the endless reams of paperwork he'd created ready for my return. Ace would be going grey trying to calm them both down.

I smothered a smile at the thought.

"We were lucky to meet MC and Sabine though," I said.

Kainen nodded. "I hope he does get his apprentice role and makes some friends like he wanted."

He had asked for that. It was the kind of offer I'd have

made to him without a second's doubt if we'd been in Faerie. But we weren't in Faerie, and I wasn't the one in charge here. I forced my legs to move just that little bit faster.

"Can I ask you something with no debt?" I called after Tirzella.

"You may ask."

Fair enough.

"You seem to know Sabine already, but will you make sure MC has something good waiting for him too? He's been a huge help and kindness should be rewarded."

Tirzella slowed her pace enough for us to catch up with her.

"The quivering boy who looked like he was about to burst into tears?"

Harsh but accurate. "That's the one."

"I will keep a kindly eye on him," she promised. "Here we are."

She opened a door and trotted us down a spiralling stone staircase. Kainen straightened himself up with one hand on the wall, his breathing still a bit laboured.

"I'm fine, you go first." He leaned toward me. "Stay close."

I let my warding merge with his, wondering if my doubt of him would ever fully fade. A swell of guilt echoed in my head that I should forget as well as forgive, but it was always easier said than done.

The walls were narrow around us and I pressed a hand to my chest with the other brushing the cool stone beside me.

Too tight. I tried to keep my breathing steady. *I can do this. I've braved being locked in a cupboard and a trial chamber tunnel. I'm a freaking queen.*

The words made no difference to my pounding heart as the walls closed around me and the panic grew, thundering in my ears.

"Is it much further?" Kainen asked. "And what exactly are we facing?"

Something I should have asked.

Tirzella didn't answer, her steps increasing pace. I stumbled after her with the mad realisation that the only thing I could trust right now while torn up with panic was Kainen's warding firm around mine.

"Almost there," Tirzella called back.

I continued on with my fingers clenched tight around the strap of my satchel and my entire body shaking. I tripped when the steps ended but Kainen had an arm in front of me before I could fall. The room opened out into a small square, stone floor, stone walls and a small gap at the bottom leading into the darkness of what looked like a tunnel.

"We don't rely on gifts as the Fae once did," Tirzella said. "They never understood that. Gifts are powerful but the land will endure and we can harness it."

I blinked while huffing in ragged breaths as she lit a candle and pressed it close to the stone where it cast shadows into the corner. Then she held out two mice, one wriggling in her left hand and the other still in her right.

Light and shadow, life and death.

Kainen looked doubtfully at the dark gap. "Well, I guess we're lucky at least to have rescued you from the same place as our route home."

Tirzella laughed. "Ah routes are everywhere, young lord, if one knows how to look. Or how to conjure. But that is not information I will be sharing."

"Not information I want anyone to know either," I

muttered, thinking of invasions when we got back home.

Kainen folded his arms across his chest. "So, to get this entirely clear, you expect us to go into the tunnel? What's in there?"

I looked from Kainen and his incredulous disbelief to Tirzella's serenity.

"It is your way home," she insisted. "Crawl through, think of home and you will make it."

Kainen glanced at me doubtfully. "Do you want me to go first?"

I had no idea. If he went first and something happened then I'd be left with my guilt. If I went first and something happened to me, I'd have no way of telling him not to risk it. Even Betty wouldn't be able to get back and warn him if I went first and took her with me.

"What about Betty?" I asked.

He patted his pocket. "My life wouldn't be worth living if I went back to Reyan without her, don't worry."

"We go together then," I decided. "Wherever you end up, go straight home and find Reyan. When you're ready, come to my court. You go in first and I'll be right behind you."

He nodded. "Okay. Feel free to put a hand onto my leg if you need to, I won't tell Taz if you don't."

With a flash of that cocky grin, he dropped to his knees before the opening and eyed Tirzella warily.

"Any magic words? No incantations or funny dances?"

She chuckled. "You can if you want, but they'll only distract you. Keep crawling and think of home."

Kainen took a deep breath and inched inside, his body disappearing until all that was left was his feet.

"I'm waiting until you're behind me," he called back.

I dropped to my knees and realised I hadn't quite

thought it through. Although me having to stare at the back end of him was probably better than him staring at the back end of me. My fraught brain tried to guess which one Taz would freak out about the least.

"Remember our agreement, queen," Tirzella said, her tone dropping deep with warning. "Stay out of our land and we will leave you to yours."

I nodded. "Gladly, and I'll do what I can to keep my enemies away too. Might be worth checking that your enemies, whoever they are, don't have some way of communicating with our side though, just in case."

"That is an adventure for another time," she said, her voice softer again. "Travel safe and swift."

I took a deep breath and with my insides roiling, I tapped the heel of Kainen's boot to send him forward and started crawling after him into the darkness. Almost immediately, the solidness of the stone began to flex.

"Can you feel that?" Kainen called back.

"The floor not being a floor anymore? Yeah."

Thoughts of us crawling into some kind of pit or ancient demon mouth filled my head, but each movement had my fingers brushing the sole of Kainen's boot.

"It feels like the nether." He crawled faster. "Think of home!"

His foot disappeared from my reach.

"Kainen?"

I waited, but nobody answered.

CHAPTER NINETEEN
REYAN

Reyan wiped a speck of blood from her face and eyed the room, waiting for another challenge. None came. She flinched as the air shivered but Ace appeared a moment later and she sagged with relief. She didn't dare ask about Blossom, but his expression wasn't encouraging. She wondered if he'd be safe enough to get Emil back to Arcanium or the Forever mountains by himself when a round of gasps filled the air.

Tension twisted through the shadows as the crowd's eyes collectively widened. Reyan waited for the next inevitable challenge, firming her warding around her. It tingled though as someone approached from behind, oddly reminiscent of-

"Throwing a party without me, sweetheart?"

Shock reigned for several moments and she couldn't move, couldn't breathe. Couldn't let herself believe it.

Then a sob slammed into her chest, the subtle scent of familiarity and ripeness swirling around her until she was sick with longing.

Without stopping to check first, Reyan shoved Emil into Ace's waiting hands, twisted around and leapt.

Kainen caught her mid-leap, laughter plastered across his face as she wrapped her legs around his waist. She didn't care the court were watching, didn't care that their rule of it was still on a tipping point.

Didn't even care that their relationship was *technically* still a fake.

He grasped her tight to him and dropped kisses over her face, her neck, any part of her he could reach. Tears rolled down her cheeks as she bunched up fistfuls of the grubby t-shirt under his leather jacket and clung on, her gaze drifting over the rainbow bracelet on his wrist and the utter feeling of belonging zinging through her as the essence of their court wrapped around them both.

"Missed me, did you?" he asked, delight singing in his tone.

"I hate yo- you- how much I've missed you," she cried, clinging on tighter.

He chuckled. "Well then, I love the way you hate me."

He manhandled her so that she was standing in front of him, but even then she lifted a hand, fingertips smoothing over his face, memorising it.

"What state are we in?" he asked.

He didn't look at the court but she knew that's what he was worried about. There'd be time to tell him what state they were in personally, maybe once she'd shouted at him for a long while, but their court had to come first.

"Insurrection handled as of about a minute ago," she murmured. "Now you're back, it'll be okay."

He folded one arm around her waist and pulled her tight against him. In that instant the truth fell from his face, his lordly mask taking over. Gone was the bright smile and the shining eyes, replaced with the wicked grin and devilish darkness everyone knew him for.

But Reyan pulled on everything she'd learned. Everything she'd fought to earn from *their* court.

"Don't you recognise him?" she asked silkily. "KNEEL."

Kainen shot her a horrified look and she smiled back as the court dropped under the weight of the compulsion, some extremely reluctantly, to their knees.

"You have them well trained in my absence I see," he crooned, that soft fondness for her alone. "I'm impressed."

"Well I had to do something while you were off gallivanting. We've had a challenge to my leadership by him over there," she pointed at Emil with a look of disgust. "Then some of the Forgotten dropped in. We had one casualty, but you wouldn't believe me if I told you. I should check if she's alright."

Ace grimaced. "I handed her over but it didn't look good."

Before Reyan could express any sorrow, Ace yelped and stumbled back.

Emil retracted his elbow from Ace's gut and launched to his feet, lurching at her with both arms outstretched. Reyan lifted her hand to defend but a loud bang sent Emil flying backwards before she could call any power behind her. He hit the nearest stretch of rocky wall and slithered down, his head lolling as he tried to lift it.

"You shouldn't have done that," Kainen said, his tone entirely conversational. "Attack me, fine. Attack my court, I'd deal with you fairly. But attack my fiancée and I will show absolutely no mercy."

Reyan's heart swelled to hear that, but several of the Forgotten had taken that as a chance to try the same thing. She winced as Amba's fist arced back into a man's head, a man who was bizarrely wrapped at the throat with a towel. Meri was hitting some random woman with a ridiculously enormous clipboard that couldn't be in any way practical.

Reyan choked over an ill-timed giggle. Her court was entirely mad and she loved it.

"Oh for the love of-" Kainen muttered.

Reyan flinched closer to him as he lifted his orb, but the

face was shadowy and too busy moving fast to be clear.

"I'm good," Kainen insisted before anyone could speak. "We'll be there in a bit."

"Is the traitor-" The voice was female but too muffled to make out.

"Reyan's sorted him, don't worry." He ducked as a small ball of steel whipped over his head, missing him by inches. "Oops."

He shoved the orb in his pocket and Reyan scanned the crowd, her strength rising. Kainen was back at her side, and now she felt she could survive anything.

"This ends now!" she shouted.

The scuffles slowed, hesitation and doubt warring through the crowd. Several noble faces peeked out over balconies, and Reyan decided she would torment them for not standing up for their court for a long time to come.

She collared Emil again before he could recover from Kainen's previous attack and pushed her hand to his head. Shadow and smoke obscured his face and swarmed up his nose until he coughed. She didn't relent. It wouldn't kill him but he would suffer if she had anything to do with it.

She lifted her head to find Kainen staring at her, wide-eyed. She couldn't remember if he knew about the court claiming her. The last brief time they'd seen each other had passed so quickly.

"You look divine with our gifts, sweetheart," he said, loud enough for the court to hear. "I'll have to ask you for a place in your court now it looks like."

She searched his face but his eyes were shining with adoration and she wondered how she could have ever doubted his devotion to her as he turned to face the court.

"Well, take that as a lesson," he announced. "Together we are even stronger. But while my lady is pure strength and power, I would counsel kindness. This court supports our queen and anyone else who doesn't should leave. You have fifteen minutes to get your stuff or declare loyalty. After that, your lives are fair game for sport."

Reyan held her tongue, even though she wanted to tease him that she'd already made that speech and he'd missed it.

"I won't let you upstage me entirely though," he murmured.

She frowned as he dropped to one knee and took her hand in his, regardless of the black smoke weaving around it. Her skin buzzed happily the moment it touched his and she sucked in an exhilarated breath. She still had one hand on Emil's collar, but it would take him at least a few minutes to recover from the pain she'd put him in.

"My lady," Kainen bowed his head. "Not my consort, not my future bride, but lady of the court I will pledge my life to."

Her cheeks flushed bright red. "Kainen, get up."

"No." He grinned. "You own this court in your own right now as surely as you own me."

He kissed her hand, his lips lingering over her skin until tingles burst in her gut and she had to fight the urge to make their excuses and drag him back to his room.

Our room. She smiled.

"It's our court, love, yours and mine."

His eyes sparkled even more as he got to his feet.

"As you wish, Lady." His expression twisted into pure fury as he eyed Emil. "As for you, we'll finish this war where it began. With the queen and the king consort, and Arcanium."

CHAPTER TWENTY
DEMI

Crawling through the darkness brought back too many awful memories. The air smelled ancient and chilled the sweat on my face as my palms began to slip, the floor underneath my hands soft and moveable.

"Kainen?"

Still no answer.

I stopped crawling, my insides pounding a deafening rhythm. I couldn't feel nether, only the suffocating embrace of whatever I was swamped in.

Think of home. I can do this. Taz. The common room. Our room. The library. The atrium. Milo glaring at me over papers and Ace laughing at him. Beryl, Meryl and Cheryl making things explode.

The image of Taz's face swam in front of me. I reached out for it through the darkness but it dissipated.

"Kainen?"

Still no answer. He was gone, hopefully home to his court, or mine, or somewhere in Faerie at least. Stifling a frantic whimper, I forced my hands and knees forwards.

I need to get to Taz. To Faerie. I need to get back to him.

My cocoon of nothing tightened, the brush of it wisping my skin. I closed my eyes as it whirled up my nose, permeating my skin and reaching right down into the very bones of me.

Taz.

I repeated his name over and over, lodging his face in

my mind as I started to choke and everything around me felt like spinning.

An almighty thud cracked through my knees and my forearms. I winced, gasping lungfuls of crisp, sweet air. I scanned my body the way I'd been taught during FDP training, assessing my connection to my gifts. My energy gift sang inside my arms but beside it was every note of my queenly essence chorusing together in perfect harmony.

A series of crashing noises hit my ears around the time I heard voices shouting.

Please let me be home. Please.

I opened my eyes and let out a pained wail.

The Arcanium atrium was on fire. Gifts whizzed back and forth from what looked like two sides corralled on opposite ends of the hall. Several of the golden gates to the lifts were still in place but a couple were missing.

Belladonna loomed in the enemy crowd furthest from the lift to the human world, her voice screeching things I couldn't make out. She didn't seem to be attacking but there were enough Fae around her to more than make up for it.

A guttural roar filled the air as I turned to check over my people next. I managed to clamber to my feet and throw up a shield warding behind me with my back to the enemy as Taz barrelled into me from the front and knocked me back to the floor again, his hand cradling the back of my head.

"Is it really you?" He all but screamed it, even as my warding curled around his with irresistible familiarity.

I choked over a sob and threw my arms tight around his neck, not caring that I was lying on the floor with him on top of me in the most unqueenly manner possible.

"It's really me, Queen Demerara present for duty. We know what they're after now and they won't get it."

He nodded against my shoulder. "We've been holding them back but Reyan's court is under fire from Emil. Ace is there."

"Oof, and Milo agreed to that? Is that wise?"

He hefted me up and brought us both to standing with an almighty sweep of his wings.

"I think so, although he's threatened to move all the books to the Word Court twice. Duck."

I ducked without questioning it, his hands pulling me down. Moments later, a fireball shot over our heads, exploding against the warding protecting the rest of my court.

"Discuss it later?" he asked, a wry grin breaking over his face.

I nodded, pressing my hands to his cheeks and my lips to his. His arms tightened around me, the one home that kept me anchored to everything else I was responsible for. He broke the kiss some moments later, his cheeks pink and his turquoise eyes dancing.

"What happened to the Di- Kainen?" he asked.

I caught the subtle tone of wariness in his voice, that residual fear that we needed to put properly in the past now, as he led me toward our group. The enemy attacks were raining down against our warding but our side kept their defences still, waiting for us to join them. Several of them were down on one knee, Arcanium outsiders, I noticed. My lot had given up bowing and kneeling early on, mainly because you never knew when one of the Eastwicks or Hutchinsons would take it as an opportunity to swoop up and use you for a game of leapfrog.

"He's not here?" I grimaced. "Orbs, I should have

checked. He's been loyal the whole way through, don't worry." I pulled my orb out of my pocket. "Kainen?"

His face hovered in front of me moments later in pearlescent grey.

"I'm good, we'll be there in a bit."

I huffed a relieved breath. "Is the traitor-"

"Reyan's sorted him, don't worry. Oops."

He ducked and the vision of him vanished, no doubt still fighting any insurrections in his court. He and Reyan would handle theirs, but I had my own to worry about now as we passed through the communal warding protecting our side from the enemy.

"Thank Faerie!"

Milo threw his huge arms around my neck and all but strangled the life out of me. I patted his back gently as Taz bundled in with us, rocking us back and forth in an unsteady wobble.

"I know, I know, there'll be paperwork," I joked.

Milo let me go but he looked like a huge weight had been lifted off his shoulders. Probably because now managing Taz without me there wasn't his problem anymore.

I surveyed the assembled people, some injured and still standing to fight. A swell of hope filled my heart as I saw people from the other courts looking back at me. Lolly and Tyren stood near the back in a cluster with a group from the Flora and Revel courts, while Sannar and Odella were surrounded by a smaller group of what looked like people from the town beneath the Nether Court. I didn't miss Tira standing with the Eastwicks either, her little finger curled sneakily around Meryl's.

"I've been away," I announced to the crowd, letting my voice ring out to state the obvious because it beat having to be formal about it. "Now I'm back. We finish this today."

A cheer went up at that which startled me a bit. Taz wrapped both arms around my waist from behind while Milo stood muttering about official slogans.

"Is that it?" Taz teased, his breath soft on my ear. "Milo may have a point. We need a battle cry of some kind. Something to go down in the Book of Faerie for the ages."

I raised my hand, my energy gift crackling to my fingertips and lighting them with an icy-blue glow.

Tirzella was right about gifts being less than the land we lived in. Faerie would endure long after queens and lords and ladies and folk were gone. I'd grown reliant on my new gifts as queen, but attacking Belladonna required a personal touch, something wholly me.

"No more Forgotten, no more suffering!" I yelled, magnifying my voice so it'd be heard across the realms.

I threw out my arm without looking and sent the jolt of power sizzling across the hall. It crackled over the surface of the enemy's warding, picking out those who were determinedly warding themselves, piercing through it. As if I had *metirin* iron inside me, as though the essence of the Prime Realm was somehow embedded in my skin, or more likely the mass of dirt covering it, the attack shattered several holes in their protection.

"Whoa."

Taz warded us both as our side charged forward to attack, but I hung behind to check the boundaries of the court and strengthen our protection. Whoever had managed to get inside wouldn't be leaving again, except to be taken straight to the forever mountains.

"She's mine," I nodded to Belladonna. "Don't mind if you help, or if Lolly gets involved before I do, but I have to end this now. Any objections?"

Taz clasped my hand in his. "Nope. She may be my sister by blood, half-sister technically, but she attacked my family. We do what we have to do."

We jogged through the battle side by side, dodging flying gifts and fighting sections. Call-Me-Henry, Arcanium's long-suffering Head Receptionist and Stationery Organisation Director, saluted as I went past his reception desk, but I knew better than to ask if he needed any help as he stood launching staplers with lethal precision using a rubber band and a ruler.

"Heads up!"

Beryl darted past with Harvey holding a metal tray. I didn't dare stop to ask but followed her finger pointing through the thick of the enemy. Belladonna was fighting through them, screaming orders but definitely heading for one of the lifts.

"Oh, you won't have seen," Taz said as we rushed after her. "Blossom did something and Reyan got Belladonna's gifts. She's got none."

That's why she's running now I'm here. I can use that to my advantage.

Summoning my connection to my court, I twisted the already broken golden bars of the lift's grill into a barrier to block her exit. She skidded to a halt inches away from getting a face full of metal, twisting around with her eyes rolling wild.

"Surely she'd have found a courtier to gift her with things though? Blossom even?"

Taz shook his head. "We weren't given the ability to gift people as we weren't sworn to my mother's court as children, remember?"

And she wouldn't want anyone close to her knowing she

was vulnerable.

I would be capturing her today and putting an end to this. There was no other way to avoid her rising against us again and again, inciting the remnants of the old ways against us and stirring up discord. We all knew a ruler had to make harsh decisions for the good of their people, but targeting her when she didn't have gifts to defend herself with still seemed unfair somehow.

I released a wave of frost and fire, building a cage to hem her in. She rattled her hands against it and pulled an arrow from her back, lashing it through the bars.

We had no gift that could overpower *metirin* iron, but she would tire eventually.

"See if you can get her unawares while I keep her distracted," I muttered. "Get the iron off her."

Taz nodded and took to the air in a flap of fiery wings, leaving me to face Belladonna alone. Without gifts to rely on, she was warding herself with everything she had. Taz had a sword of metirin iron he could use to pierce through her protection, but with the iron arrow she could defend herself against most things Fae.

"We're at an impasse," she shouted.

I shrugged, playing for time. "I don't see how. This is my court, my crown, and these my people to protect. We both know you have no gifts to fight with, and you're not getting any more iron from the Prime Realm. That's why you wanted to get in, wasn't it?"

The hatred on her face quivered but she held herself steady to face me. I didn't dare lift my gaze from hers, forcing myself to hold the eye contact, but as Taz dropped down and speared at her protection, she darted to the side and fixed it just as fast.

He took swipes but she sent the iron arrow out to meet

209

his blade, his combat skills far outmatched by her own.

Pull back, don't get yourself hurt, I warned him. *Sneak attacks while I distract her.*

He grimaced and took flight again. Belladonna wiped a hand over her forehead to shift errands strands of hair.

"You can't hold off the old ways forever," she seethed. "They will always be there. They will always return."

"Be a bit boring if they didn't."

I threw my hand up to clear a wave of glass shards heading for a group near us, the sharp edges turning to raindrops. Not once did I look away from her, determined to give Taz his opening.

"So, we wait," I added. "You hide in your protection and I'll wait for you to come out. Was it your idea to find the Prime Realm, or another of Emil's "brilliant" schemes? Last few haven't worked out so well for him."

She snorted, arrogance overtaking sense. "This was always the plan. Resurrect the Old King, have him hold court over Faerie and relax the protection on the human world so that we could use it to find the Prime Realm. There's a wealth of resources over there and it was our land rightfully long before we were banished."

She hesitated, her face descending into a furious scowl as she remembered who she was talking to, but I had my answer.

I'd stumbled into an ancient grudge being wielded long before I became queen, perhaps even before I even knew I was a fairy, before I was born. I thought back to my enemies in the past war. The Old King with his unshakeable arrogance, now dead. Elvira still in the Oak Queen's keeping, a mere pawn of Emil's greater plan. The Apocalyptians with all their essences of power, now all diminished.

And Belladonna standing before me, ready to try and best a queen of Faerie simply because Emil had convinced her that this was the 'right' thing.

Even I didn't see Taz swoop the second time, his blade slicing through the top of Belladonna's protection. She lifted the arrow in an attempt to spear him right through and I launched forward with energy searing my entire body as his fingers closed around it. And slipped away.

Belladonna dropped to the floor and sealed herself before he could drop after her, and he swooped away with a curse on his lips.

As iron fought iron, I remembered again what Tirzella had said about land over gifts.

One more time, I sent the mind-speak out to Taz. *I know what I'm doing now.*

I summoned my connection and wrapped the comfort of my court around me, ready to pounce. I hadn't answered Belladonna but perhaps it didn't matter. There would be time to talk yet, and if Reyan and Kainen had Emil in their keeping, we might get another shot at ensuring lasting peace in Faerie.

"So he's used a lot of people for the cause," I said. "And you're the latest. Congratulations. Self-confessed Queen of the Bag of Bones Court or whatever, ex-royalty who lost her gifts and plays puppet for someone else."

"You think you can trick me into doubting him?"

I grinned. "He's promised so many things to so many people, why are you any different?"

Before she could answer, Taz attacked again. I sent my will out to the court and a strand of ivy peeled away from the wall, whipping down into the gap Taz created in Belladonna's warding. She swung the arrow toward him and dodged his attempt to grab it, but she had no hope of

211

releasing it from the thick strand of semi-sentient ivy. Her screech echoed over the chaotic battle noise behind me as the ivy threw the arrow while Taz sneakily grabbed the remaining ones on her back.

The arrow sailed through the air and Taz surged after it like Leo chasing a tomato, rolling his body around it and swooping away with the lot.

Belladonna re-firmed her warding but she had nothing to attack with now and stood frantically eying the crowd as if she could summon one of them to fight me for her.

Are there people ready to fight for us on other floors?

I sent the thought out to Taz, flinching as he dropped down beside me.

"Absolutely. I put Cheryl and Hutch on it."

I blinked at him. "Will I have a court left after?"

"Um, maybe?" He grinned guilty. "What you going to do?"

"Meryl!" I shouted loud enough for the whole hall to hear.

People twisted to look and others paused fighting before renewing the fray, but Meryl jogged toward me with Tira hurrying alongside her.

"Hiya." Meryl beamed, looking livelier than I'd seen her in months. "Welcome back."

"Thanks. Can you pull a couple of lift grills free and make a cage?" I pointed to Belladonna.

Meryl nodded. "Can do. Glad to have you back, although to be fair to him Taz only threatened to kill three people and dissolve one court."

"Hey! I did pretty well all things considering," Taz muttered.

"Ouch." I stuck my tongue out at him, not quite able to pull off a disapproving look. "Who needs an official apology?"

Meryl's focus turned to the task, two of the golden lift grills beginning to sever from their hinges and crunch into the form of a cage but Tira gave me a shy smile.

"It was mine but he's already kind of apologised so it's fine."

I feigned astonishment, dropping my jaw as Meryl's makeshift cage crowded a glaring Belladonna onto her knees.

"Is the king consort finally showing some sort of emotional growth?" I teased.

He slung an arm around my neck and squished gently, his other hand on my hip to hold me steady.

"All because of you, my queen. Your glowing influence is a shining beacon to every- *ooof.*"

I retracted my elbow from his ribs with a smile. Now was the time to make things clear once and for all. The enemy were still fighting but their efforts were fractured and without a leader, they would crumble quick enough.

Tira and Meryl darted back into the fight, and I spared a brief moment of curiosity as Tira seemed to have all of the Arcanium butterflies that usually nested amid the ivy and holly on the atrium walls flying in formation behind them.

I sought through the faces in the chaos of the crowd, looking for troublemakers, but a blur of struggling colour popped into existence in front of me and changed the plan.

"One traitor for you, my queen," Reyan said, her cheeks pink and her hair a complete mess. "Welcome home."

She hesitated and eyed the state of the crowd, several of them now faltering. I noticed her beginning to lower and scowled.

"Don't you dare kneel," I muttered. "Can someone get

the court lords and ladies behind me?"

I saw Milo hurrying out of one of the lifts and knew immediately he'd gone to hide out and defend the library, but he heard me and set off to chivvy the others about. Which left me with the one person I hadn't had the delight of dealing with, not for a long while.

I dropped my gaze to where Kainen had Emil hunched over, one hand pressing swirling black darkness into his shoulder to hold him down.

"I'm just giving him a little dose of what he's done to others," Kainen said. "Nothing too lasting."

I shouldn't technically approve of that but I let it slide as Kainen made the smoke recede into his skin. Emil lifted his head. The last time I'd seen him in what I guessed was his original form he'd been bald, but now he had a short buzz of greying hair. I'd seen him since glamouring as his Lorens persona, but it had taken me a while to realise they were one and the same.

He tilted his head enough that he could look up at me, his gaze calculating his chances even now.

"We'll take him to Queenie's office." I stepped forward, glancing from Kainen to Reyan. "Stand together."

Taz looped an arm around my waist and clamped a reluctant hand on Kainen's shoulder as I did the same to Reyan. I was exhausted but didn't even have time to consider it as Taz skipped us through the purple-grey swirl of the nether and into the more gothicly dramatic purple-grey aesthetic of Queenie's office.

"Fitting it began and ends here," I said. "Don't you think, Emil? I'll be compelling you to answer honestly, so no point going for the theatrics."

The door swung open before I could think about which

question to ask first. As Queenie strode in with Ace behind her, I fought the innate urge to apologise for commandeering her office. She stared at me, wide-eyed, then dipped her head and shoulders.

Ace shoved past her and Taz let go of me as I let myself tumble into his arms.

"I knew you'd be okay," he murmured. "I knew it."

I stepped back, red-cheeked and brimming with relief. Taz reclaimed me immediately with his arm around me, his hand resting in the pocket of my jeans.

I looked up in time to see Kainen frowning at Reyan then looking at Ace.

"Thanks for looking out for her," he muttered.

"No problem." Ace nodded then glanced at me. "Likewise."

The swell of masculine awkwardness filled the air until Queenie stalked through the middle of them with a huff.

"Well, thank Faerie you're back, Demi," she said. "Milo's been worse than Taz. *Six* new protocols for things that have never even happened in Faerie's history. *Six*."

I grinned. "He takes his job very seriously. But that has to come later."

"Yes, the atrium is under attack. The library is in tatters."

My heart squeezed in torment but Taz huffed loudly.

"It's barely got a scratch on it, don't upset her."

I soaked in the bliss of being at home, Taz and Queenie squabbling like it was any other normal day. Except it wasn't.

"Kainen, or Reyan, would you mind?" I asked. "Compulsions are more your forte."

Kainen nodded. "Gladly, my queen."

You trust him? Taz's voice filled my head.

I smiled. *Actually, yeah, I do. But we both know Ace will be doing it as well without being asked, just in case.*

I glanced at Ace and he nodded, the tiniest tip of his chin letting me know he had me covered as I faced Emil for what I really hoped would be the final time.

"So Emil, here's your moment to shine. Why not tell us the whole thrilling tale about how you managed to outfox us oh so effortlessly."

He glared up at me, a prideful sneer still on his face as Kainen and Reyan both held him down by the shoulders.

"What is there to bother telling you?" he spat. "You probably know most of it. I enlisted Elvira's help to raise the Old King, thus releasing the Apocalyptians. I used the chaos it caused as a distraction to search Faerie and the courts for information on the Prime Realm. I didn't bargain with Elvira being so disgustingly clingy though, or the nether crowning you."

"Faerie knew you had to be stopped," Taz said.

Emil shrugged. "If you say so. I managed to locate an artefact from the forgotten halls of an ancient Fae line and that gave me access to someone in the Prime Realm."

"The mirror," Reyan said.

He nodded. "Yes. What I quickly realised was that the owner of the other mirror had a debt placed on his family by a Fae long ago before they were banished from the Prime Realm. I offered to release him from that debt if he gave me access to resources."

"Loth, yeah." I smiled wide. "Met him. Horrible guy. He's been banished to some distant part of the Prime Realm. Won't be seeing him again in any of our lifetimes most likely."

I had to trust Tirzella on that, but it was worth it to see Emil's face twist with horror, his eyes wide as his mouth dropped open.

"I also know you went in there because you wanted *metirin* iron," I added. "Big foundry, lots of the stuff. Would no doubt make you invincible if you could summon the stuff at will and make warding essentially pointless. But there's no way through left, not from Faerie or the human world at least. We'll be smashing that mirror of yours as well when we get to it. I'm guessing you used Belladonna's ruthless psychopath tendencies to incite another Forgotten uprising so we'd be too distracted to be hunting you?"

His face twisted with rage and he wriggled to get himself free, but Kainen and Reyan had him pinned too tightly.

"I cultivated Belladonna into the role of wannabe queen the same way I did with Elvira. Once she found out the Prime Realm had iron, it became her obsession. It was easy for me, and off she went doing all my searching for me while I skipped about trying to recruit more supporters."

"Yes, there is that. The realm-skipping. Is that a natural thing?"

Emil grinned. "Oh no. You can thank Queen Tavania for that one. There was a time she trusted me oh so very closely."

He eyed Taz with vindictive expectation. Taz stared back at him.

"What, is that supposed to upset me?" He snorted in disbelief. "Who she consorts with is nothing to do with me."

"Then you two got taken through the portal instead of me," Emil continued, his brow furrowing as his taunt didn't land any injury. "That was the eventual plan, to convince Belladonna to get everything in place to enter the

217

Prime Realm then go through before she had a chance to follow. I even had a plan for that girl from the Nether Court to block everyone out so only I could go through once the portal was open, but everything happened so fast."

"And now I'm back." I wiped a hand over my face, still half-scared it wasn't real. "And you're in chains. The Prime Realm is cut off for good. Sucks for you."

Emil's expression contorted and both Kainen and Ace took a forceful step forward.

He's fighting the compulsions.

I raised my hand to intervene, to add my power behind theirs, but Emil gasped before I could.

"Portals are not the only way." He choked the words past gritted teeth. "Anything that can travel through the nether can breach the banishment."

He sagged and I took a step back.

Anything that can move through the nether.

Trolls travelled through it every day at Arcanium, but I'd asked Trevor to try finding the Prime Realm and he had no luck.

I glanced at Kainen, realisation dawning. He pinned his lips together in a motion of secrecy and I nodded in reply. We wouldn't mention a certain creature that had brought him a message all the way to the Prime Realm, a creature that was potentially borne of the same elements as Reyan.

I watched Kainen and Reyan look at each other, their expressions twitching as they no doubt communicated through their mind-speak connection. That was a worry for another time though.

Every single film or show I'd ever seen where the bad guy was questioned over a long period of time meant they ended up escaping. Emil had slipped past us more times before than I wanted to admit. I guessed that the chains around his wrists were made of *metirin* iron or he would have realm-skipped free by now, but there would be no more mistakes.

Faerie needed an end to the story so that the new one could begin.

"Well, that's delightfully enlightening, but you're done," I told him.

I leaned back against Taz, letting him support most of my weight. I shivered in delight as his wings brushed either side of me, cocooning us in.

"What's the plan?" he asked.

I smiled, letting the wickedness creep across my face.

"We give Faerie the show and ceremony that Milo's always moaning at me for forgetting. Down to the atrium everyone."

Ace latched onto me as Taz realm-skipped us back down to the atrium, but the moment we landed in the clash and clang of the fighting, he was off toward Milo.

"I should try to look queenly, shouldn't I?" I muttered.

Taz nodded, his chin still on my shoulder. "Probably best."

"Which means you need to let go."

"Never."

He conceded to lifting his chin and stepping to my side, but I let him keep his arm tight around my waist. I took that moment to myself, to turn and look at him properly, fiery wings outstretched and his turquoise eyes full of devotion as he stared back at me.

I had the vague awareness of the lords and ladies of the courts stepping into line behind us, but I made myself a promise that I'd make Taz and I forever officially as soon as I could. Until then, I'd take the vengeful parts of being queen and have some fun with them instead.

I pursed my lips and put a hint of my power behind the effort as I whistled loud enough to cut through the cacophony of fighting. People stumbled together and apart. Gifts exploded and sizzled to nothing.

Taz grumbled beside me and shook a finger in his ear.

"I'm so glad so many of you are here to witness this." I raised my voice into the now swelling silence. "The rumours have no doubt done the rounds. I don't know if people think I died, or deserted, or had some mysterious illness. But I'm here now and this ends today."

I pointed down at Emil still clamped between Kainen and Reyan. Nearby, I noticed Meryl guiding Cheryl, Beryl, Harvey and Hutch, all very red-faced as they shunted Belladonna toward us, hissing and spitting curses in her warped golden cage.

"Many of you will know this man. Emil is a traitor and a killer. So is Belladonna here, once-princess of Faerie. That's why I'm so glad you could all join us today, because I've decided it's time we hold a public execution. Won't that be *fun*?"

CHAPTER TWENTY ONE
REYAN

Reyan stared at Demi in horror. She vibrated with powerful, queenly energy and not in a gift sense either. She held herself gracefully with total confidence, eying the spellbound crowd. Even with her black hair corkscrewing all over the place and her casual clothes all torn and dirty, her supporters and enemies alike fell still as her voice filled the hall with mention of a public execution.

She's not serious, is she? Reyan sent her voice into Kainen's mind.

They still had hold of Emil but Kainen shot her an uncertain look.

It's not her style, but we'll see. We trust her until we can't anymore.

Reyan nodded, her pulse beginning to pound as Milo vanished and reappeared with a crown and rammed it on Demi's head with a menacing "don't you dare".

With a wave of her hand, Demi cast a vision of herself into the centre of the hall, the pearlescent grey image magnified. Reyan guessed most people wouldn't catch the subtle wince in their queen as she stared at her own supersized face, but Reyan noticed.

"Citizens of Faerie, hiya," Demi began with Milo cringing beside her. "Some of you may have heard rumours recently about the Forgotten. Some of you might have thought about joining them. Perhaps they offered you riches or rewards. Perhaps you think their way of thinking, the 'old ways', are how things should be."

With a subtle crook of her finger, Demi beckoned

Kainen forward with Emil and for Meryl to move Belladonna closer in her cage. Moments later the vision widened to include them.

"I thought a good way to re-cement my rule as your queen and remind you all of how things are going to be from now on is with a public execution."

A ripple of uneasy muttering ran through the crowd but Reyan held herself steady despite her doubts.

"A couple of people very precious to me, now gone, have always counselled kindness," Demi continued. "Xavio and Petra, my mentors, were killed by these two here. I'm sure many of you will recognise Belladonna, once princess of Faerie, and Emil, a traitor."

Is this some kind of vendetta? Reyan had to ask. *What if she asks you to do the killing as a sign of loyalty?*

Kainen's shoulders stiffened. *I don't know. I have to trust she's still the person who earned her title, and that she trusts me enough now to know I'd say no if she asked.*

"The penalty in the old days was death," Demi continued. "Death for a death, a gift for a gift. Perhaps death would be a kindness. But I promised you an execution. If you're the Fae I hope you are, you'll agree that we've had enough of the old ways. We've had enough of death from the likes of these two."

Reyan eyed the other lords and ladies, their expressions ranging from a mix of disbelief to stoic resolution as Demi turned to face her enemies.

"So today we'll be executing the old ways. Cutting them out like the rot they are." She lifted her head, her voice radiating loud enough to puncture through the very fabric of Faerie, the nether and whatever lay beyond. "No more Forgotten, no more suffering!"

Half of the assembled crowd rose to the chant, echoing

it back. Some of the enemy were already aiming for the exits but they were stopped, blocked and pushed back.

"There is however the balance of punishment," Demi added, her tone turning lethally sweet. "I am queen by the choice of the nether and of Faerie, but a lot of you are governed by various courts. Today, there will be no death to our enemies, but I would have your courts work together to choose a suitable alternative fate for them."

Her grin was wicked as Taz grabbed Emil's shoulder from Kainen and set the point of his sword to Emil's neck.

Reyan let go as Kainen wrapped his hand around hers and guided her a short distance away to join the other lords and ladies. She discreetly moved the hold so that she could curl her arm around his and press her cheek to his shoulder instead.

"What do we think?" Tyren asked.

Lolly sighed. "I would have gone for death, but I know it's not the way to do things."

"I was reading some of the human fables Milo sent me," Tira chipped in. "They definitely have some interesting methods of punishment. Pushing a rock up a hill forever with no break, being chained beneath the dripping venom of a snake."

"We could chain them under Arthur but I don't like the idea of our court being sullied by them," Tyren added.

Reyan hid a smile.

Our court she says, she mind-spoke to Kainen. *As if Lolly being Lady of Revels and one day Flora makes it as much his court as hers.*

He smiled at her, the others momentarily forgotten. She blinked back at him as he lifted his free hand to her face, his thumb rubbing over her cheek.

He's a lord in his own right, titled and chosen. He

reminded her. *He's her equal exactly as you are mine, Lady. Although our court chose you whereas I only got there by blood ties. I am eternally in your service.*

She pulled a face at his teasing tone but let the fact wash over her yet again with growing confidence. She was Lady of the Illusion Court, not by marriage or a fake engagement or inheritance, but because Kainen and Demi chose her. Because the court had chosen her. Even the nobles had grudgingly respected her when she finally stepped up enough to command it.

"What about we don't punish them at all?" Odella asked.

She froze when everyone else looked at her, including Lord Bryson. Despite him being Lord of the Nether Court now, Sannar and Odella were the ones with Demi's confidence despite not being titled at all.

"Go on," Bryson said gently. "You clearly don't mean let them go free."

She shook her head. "Of course not, but their biggest punishment will be nothing. No pain, no stimulation, nothing to fight against. Give them four walls, two beds, regular meals, but no way out, no change in routine. No company except each other. Let them be insignificant and truly forgotten."

"Isolation," Kainen mused. "It's almost wicked in its nothingness. I'll agree to that. Rey?"

She nodded. "They've conspired together, now they will endure their punishment together, and nothing else."

"Revels agrees, and my mother said I might as well speak for Flora too," Lolly said then rolled her eyes. "But only if Tyren agrees apparently, which I did *not* appreciate."

Tyren grinned. "Face it, your mums like me better. I

224

agree. Punish them with themselves. Tira? Lord Rydon?"

"I agree," Tira said.

Cerys nodded, the movement firm and resolute despite her silence and the dark circles around her eyes. Demi ambled over when Kainen beckoned for her as though they had all the time in the world, but despite the live feed still being projected she looked uneasy.

"What's the verdict?" she asked.

Milo hurried up with Queenie beside him, both whispering to each other frantically as a round of nudging and shuffling ensued amid the courts.

Reyan frowned at Kainen.

Aren't you going to jump in?

Kainen grinned. *You're Lady of the Illusion Court, sweetheart. Aren't you?*

He had a point, but her nerves didn't get the message and her hands started shaking as she cleared her throat.

"We've chosen to punish them with themselves," she announced, her voice holding the shakes better than she expected when addressing the whole of Faerie. "Insolation with nothing but each other for company. No pain, no change, no notoriety or visitors. They will be nothing and receive nothing, if you agree, my queen."

Demi stood for a long moment without a single sign on her face that she'd even heard. Then a slow, brilliant smile dawned.

"The courts have decided to kill them with kindness in the most modern Fae move so far," she said to a smattering of laughter from the crowd. "Let it be known today that there will be no resurrection of the old ways. We work together. We respect each other and we make Faerie the place where everyone can succeed and thrive, not just the mindless elite."

Milo waved his arms wildly, almost knocking Queenie over. She rolled her eyes and muttered something. Moments later, the grey image of Demi's face shivered into the scene of a crowd gathered in a town square.

Taz slid an arm around Demi's waist as her knees seemed to buckle slightly at the scene unfolding elsewhere in Faerie.

The entire crowd on the projection was cheering and throwing what looked like party favours and ribbons.

The vision moved again to another crowd gathered in a large field. All cheering and throwing flowers and branches full of blossoms.

The courtyard at the Nether Court appeared, the gathered people all cheering. Reyan peered closer and balked to see one nether brother throwing his robe in the air, leaving him in nothing but a large pair of pants flapping in a brisk breeze.

Even the great citadel of Faerie seemed to be having a celebration.

The vision faded after that and Reyan bit down the bittersweet disappointment that their court hadn't been shown.

She had no idea how much trouble she and Kainen would have when she got back, how many courtiers they might have lost, but as the atrium descended into chaos, Kainen slid both arms around her waist and hugged her close with his warding firm around them.

"The FDPs will sort this lot out," he murmured. "I feel like I've not seen you properly in weeks."

She grinned into his shoulder as people trying to escape and those giving chase shunted against them.

"We should wait to be dismissed before going home though," she said.

He huffed. "Fine. When we get home, we'll weed out the ones who don't want to live by the new rules. Then it's time for us. Have you missed me?"

"Begging for validation already?"

"Absolutely." He kissed her neck and nodded. "You're lady of our court now with or without me included. I have no guarantees."

"You never had any guarantees with me, love," she teased.

He held on tighter. "I know. Is that a no then?"

So many times she'd rehearsed in her head what she would say to him if she saw him again. No dancing around the fake engagement situation, no doubts or miscommunications. She sent the words into his mind with every essence of heartfelt meaning she could muster.

It's a 'you're mine and I'm yours, court or no court'. Take from that what you want.

He lifted her against him until her feet were dangling and she shrieked as he turned in circles until she was dizzy.

"Sorry to interrupt." Demi didn't sound sorry at all, but at least she stayed outside the boundary of their shared warding, which was a concession of sorts to their privacy.

Kainen sighed and dropped Reyan back to her feet.

"I know, queen."

"Yep." Demi grinned. "And as queen, I'm ordering you both to go home."

Reyan glanced around and realised the other lords and ladies were already gone or rounding up members of their court still inside the atrium. She would have time now to form the friendships that all the courts would need to keep Demi's latest attempt at peace going strong.

Kainen nodded. "Don't need to tell us twice. You know where we are if you need us."

Demi shoved her hands in her pockets.

"I do. I appreciate everything you've done, both of you." She looked Kainen in the eye, or the face at least. "Especially you, with the whole Prime Realm stuff and everything. Taz might still take some convincing but I'd like it if we can all be friends now. A totally new start."

Kainen clicked his fingers to summon his gift to realm-skip them home and this time Demi didn't even blink.

"I'd like that," he said. "We've got our court to sort out so we all need friends now."

"Yes, although for me this is going to mean a depressing amount of paperwork." Demi lifted her head and dodged sideways. "Oh orbs, there's Milo. If you see him, you didn't see me, okay? And that *is* a royal order."

She turned away and scurried away through the crowd, her crown off centre as she ducked and dodged behind people to avoid the impending doom of paperwork that came with being queen.

"You know, I don't envy her." Kainen chuckled as Milo spotted her and set off in pursuit.

Reyan nodded and he caught her eye, his expression turning fond.

"Home?" he asked.

She smiled at the mere thought of what that one word now meant.

"Yeah. Take me home."

A wisp of the nether folded around them, leaving the chaos of Arcanium behind.

"There you are!"

Kainen groaned as Meri stormed toward them. Reyan managed to get a glimpse of the main hall and recognise that the fighting had at least ceased. Then Meri was on both of them, hugging so tight Reyan struggled to breathe.

"That is completely improper," Kainen huffed.

Meri nodded. "Probably. The court is safe. Most of the courtiers have been muttering about insubordination, but only a few of the worst have either vacated their rooms or demanded the staff come pack their bags."

She let them go and stepped back, but her eyes were almost as watery as Kainen's. Amused at the thought of leaving them swilling in awkwardness, Reyan relented.

She clicked her fingers, summoning the glittering black smoke and spoke into it.

"The entire court is to come to the main hall immediately," she demanded.

She glanced at Kainen but he merely bowed his head in deference and gave her a wicked smile.

"Drinks to be on hand?" Meri asked drily. "Or are we seriously going to punish them?"

Reyan smiled. "Drinks flowing and tabs racking up. Let them earn their privileges for a while. Let them work for it."

She flinched as Meri patted her hand and bowed low.

"Never leave me," Meri muttered.

She stalked off as the court began to file in, several courtiers eying them warily while the staff were busy bowing, or in Amba's case grinning widely.

Every court needs their ruler to play the part, Reyan whispered into Kainen's mind even as she pressed herself against his side, delighting in how quick he was to wrap himself around her. *I realised that while you were away.*

While he was mischief and darkness turned moral, she could be the smiles and playfulness that bit hard.

What's my part then, Lady? he asked.

She grinned. *You're mine.*

Before he could process that, or hide the look of awed

delight sparking in his eyes behind his usual lordly mask, she faced the rest of the court.

Once she was sure most were assembled, she led Kainen toward the stone stairs leading up to the hallway that led to their room and paused at the top.

"The queen won today. *We* won. Let this be the last word on the Forgotten, the old ways and any nastiness. We will always be the Court of Illusions, of secrets and trickery. We throw the best parties."

A smattering of laughter grew and she thought a large portion of it even sounded natural rather than forced.

"We won't be getting rid of every tradition though," she added. "So kneel, and accept your place in the new world, and our new court."

She didn't put any compulsion behind her words and knew Kainen wouldn't undermine her by doing it either.

Her heart pounded, her stomach tangling as she waited.

The crowd dropped, some more hesitant than others, but they were down. She spied Lord Marquest in the midst of them with his wife. She saw a few others whose presence surprised her. And she saw Ciel, his head bowed low enough that he had no risk of catching her eye.

"Rise and go have some fun," she finished, grinning with devilish intent in Kainen's direction. "I know I'm going to."

The crowd laughed then and the noise picked up. Many of them would start to insist it could have been worse, and the situation wasn't too bad really, and even lords and ladies could be manipulated to see sense with careful handling. She would face all of that another day.

As she gripped Kainen's hand tight and dragged him into his bedroom, a ripple of uneasiness filled her mind.

"I've been using your room while you were away," she

said, hesitating the moment the door was closed behind them. "Ace took mine." She looked down. "I've been kind of wearing your shirts too, but we can always wash them, or get you new-"

"Come here, sweetheart."

He held his hands out to her, a wordless request. She could refuse it but she had no desire to be anywhere else than as close to him as possible. She pressed her face into his chest, wrapped her arms tight around his neck and held on. He nestled her even closer, his arms tightening around her waist.

"We have so much to sort out," she mumbled.

"You've not been doing this long," he replied. "But once a wise woman told me that I should take a day off."

Remembering that from what felt like so long ago now, Reyan grinned and lifted her head so she could see him smirking down at her.

"And you said court lords don't get breaks, that some of them are just clever enough to play the game and take what they want."

"Not exactly what I said, but it'll do." He ignored her indignant huff. "Today, we're clever enough to take what we want, and what I want is a day off with you."

"What about what I want?" she teased, knowing he'd give her anything and everything, and that all she wanted for the rest of the day at least was alone time with him.

He frowned, pretending to think. "I think you want what I want. The decks? I get the feeling it'll be warm out there now. We can talk. Or not talk. Lady's choice."

Exhausted from so much time spent worrying and fighting, she knew the sensible thing to do was agree. To take his hand and walk quietly through their court, giving anyone passing the impression that they were calm, respectable and in control.

She let the wicked amusement drift across her face instead, then dropped all but her head into an outline of shadows.

"You'll have to catch me first."

She dissipated into the shadows darted to the door, slipping under it as his footsteps echoed behind her. The hall was deserted as she swept along, keeping just out of his reach but visible as a shadowy outline so he wouldn't lose sight of her. There would be many court issues to come, but they could finally face them together now.

She almost stopped as she passed Ciel with a small group of courtiers. He saw Kainen first and backed against the wall with the others to let him pass, his eyes lighting on Reyan when she got close enough to be seen. There was resentment there on his face, and the same for the others he was with, but Reyan refused to let it mar her day. They would deal with it all tomorrow, and the next day, and the next.

She sped up as she reached the door to the decks and reformed her physical body with Kainen laughing behind her. His fingertips wisped over her hips as she wrenched the door open and dashed outside. The warm sunshine of imminent summer hit her face and she breathed in deep as she dashed down the rocky stone steps.

Kainen would go slower to be careful, but he'd find her at the end. She tumbled down toward the decking that was tied over the pounding swell of the river between the two cliff-faces, her cheeks burning and her breath huffing out of her.

Hitting the decking, she collapsed panting on the nearest padded bench. Kainen appeared a minute later, looking wholly unflushed for someone who was meant to be chasing her down.

"It gives me palpitations when you run down like that," he grumbled.

She grinned as he sat beside her. After a second of hesitation, he reached out and pulled her legs over his thighs, his arm sliding around her hips. She nestled her head on his shoulder, shivering in delight as he started to trace patterns over her back with his fingertips.

"So, Lady, have you finally had your fill of Faerie and adventure?" he asked. "Are you ready to come home now?"

She nodded. She was more than ready, more than done with adventures outside their court. There would be several to come yet no doubt, but her place was at their court with him.

"Yes, so I suppose it's time we dissolve the fake engagement," she suggested.

His body tensed against hers. "I actually liked the idea of keeping it going to be honest. Knowing that the whole of Faerie thought you were off-limits made me feel safer somehow. Besides, they'll make up all sorts of scandalous rumours about my reputation if you reject me now you're a lady in your own right."

Her insides warmed and set flight. He'd proven his feelings over and over, but they had time now to take things steady and let them grow naturally.

"I am off-limits. Just because we don't need the ruse any longer doesn't mean I want anyone else." She hesitated, then forced the truth out to make utterly sure. "If you feel happier keeping it going in front of others, that's okay. And if you were to ever consider asking me for real one day, a long time in the future when we're ready, I'd *probably* consider saying yes."

Despite her teasing tone it was as much as she was willing to give, but the way he pulled her close and all but tried to become a part of her said it was enough.

I'd ask you right now, sweetheart, if that was what you really wanted. His voice murmured into her mind and left her with excitable tingles rippling right through to the bone. *But we have time to take things slow. I'll just have to give you everything you could possibly dream of until the time comes for you to say yes. As long as you're mine, we can call it whatever you want.*

Amused, Reyan twisted so she could see his face.

She'd never even properly kissed him, not really. They'd almost kissed at the Nether Court twice, and kisses on the cheek barely counted in comparison to how madly she'd wanted him for a long while now. He'd kissed her on the lips when he gifted her with transmutation which technically didn't count as a proper kiss, then properly before he got sucked through the portal to the prime realm, but she'd not even had time or space to process that one.

Perhaps he was thinking the same as his tongue darted out across his bottom lip, his arm firming as if to lift her shoulders that little bit higher, his gaze darting to her mouth.

Reyan balanced her hands on the bench behind her and leaned forward, brushing her lips against his. Ripples of desire erupted inside her at the contact, and she squeaked as he pulled her until her legs were either side of his, her hands pressed against his chest. Dizzying thoughts filled her head of futures they might have, but right now the only thing she could grab was that she never wanted to stop kissing him.

"So, that was a definite yes to the whole being mine thing?" he asked hopefully.

She grinned and dropped lingering kisses on his lips, stopping only long enough to reply.

"Where would be the fun in that?"

CHAPTER TWENTY TWO
DEMI

The atrium was winding down and most of the courts and non-Arcanium people were gone. I'd never tried translocating out of a moving lift before, but managed to reach the storeroom at the back of the atrium without losing any limbs. I wouldn't avoid Milo forever, just until I'd been able to grab some quiet moments with Taz.

I'm in the atrium storeroom. I sent my mind out to his. *But don't let Milo catch you.*

I leaned against the sofa in the middle of the room while I waited, exhausted. I'd have to do an official visit to the courts in the coming days but my mind kept jumping back to the Prime Realm.

Despite Belladonna and Emil finally being in our keeping and unable to machinate any more evil plans for Faerie's future, I couldn't help wondering how safe we were. I could ask if they had any other schemes planned or minions out there biding their time, but that would be a task for another day.

The storeroom door opened and I jumped as Taz strode in, swung it shut and shot across the room to hug me. Unable to be vulnerable in front of anyone else, not even Milo or Ace, Taz was my exception.

"They're locked tight in the forever mountains, I made sure of it myself. Now, what do you need?" he asked, his hands getting snarled in my tangled hair. "Crying, distraction or punching things?"

I snorted as the tears I'd been holding in for days spilled over, burning hot and angry down my cheeks.

"When do I ever punch things?" I sobbed, gently punching his shoulder. "Idiot."

He laughed, holding me tighter. "You know what I mean."

I took a shaky breath and forced myself to tell him the whole story, from being sucked into the Prime Realm, to MC and Sabine, to Tirzella, to Kainen being a real support, and my new theory that perhaps I should ask Reyan to send Betty into the Prime Realm now and then, just to keep an eye on how safe we are from them.

I tried to pull back when I'd finished but he clung on, knowing me better than I knew myself. Even when I was trying to work, to fix things, he held me still to face what I was avoiding.

"You didn't do anything wrong," he insisted. "We can't control everything, and you and Kainen getting taken was awful, but it wasn't your doing. You were as careful as you could be in the circumstances and almost everyone survived."

I froze. "Almost? What happened?"

"Blossom. She was fighting on our side in the end, but I sent her to support Reyan as a test and she got taken down. Reyan brought her here and I took her to Marthe but it was too late."

My insides plummeted, shock filtering through my head.

If I hadn't asked her to spy for us… If I had thought of her as more than a pawn…

"Oi, stop it." Taz finally loosened his hold and grabbed my chin between his finger and thumb. "She made her choice and she stood by you right to the end. We all carry guilt but we owe it to them not to let it ruin the lives they died to gift us. Also, Betty's the shadow-snake, right?"

Reassurance and a swift distraction in one breath; the boy needed a halo. He knew I was thinking of Xavio, Petra, and even Blossom, all the people who died helping our side.

"We'll find a way to honour them properly." I wiped my eyes with my sleeve. "And yes, Betty's the snake."

Taz smiled softly. "You realise you'll have to speak to Milo for that right? The honouring thing?"

I pulled a face before pressing it against his chest again.

"I should ask Reyan now while it's still fresh, but I think Kainen will probably strangle me if I visit unannounced one more time."

The most peculiar shiver of revulsion passed over Taz's face.

"I should probably... *thank* him, for looking out for you," he said, grimacing at the mere thought. "Now, before I change my mind or the opportunity passes. Then it's not your fault that I've got no manners. Lead the way."

I wrapped my hand around his and stepped back. My court felt safe, broken in places and weary, but safe. I could risk leaving it for an hour or two. I was technically supposed to tell Milo when I was leaving, but I wouldn't be pulling at that teetering pile of books until I absolutely had to.

"Milo will understand," Taz insisted. "He's handled things brilliantly while you've been away and I've been... yeah. I don't cope too well without you."

Not needing to think of anything because apparently my friends had it all covered, I thought of Kainen and Reyan, of the Illusion Court, and my power sent us wisping through the nether. We dropped onto the decks, the outside area between the mountains their court was set in, the loud rushing of the river filling my ears.

I opened my mouth to announce us but the words slid from my lips. Taz clamped a fist to his mouth and turned away to hide his laughter.

"Um, hi."

It wasn't the most eloquent thing I could have said, which only made Taz laugh even more. There might well have a been a touch of grief and exhaustion-fuelled hysteria in there, but I was too busy facing the most irate version of Kainen I could ever remember seeing with Reyan draped over his chest. I half expected her to jump up, go bright red, make excuses, but she only shrugged her cardigan back over her shoulders and gave me an amused look.

"When we said we're here if you need us, it was more of a 'in the coming days' sort of thing," Kainen muttered.

Taz finished laughing and slid his arm around my waist with a wicked grin.

"I decided I should thank you for looking after Demi in the Prime Realm," he said easily, as though it was no big deal.

Kainen frowned. "And that couldn't have been an orb message? Or a call? I'd have happily accepted some kind of pastry basket."

"Ignore him," Reyan insisted. "Are you passing through or should I get drinks?"

I hesitated. "There's something I wanted to ask you actually. You can say no though, of course."

Reyan slid off Kainen's lap with a groan and sat beside him. The moment she was sitting still again, he had his arms around her, and I could feel the last twinges of my reservation finally slipping away.

"I'll get the drinks," he muttered, clicking his fingers. "Hospitality for four to the decks, please."

I sat down on the opposite bench to them with Taz beside me. We wouldn't stay long, mainly because I owed Milo so much time and attention after this. Maybe I'd find some kind of honour or award for him too, although Head Librarian and access to the whole of Faerie for books was probably as good as any award would get for him.

"I haven't had time to explain much about the Prime Realm," Kainen said. "We addressed the court then got distracted."

Taz smirked at him and Kainen returned it with a small flicker of a smile.

Today really is a day for new things.

"The Prime Realm will be left alone as they requested," I said. "The fight today and the truth of the past will be written into memory so that everyone can learn from it. No more hidden skip-ways or veiled legends. I'm sure we'll find many new horrors to deal with, but this one is done."

Kainen nodded. "Agreed. If the Prime Realm keep to themselves, so should we. Are you going to do anything about the iron thing?"

"No." I noticed Taz and Reyan exchanging confused looks. "The fact that the Fae were banished into Faerie from the Prime Realm for gift misuse is the past, and them having access to unlimited *metirin* iron can't hurt us if we stay on our side."

Reyan's eyes narrowed. "But I imagine you'd want to keep an eye out all the same."

"I- kind of."

"You want to send Betty between to find things out."

Kainen frowned. "But she couldn't get back, we couldn't send her or any messages back."

I hesitated. In this moment I trusted Kainen and Reyan, but things could always change. Minds could warp just as easily as they could mature and evolve. But I was a queen. Not killing was one thing, but vigilance for the good of my people was something I had to do if I could.

"While you were running with the wolves, Tirzella said that the tunnel we went through has been used by shades, their version of Reyan I think, for ages. I wouldn't ask you to go and we have no way for you to get in now anyway I don't think, but if you were to consider Betty going, she would pass by unseen by most."

Reyan sighed. "I'll consider it. She's not a pet so I don't control her, but I'll ask and see what vibe I get."

"That's all I can ask for," I said.

A woman materialised beside Reyan without warning and made me jump. She noticed us, gave Kainen a despairing look and dropped a tray of drinks and pastries on the table before bobbing a bow in our direction.

"Forgive me, I didn't realise we had royal visitors," she said, her tone dripping with irritation.

"They don't have a habit of announcing themselves," Kainen muttered, grunting when Reyan elbowed him in the gut.

The woman's lips lifted. "I've stayed all necessary matters for a short while, Lady, Lord, but it'll soon pile up. You have two days."

She vanished and I stared in astonishment as Kainen gave Reyan an accusing look.

"I told you she likes you better," he grumbled.

"No she doesn't."

"She does, she *always* titles you first."

"Because she's seen me do a day's work in my life before."

"Ouch, sweetheart."

I grinned to see it, relieved beyond belief to know that

things were working out for them.

"Did she kind of just order you about though?" I asked.

Kainen nodded. "She's in charge here. Second in command technically and she served my mother for a long time, then her family for a while before I took over the court. But I know better than to challenge her because I always end up being wrong."

"Kind of like me having Milo," I conceded. "So, no more fake engagement now then?"

Taz huffed beside me. "I still can't believe you never told me about that. You're supposed to tell me everything."

I grabbed a bottle of *Beast* because I'd be damned if I wasn't celebrating at least a little bit before facing Milo.

"But you knew anyway."

"Yes, but you didn't actually tell me. I had to find out on that human train thing like everyone else."

"Because you meddle."

He gasped, outraged in an instant. "I do not!"

"Sannar and Odella."

"I merely gave him a nudge in the right direction. Besides, you took them both on at court so they could be together."

"Lolly and Tyren."

He scowled, a full-scale royal tantrum brewing. "If I remember right, it was *you* who titled him and *you* who suggested I have a quick word with him, and *you* who decided to merge their courts together."

"I never said I don't meddle too." I grinned. "I don't think I had anything whatsoever to do with Meryl and Tira though. By the looks of it that one they did on their own."

He inhaled then stilled. "Ah. I might have had a few words with Tira after apologising for threatening to disband her court. I vaguely remembered Cheryl saying

242

something about Meryl being too hung up on the old to fully let herself embrace the new, and I think I shouted at her. So yeah, that one might actually be me."

Orbs alive, it felt good to be ridiculous for a while.

Reyan and Kainen were looking at each other, expressions twitching so I guessed they were communicating in mind-speak. After a few moments of silence, Kainen sighed.

"Fine. Would you two like to stay a while and we'll invite the other courts too."

It wasn't an invite, more a reluctant insistence under force of whatever Reyan was threatening to do to him. Or not do.

She rolled her eyes. "I can ask Tira, Lolly and Odella. Not entirely sure about Lord Rydon, doubt he'd accept, especially if he sent Cerys in his stead to Arcanium. Maybe she'd like to come instead?"

I tensed as Taz grimaced and leaned forward.

"I'm not sure about the facts, but Blossom told me that Lord Rydon is dead and she became lady of the Fauna Court. She insisted it go to Cerys though."

I wiped a hand over my face, my insides plummeting. I couldn't forget Lord Rydon, gruff and stubborn, but he'd trusted me enough to let me know the Forgotten weren't just storming his court when they attacked it but also hiding there too. Another failure of mine I'd have to bear, that I sent Reyan and Kainen in knowing that with only a scant warning about being careful. Not that I'd known it was Belladonna herself there, but it would haunt me all the same.

"The Fauna Court is hers," I insisted. "Invite her too, please. She might not want to come, but she's lady of a court just as any of us are."

Reyan nodded. "Of course. It's been a while since our court has had a whole group of friends to visit. We'll make a thing of it."

Kainen clicked his fingers and soft lights flickered over the side of the mountain and the decks. It reminded me a little of the library, the soft hue of the lamps but with the sound of rushing water added in.

"That sounds lovely." I grimaced. "I should probably check in with Milo though. It might take a while."

Reyan grinned. "Stay here where it's private then. We'll get in touch with the others and come back in a bit."

Before we could say a word, she and Kainen vanished to another part of their court. I curled into Taz's side when he held out his arm, took a deep breath and held up my orb.

"Milo?"

His face loomed in front of me, even larger than normal as he squinted at us.

"You're at the Illusion Court?" he asked.

I nodded. "Yeah, and I know I should have checked in and that there's going to be an entire realm of paperwork-"

"It doesn't matter."

"I- what?"

He laughed and I heard Ace's deep chuckle echo behind him.

"It doesn't matter, for now," he amended. "The paperwork will keep and you've had a tough time of it. Go do something fun."

"I slipped some *Beast* into his coffee when he wasn't looking," Ace shouted.

"You did not." Milo giggled, actually giggled, then his eyes widened. "You didn't, did you?"

Ace's face appeared over Milo's shoulder. "Go, have

fun, stay out all night. Arcanium is safe and happily revelling your victory so you should be too. We'll say you're touring the courts if anyone demands an answer."

They disappeared, leaving me both touched by Milo's supposedly *Beast*-induced rebelliousness and worried that I was suddenly surplus to requirement.

"Stop it." Taz teased, his fingers rubbing the back of my neck. "You're still queen and it'll still be there when we get home. I should orb back and ask him to send you a dress for the occasion though."

"Don't you dare," I growled.

He grinned as I shoved the heel of my hand against his shoulder and dropped my lips against his, revelling in the one thing I'd missed that I would never ever get tired of.

"Ready to party, Sparky?" he asked a while later.

The sun was going down fast and further up in the mountain there were lights and sounds of other people at the court celebrating on their own deck, with what sounded like thumping heavy metal music filling the air.

I snuggled deeper into Taz's arms. "Ready to sleep for a week more like. At least I don't have to be queen today. I can just be me."

"You're always you. You'll always be the same girl who walked into the arcade and into my life like a demolition orb, seduced me in about two hours and went on to overtake my family and rule the whole of Faerie pretty much."

I scowled. "I did *not* seduce you."

"You did. Maybe about three hours. I was hooked from the very first withering remark you shot my way."

"Makes you kind of easy then, doesn't it?"

With our backs to the mountain and the stairs leading back up to court, neither of us heard the footsteps over the rushing water.

"Who's easy?"

We twisted around to find Beryl, Cheryl, Hutch and Harvey clambering onto the decks with Meryl and Tira lagging behind them.

"Who's easy?" Beryl repeated, clapping a hand over Harvey's mouth. "Don't you dare say me."

"You me or me me?" he asked when she released him.

"Where's Reyan and Kainen?" Cheryl asked.

I shrugged. There was more than enough room for all of us and the wooden platform didn't even twitch when Hutch and Harvey started jumping up and down to see if they could dislodge it. Or when Beryl gave in and joined them.

Tira and Meryl sat beside us, but Kainen and Reyan appeared with Sannar and Odella before anything could be said. By the time Lolly and Tyren appeared, the situation was looking decidedly raucous.

I noted that we were only missing Cerys from the Fauna Court, and I knew I'd have bridges to build with her in the coming days. I also had to deal with Taz's mother at some point too, a self-imposed fading regent who was no doubt grieving for most of her daughters.

"I did ask Milo and Ace as well," Reyan whispered. "But there was just some snoring and then Ace said they were having a night in. Then there was a huge crash, some swearing and he disappeared."

I grinned. If I was really lucky, Milo might be the one needing a day off from paperwork tomorrow.

When everyone had settled down Taz stood up with his drink, his free hand curled around mine.

"I want to say a toast," he said. "To those we've lost who will be always honoured and never forgotten. To friends, both old, new and unexpected. And to us, for finally getting the job done."

Everyone raised and drank as Taz sat down.

"Not too shabby with the words, are you?" I teased.

Nestled back against him, I could relax. I could let the grief and the exhaustion and all the stress wait outside a while. I could smile at my friends and join in the odd joke, cheering when Hutch challenged Beryl to a drinking contest and sulked when Lolly ended up winning, much to Tyren's horror.

And when my eyes wouldn't stay open any longer, I could lay my head on Taz's chest and finally let go for a while.

Only a while though because we all know that in Faerie, anything can happen.

EPILOGUE

One year of peace later

REYAN AND KAINEN

"We're going to be late!" Reyan huffed.

Kainen patted his pockets. "Well, if you weren't so intent on finishing paperwork until stupid o'clock, you wouldn't have overslept."

"You could have woken- okay, it takes a land-shake to wake you on a normal day, but you could have taken some responsibility for this too."

She wriggled as his arms came around her waist, holding tight as he dropped a gentle kiss on her cheek.

"Stop fussing. Anyone would think it was our wedding the way you're carrying on."

She grabbed her favourite shoulder-wrap and bundled it under one arm, glaring absolute murder at him. He grinned wider.

"We won't ever have one if you keep stressing me out," she threatened.

He chuckled. "Ouch, sweetheart. Wait... does that mean we might have one if I'm on my best behaviour? How dull."

She stepped in front of him, her head tilting back so her face was more aligned with his. He put a hand on her waist, the movement small and instinctive, like hers was as it landed on his shoulder.

"Will we be safe to leave the court?" she asked.

"With Meri in charge of it?" He nodded. "Absolutely. It's been a year of extremely un-Fae-like peace, and now I'm looking forward to some harmless revelry with my fiancée."

Her lips twitched. "Fake fiancée. And don't get any awful ideas about hijacking the event by proposing either."

He inhaled, then froze. She grinned, happily pretending she hadn't gone through his jeans looking for their invitation and found a suspiciously square jewellery box instead. She hadn't opened it because some things were best left a surprise, but if he *was* going to ask anything, she wouldn't torment him for too long before saying yes.

"You spoil all my fun," he grumbled. "I wasn't going to, but teasing you about it would have been hilarious."

She smiled and tugged on the lapel of his black jacket. "We're late, remember?"

He leaned closer and pressed his lips to hers instead of realm-skipping, and she lost all urgency to leave. Even when his fingers teased through her hair, threatening to unravel the pinned creation Meri had spent ages on, she didn't pull away.

"I thought we were going to be late," he murmured.

She grinned. "We're not exactly known as the court of punctuality and manners though. But yeah, let's go."

Kainen's arm slid tight around her waist and a soft hiss from somewhere around his hip region suggested Betty had every intention of tagging along to terrorise Demi's chameleon, Leo.

The nether swirled around them and dissipated to reveal the atrium of Arcanium that had swelled to enormous proportions.

"Wow." Kainen turned his head, his mouth dropping in awe. "I've never seen the atrium look this fancy."

Reyan had seen it a couple of times, once during battle and the rest of the time it had been a hive of chaotic activity. Every surface of wall was covered with ivy and holly, the maroon beams adorned with red, green and silver ribbons full of sparkles. High above the gentle light sent small flurries of snow cascading down, the flakes fading before they could settle onto heads or shoulders.

Rows of delicate chairs painted silver created an aisle down the centre of the atrium, leading to the reception desk that had been decorated as an altar with an archway adorned with winter flowers, aside from an enormous cherry blossom tree in a pot that looked like it was somehow growing willow fronds out of it.

"Fashionably late, as always." Ace strode toward them and bundled them both into a hug. *"Save me."*

Reyan glanced over his shoulder and stifled a laugh. Milo had reams of paper in his hands, the whole essence of him flapping as though he might be able to take off and fly through sheer power of nerves.

"We could glamour you," Reyan suggested.

Ace sighed. "Milo would know somehow. He always knows. Besides, I need to be with Taz."

He let them go and nodded toward the reception desk and the archway. Taz stood in a royal purple suit with gold stitching, his fiery wings on display and his honey blond hair swept back from his face. Even though his mouth was wide with amusement, his turquoise eyes were sparkly and he had his hands in his pockets as he slouched against the desk.

Kainen raised his eyebrows. "That is the most chilled out groom I've ever seen."

"He's literally glowing, and not just the wings," Reyan agreed. "He looks like he's been on some kind of magic spa retreat that gives you-"

"Okay sweetheart, calm down. He's taken, remember?"

Reyan snorted loud enough for a couple of courtiers from one of the other courts to hear. She ignored the scandalised looks as Kainen tightened his arm around her waist.

"No need to get possessive. The king consort is definitely not my type."

"Good thing too." Beryl Eastwick hurried toward them. "His lordship probably won't find anyone else to put up with him."

Kainen grinned as she nodded in his direction. "I won't argue with that."

The crowd around them grew and Reyan shuffled a tiny step back. Kainen stood joking with the Hutchinson brothers like they were old friends, while the other ladies and lords of courts caught their eyes with smiles and waves.

I never thought I'd be back here like an equal, Kainen admitted into her mind.

Reyan smiled. *You did well to redeem yourself though, and they respect that. They like you for you now.*

As the others hurried off to their places before Milo's increasingly red face popped, Kainen slid his hand over Reyan's, his fingers weaving through hers.

"I never imagined I'd ever be liked for myself," he admitted. "Until you."

She gazed up at him. "I don't know about 'like' half the time because you're the most infuriating person I've ever met, but-"

"I swear to Faerie, if you two don't take your seats…"

Milo appeared beside them, glaring and pointing with a defined jab of his finger to two vacant seats in the front row.

"Sorry Milo," Reyan said, keeping her tone meek.

Kainen led her to their seats but slid his arm around the back of hers as they settled, his fingers curling around the nape of her neck. She shivered.

Go on, he reminded her. *You were saying I was infuriating, but…?*

She grinned. *I was going to say but that just makes loving you all the more fun.*

He blinked, his eyes wide.

"You've never said… *that* before."

She shrugged. "Neither have you. We've been focused on running the court and it's kind of a given these days. But someone had to go for the L word first." She saw his hand going to his jacket pocket. "*Don't.*"

He grinned, his face a picture of total wickedness as he pulled out a dark grey handkerchief.

"Don't what? It's a wedding, you might cry."

Before she could take the hanky and possibly hit him with it, the music swelled and the crowd hushed. Everyone turned in their seats and Reyan clenched her fingers tight as Kainen tucked the hanky between them.

Demi's dress was exquisite, trails of ice white silk peppered with silver snowflakes. A flash of berry red and holly green peeked from beneath the hem and the ribbons holding the strapless bodice to her body.

But Demi herself, walking carefully down what was probably the longest aisle in all of the history of Faerie and beyond, she was breathtaking. Her holly crown glinted amid the elaborate hairdo, the oil slick black curls already fighting to unravel, her cheeks pink and her piercing blue eyes bright with intent as she focused solely on Taz.

"Told her she should have practiced in those shoes," Beryl muttered behind them.

"Shh," Cheryl hissed. "Although she is about to step on the train."

"Fifty percats says she trips," Hutch said.

Harvey snickered. "I'll take that."

Reyan glanced over her shoulder to grin at their squabbling.

"Stop it, you two," Tira piped up.

Meryl grinned. "Yeah. Double or nothing the shoe comes off and she keeps going without it."

"Meryl!"

"They should have had Trevor wheel her down the aisle in the rickshaw," Reyan suggested.

"Milo suggested it." Beryl giggled. "Demi threatened to elope."

"How many times is that now?" Harvey asked, eyes glinting.

"Sixty three."

"Crud."

Hutch held his hand out and Harvey grudgingly dropped a clinking coin pouch onto his palm.

Demi reached the end of the aisle with both shoes and no tears on her dress, but she could have been in a bin bag and Taz clearly wouldn't have cared.

As they faced the Oak Queen of Faerie standing stiffly in the centre of the archway, Taz and Demi joined hands.

"I promise you everything that I am, and all that I have," Demi vowed.

Taz beamed. "I promise you all of that and more, for always. There's no life without you, and I vow I will be yours until Faerie and the nether reclaims us."

"Did Milo help him write that?" Lolly whispered.

Hutch shook his head. "Nope, all him."

"Together," Demi said, her eyes glistening.

Taz nodded. "Together."

As the Oak Queen united them as one, Reyan glanced sideways at Kainen and smiled. If there was any speck of her heart that was still her own, she lost it to him in that moment. Then she passed him the hanky to dry his eyes.

I'm not crying, he insisted.

She smiled. *You are. It's sweet.*

She didn't need to ask if the tears were from any lingering crush he might have on Demi; that part of their life quashed and done after the final battle with the remnants of the Forgotten. Kainen was wholly hers and the rest was pure formality.

I'm merely calculating how much it's going to cost us to beat this, he countered with a delicate sniff.

Reyan nestled against his side, both of them cheering along with the crowd as Demi and Taz faced everyone, hand in hand, united as one.

Taz's suit changed colours to match Demi's dress as the crowd stood, while the chairs vanished to make way for a dance floor and fancy tables at the far end of the atrium. Milo and Ace came to join their group but the lords and ladies hung back while the rest of Faerie surged forward to congratulate the happy couple.

"Where's the honeymoon?" Reyan asked.

Milo beamed. "Top secret. Nobody knows and it's going to stay that way."

He looked so relieved that the whole thing was over, his cheeks pink and his eyes bright, his burly shoulders finally sagging. Reyan couldn't help laughing.

"Probably best. You'll give the others a complex about having to keep up with them."

Kainen wrapped his arm around her shoulders from behind.

"I already know where we're going for our honeymoon. Where we're going to have our wedding. What you'll be wearing. Everything."

Reyan gasped. "Don't I get a say in it?"

"Of course. You're the one who has to tell me when I can propose. You keep telling me not to."

"I-" He had a point.

He kissed her cheek with a chuckle. "Not here, sweetheart, don't worry. This is Taz and Demi's day."

As the music started up again, their friends cascaded onto the dance floor to show the rest of Faerie how it was done. Or in the case of the Eastwicks and Hutchinsons how it was absolutely *not* done, at least in polite society circles.

"How about a dance to start with then?" Kainen suggested, bowing low with a wicked twinkle in his eyes.

Reyan curtseyed with a smile. "To start with."

He led her to the dance floor and pulled her close, his hand warm on her bare back and his lips inches from hers.

"And after that?" he asked.

She smiled. He was the kindest, most frustrating man she'd ever known, mainly because his biggest enjoyment in life was caring for and tormenting her in equal measure. But she had realised one thing in the past year. She'd more earned her place as his equal, his lady and the lady of the court they shared. She could care for and torment him just as wickedly.

"After that?" she frowned, pretending to think. "After that... will you marry me?"

He stopped dead, his jaw dropping and his eyes widening in horror.

"You can't ask me that!" he hissed, glancing around to see if anyone had heard.

"Why not?" She laughed. "You don't want me after all? That's going to make running the court really awkward. Will we get joint custody of Meri?"

Kainen seemed to be struggling with the concept of

words for several seconds, his lips twitching over various stunted sounds.

"I had a whole thing planned! No, I'm not having this. Take it back."

"You want me to *un-propose*?"

He nodded frantically and she grinned, wicked thoughts of refusing filling her head.

"Fine. I take it back. I won't offer again either, so you'll have to do it."

He pulled her close, his eyes full of darkness and sparking shadow as he pressed his lips to hers, inciting her into kissing him back.

"I can't believe you upstaged me," he grumbled. "I will never forget this."

"Just keeping you on your toes."

He huffed and lifted his hand, the backs of his fingers stroking down her cheek. Even as he frowned at her, he was fighting a smile.

"I'm in love with a wicked woman," he said.

She smiled. "Fits kind of perfectly then, if you think about it."

"Don't need to think about it at all, sweetheart. As long as you're mine, it's perfect for me."

****

The wedding goes on late into the night, and the tales that make it into the Book of Faerie soon become part of Faerie's more scandalous history.

Lolly had to be retrieved from Arcanium's quarantine floor after hearing that they had some kind of rare sentient

257

plant-life growing. Tyren was decidedly not impressed but also rumoured to have had a suspiciously pot-shaped bulk under his jacket on their way home.

Tira left early with Meryl in tow, but nobody needed a rumour mill to learn that they were very much involved and dating after Beryl had one too many cups of *Beast* and compelled Harvey to serenade them with a wholly inappropriate choice of song that would not be allowed to be aired on *Siren-Sing-Along*. Even the cast of *Demolition Ducks* were said to have given that particular tune a wide berth.

Odella and Sannar were in attendance until the end, both astounded to hear that their service to the queen's court was finally no longer required because they were being titled as part of the Nether Court nobility in their own right.

Milo celebrated the relief of having single-handedly (according to him) pulled off a royal wedding by having a long lie-down and sneaking out his super-secret advance copy of the latest *Carrie's Castle* book that Marinda made him swear not to show anyone. He and Ace have also been talking about expanding the library. At least, Milo has been talking, Ace has been gently suggesting nobody would probably notice either way. Although, Ace is apparently still sulking because Milo brought an orb-reader to the wedding reception.

Kainen has a week of events coming up soon, all planned to the minutest detail such as a lavish revel for the court, a private dinner on the decks while the weather is warm, and the promise of a tour of the best locations Faerie has to offer. Once he's finished being on bended knee, that is. As for Reyan, she's still pretending to be blissfully aware of any of it, despite the fact she's now the one who oversees the court accounts and is trying not to interfere until he officially bankrupts their court with his plans for the proposal, let alone the wedding or honeymoon.

And finally, rumour has it the queen and king consort have left Faerie for a week. As far as anyone is aware, both Milo and Queenie have promised that the royals will be back in one piece, although Hutch and Cheryl both insist they heard Taz enthusing something about doughnuts which would suggest a visit to the human world.

So, if anyone sees us out and about, definitely come and say hi. You never know, we might even let you know where Arcanium's arcade entrance is and invite you on an adventure.

Because as we all know, in Faerie, anything can happen...

ACKNOWLEDGEMENTS

A huge thank you to every reader who has joined Reyan and Kainen the various courts of Faerie on their journey! To those who've shared on social media, done ARC reads or just given me compliments about the book to keep me going.

To my family and also my writing family as always, your support means everything to me – Anna Britton, Debbie Roxburgh, Sally Doherty, Marisa Noelle, Emma Finlayson-Palmer, Katina Wright, Alison Hunt, Maria Oliver, Loz Doyle, Estelle Tudor, Aerin Apeltun, the amazing ARC readers (who have caught so many printing blips it's not even funny…), writing Twitter, everyone who joins #ukteenchat, the WriteMentor crew, libraries and schools who took a chance on this series, shops that are still stocking these books and giving this indie author a chance to reach more readers, and to the readers who will find these books in the future.

THANK YOU!

ABOUT THE AUTHOR

While always convinced that there has to be something out there beyond the everyday, Emma focuses on weaving magic realms with words (the real world can wait a while). The idea of other worlds fascinates her and she's determined to find her own entrance to an alternate realm one day.

Raised in London, she now lives on the UK south coast with her husband and a very lazy black Labrador who occasionally condescends to take her out for a walk.

Aside from creative writing studies, an addiction to cake and spending far too much time procrastinating on social media, Emma is still waiting for the arrival of her unicorn. Or a tank, she's not fussy.

For the latest news and updates, check the website or come say hi on social media:

www.emmaebradley.com
@EmmaEBradley

Milton Keynes UK
Ingram Content Group UK Ltd.
UKHW041944090224
437558UK00004B/182

9 781915 909152